STORY
OF MY
LIFE

a novel

VALERIE BAEZA

STORY OF MY LIFE

Copyright © 2021 by Valerie Baeza

ISBN (paperback): 978-1-7370134-0-2
ISBN (ebook): 978-1-7370134-1-9

First paperback edition October 2021

Book design and typesetting by Domini Dragoone
Author photo © Tim Nenninger

Cover images: main image © Athena/Pexels, cradle © Curtis Adams/Pexels, couple © Olya Kobruseva/Pexels, forest © Johanna Mary Pauline Cuomo/123rf, letters © Pixabay/Pexels, suitcase © Dan Eger/iStock

Learn more about the author by visiting
www.ValerieBaezaAuthor.com

To Veronica.

My first reader.

In the dark I was lost.

In the light, I found myself and you.

Chapter One

PRESENT DAY

Death came swift and unexpected, but Garence Leitner had reason to believe otherwise. With each box he filled, he was building a ladder from which he would jump off and end his life.

He hoisted the last of the kitchen items into his arms, exited the cottage and handed the box to a man outside, thanked him, then left him. Garence's house possessed every charm of a typical cottage, a slate roof, several fireplaces, wood beams, cobblestone detailing, and it had sold as soon as it was on the market. Now, he had to pack up his eighteenth-century abode in Bourton-on-the-Water, England before the new homeowners had their final walk-through on Monday. Three days away. That was enough time for him to go through two bedrooms, a living room, and a study. The new homeowners, a newlywed couple, wanted the holiday let as is, and they had purchased a number of the furnishings in his home. These purchases turned the house into a comfortable containment for his torments.

The November morning sun came through the lead window, casting a silver glow over the apron sink. Garence slouched over the kitchen island, avoiding the rays that had landed on his top-grain leather binder. The surface of the binder was worn with a unique patina from extended use and travel. He pulled on the tie-strap and opened the binder. In the left slip-in sleeve were a sketchpad, a graphite drawing pencil, and a Montblanc fountain pen with platinum-coated fittings. In the right sleeve was a pad of heavyweight writing paper.

His writing hand had three fingers in a splint where bruising around the knuckles was still evident after one month. The bases of the fourth and fifth fingers were fractured in several places, as were the bones from the knuckle to the wrist of the small and ring fingers. Garence had opted out of surgery and was ordered to wear a splint for two more weeks. He tossed the splint into the rubbish. He had no intention of doing that either. This letter would be his final act, and he needed to be rid of this godforsaken contraption. Growling from the pain, he curled his discolored fingers around the fine pen. His handwriting was once graceful and neat, but the reduced use of his left hand had transformed it to an ungainly and bumpy sputter.

Dear Unbeknown Reader,

If you think this is another love story about a guy falling for a girl, you are sorely mistaken. This is about everything that made my life worth living; my profound pleasure to have held three lovely ladies. In truth, I did fall in love. Twice, actually, but that's beside the point. My life was filled with perfection followed by a series of heart-wrenching events that have made me want to take my own life.

Garence ran a hand through his hair and thought of which room to tackle first. His bedroom meant packing Sabina's things, which would be a nightmare. He had dreaded touching her possessions, so he'd left this room and the next—and the study—to the last minute. With any luck, this Monday's looming deadline would force him to have everything packed and dropped off at the donation center as soon as possible. He shut the binder and carried it with him.

His steps narrowed as he approached their main bedroom. His binder felt heavy, shield-like, and his pen like a sword. The perspiration on his chest and forehead cooled his body. When he reached the threshold, he saw Sabina lying on the bed, nude, with her back toward him. The white sheets were pulled over the leg she was lying on, and there was blood coming from between her legs. He stumbled backward and hit his head on the ledge of a window. He dropped the binder, and the pen rolled into the room toward her. His ears pounded. He rubbed the back of his head, and his eyes locked on the pen.

Cold and stiff, he was terrified at the thought of entering the main bedroom, but he had to retrieve his pen. It was the only one he wrote his letters with. Garence managed to get onto his hands and knees. Focusing on the pen, he shuffled forward, one hand and knee at a time while putting little pressure on his deformed hand. When he was close enough, he wondered if he should use the right or left hand to grab it.

For fuck's sake, grab the bloody pen and get the hell out of here. The disrupted concentration allowed curiosity to encourage his eyes up toward the bed.

She was gone.

The crisp white linen was void of any trace of her body ever being on it. He sighed in relief, then grabbed the Montblanc. Garence headed for the living room. He tossed the binder and pen on the coffee table, sat on a plaid armchair, then dropped his head in his hands.

His eye twitched.

He missed her.

Garence cleared the lump from his throat. His Adam's apple glided up and down behind the unshaved look he had maintained most of his life. The overhead light caught the speckles of gray nestled within the coarse hair. There were two flat moles above the hairline on his right cheek that Sabina had liked to tap her fingertips against whenever she cupped his face. Garence could almost smell her signature scent now. Hibiscus and coconut.

At his bare feet was a massive, arched, stone fireplace wide enough for his six-foot-two stature to lounge in. The cottage was cold. A stark contrast to the once beloved home, now more like a rotting waste-land. The radioactive consequence of losing yet another love. There was a wall full of chopped wood, so he grabbed a few logs and used them to start a fire. He grabbed a box of matches from behind a photograph on the mantel and looked around for a candle. Sabina always had candles scattered throughout the house, so there had to be one within arm's reach. From the corner of his eye, a woman's hand motioned to a nearby candle. Then, as if by his own observation, he grabbed that same candle, lit it, and found another.

Stacks of books, notebooks, pictures, and trinkets were nestled on every surface and in every corner. Garence sighed. He brought in a large waste bin along with some packing material, assembled four boxes, and secured the bottoms with tape. He grabbed the books on the coffee table and discovered two more underneath the table and another under the couch. *When did I lose these?* he wondered. He dusted the books with his hand, sneezed, then placed them into the first box.

By the end of the armchair was a basket with home and travel magazines. He grabbed as many as his left hand could hold and flipped through them while glancing at the dates. Spring two years ago. Summer two years ago. Autumn three years ago. Fuck, these were old. He tossed them in the bin with an unenthused underthrow. It was a score, but there was no applause or recognition. Just silence. He dumped the rest into the bin.

He reached for his pen and binder of paper and sat in the armchair. The fountain pen's extra-fine nib was rounded, but it was bladelike. This instrument had scratched many inspirations to Sabina, and it was one of the loveliest sounds to have pierced his ears. A minuscule grin tainted his lips as he motioned the pen like the therapeutic sword it was, and in his hour of great need, Garence yearned for the solace this pastime brought.

Judging by the thickness of the pages, he guessed there were twenty or so left. His fingers drummed on top of the stack to the beat of an imaginary leaky faucet. He was an ordinary man who'd lived an ordinary life with an extraordinary woman. Time had granted him the gift of supergluing his shattered heart several times, if only to survive the day, but the gift of life was bittersweet in that it left behind the vivid memories of what once was.

He resituated himself in the chair, pulling the letter close to his eyes then away from him. It was blurry even if he shifted his head back. The living room was brightening with the rising sun, but that wasn't the problem. He placed his horn-rimmed reading glasses over his face and carried on.

Over the years, I've learned that stories are the chapters in one's life, and letters are the pages detailing the elasticity of time. Some moments are so perfect that when the spell breaks, you are incapacitated by their loss and inebriated with such grief that time stretches into misery. Then, misery dissolves into an emptiness not even you can decipher, whether you are dead or alive, while other moments are all too cruel and evanescent.

Until a few years ago, I believed everything happened when it was supposed to, but I still believe the universe sends messages or signs to guide us along our travels, like tiny nudges in the right direction. I believe in something greater than me, than all of us. Whether this greatness is called God, Buddha, Jehovah, Krishna, Source, or anything else matters not to me, so I'll refer to it as the Divine as much as I can. I am only one man in a world saturated with many practices, and who am I to say that any of them is the true one? I know there is an energy within all of us that goes back into the universe when our bodies die, and what occurs afterward, I do not dwell upon.

My unbeknown reader, however you found this letter, know that I am not procrastinating my suicide. Yes, I could have jumped off a bridge or swallowed a bunch of pills and have been done with it. But I had to ensure my Sabina's home obtained deserving occupants and that her belongings weren't tossed in the bin. As you may have already guessed, if not, then you will soon discover, composing letters is what I do. I have to write this last one.

He pinched the bridge of his nose as his thoughts switched channels like a static tube television as soon as he realized the ache. He dropped the pen and extended his left hand. Tension caused him to crave space, so he sat on the rug. He retrieved his phone from his back pocket and turned on his favorite music app. He pressed the shuffle setting, and "To Your Shore" by Jesse Cook played. The acoustic guitar warmed the room with its tender emotion, while the violin stirred in and out with sentiment. It was a musical dance, with both the guitar and the violin taking turns leading. This song was a frequent source of solace—even if it was his and Sabina's song.

Garence stood, eye level with a large photograph on the wooden mantel of Torres del Paine National Park in Chile, where he'd met Sabina. At some point he would figure out what to do with these photos. In the meantime, he removed photographs from four other frames and set them on the mantel, swathed the frames in bubble wrap, then placed them in a box.

On the coffee table was a picture of Sabina in a wooden frame, beaming as if she were in a toothpaste commercial, wearing a carnation-white, halter shift dress. This was his favorite photo. The day she had said yes to his marriage proposal. Garence tapped the picture frame. Was it possible to feel less agony if he replayed his memories? Could they be good company as he packed their possessions?

No. He would not play this game. He put the frame down.

A few paces away, the standing lamp flickered bright white light from a vintage bulb that was supposed to emit a golden light, but Garence missed the phenomenon. His head ached like a bitch, and he was, as always, intoxicatingly disheartened by the ever-present crippling emptiness that had plagued him.

"Read the letters," whispered an eerie voice that resonated with itself.

That voice had first spoken to him two years ago, in a tone Garence never placed, but it had never mentioned anything about letters before.

"Return to the light," it said.

A flash of white caught his attention, and Sabina walked past, wearing the white dress from the photo. The hem billowed behind her as if there was a breeze beckoning him as it rounded the corner. He pursued her hibiscus and coconut scent down a dim hallway, paying no attention to the collapsed cardboard boxes leaning against the wall, hiding a box of matches, duct tape, and a hunting knife.

He passed through a broad opening where arched doors were half-pocketed within the walls. The sunlight flooded the high, arched windows and skipped along the edges of the ten-foot groin vault ceiling. The study had been built soon after acquiring the property, and no time was wasted in filling the built-in bookcases with books, cherished mementos from around the world, and framed photographs capturing holidays.

Sabina kneeled in front of a corner shelf unit where a hefty set of photo albums resided, with gilded spines. Next to them were canvas treasure chests of memories in vintage luggage, flaunting their age and regular travel unabashed.

He peered into the windows of her soul where nothing but light existed. His cheeks burned like fire for wondering if she was really here or if his imagination led him to this personal archive section. He had become emotionless, but he had loved this woman with such ferocity that he was on the precipice of wishing she weren't here. He received a consoling smile, then her suggestive eyebrow motioned toward the items in the bookcase.

He glanced at them, but when he looked back at her, she had vanished. The persistent emptiness that had become the life source of his existence seized him. Contemplation tapped upon the forefront of his mind as his fingers twiddled on his forehead. So much had happened in the past five years. It was all here, nestled safely behind brass locks.

He pulled the luggage off the shelf with his right hand and unfastened the latches. Tucked inside was a small rectangular box dressed in green linen, and a turquoise box. He set them aside, where he absorbed the enormity of the task before him. Hundreds of long envelopes, including some greetings cards and postcards, captured specific moments in time, written by Sabina and himself. The thought of reading these letters had crossed his mind several times over the years, but he never entertained them. In fact, he hadn't read any of the letters since the initial readings as far back as five years ago.

He swallowed hard. If his reality hadn't been hard enough, reading the letters would propel his suicide. He gave into the letters' bidding with only a glimpse. He wanted to read them, but untying the thin jute rope that bound them would release a whirlwind of long-lost love and terrors. Then again, reading her words and seeing her emotions as plain as the ink she used would make it possible for him to hear her voice. Bring her back for the weekend.

There was a high-pitched ring, and the lamp flickered white from the golden bulb.

"Read the letters. Return to the light," said the voice.

"Fuck me," he said, indignant.

He closed the luggage and stormed it into the living room as if he were going to throw them in the bin, but he set it on the couch. He had no intention of doing anything else with it, so he returned to his packing.

He shoved more books into a box, rearranged them so they fit better, and squeezed in one more. From the corner of his eye, the luggage stared at him as the shadows of his past danced upon its surface. He filled one box and another, all the while resenting the luggage. The weight of the letters on his unbalanced mind was maddening. Before the eerie voice said another word, he sat on the floor and resumed his letter in haste.

As human beings, we have many spectrums of light, and reading these letters will be like traveling back in time, reliving experiences of my life. I know there are moments, stunning facets in time within these bundles of letters, that will be a welcomed release, but not those that occurred between and afterward. Sometimes I don't understand what happened. Maybe the letters will help fill in the voids I am incapable of filling myself, for one reason or another.

As I've said before, this is not a love story, but a collection of chapters I, Garence Leitner, will revisit. So, I guess you could say these letters are the story of my life.

He opened the first suitcase, and there they were. A collection of envelopes bundled together in stacks of eleven. Sabina's envelopes were opened from the round corner flap where she took the risk of cutting her finger every time she slipped it under the flap and glided it underneath the seal, whereas his letters were opened from the top with a sterling silver letter opener. The edges were frayed but, otherwise, the entirety was in excellent condition.

He pulled the jute strand that bound them and let it fall to the floor. He held the top letter and placed the remainder of the stack on the table, where they cascaded like dominoes. His thumb swept over her name as he recalled the trip that had led to their meeting.

PART ONE
PERFECTION

Chapter Two

FIVE YEARS AGO

— OCTOBER 8TH —

Garence was on the prowl to rediscover a remote location in Torres del Paine National Park. It was an unmarked route, and, although it had been a few years ago, he was certain he was on the right one. With his left hand gripping a canvas binder, he pulled back a branch to circumvent a rock he couldn't scale. His face brightened as his destination loomed overhead—an immense stadium of granite peaks with snow-packed crevices and a scuttling river cutting through the emerald dene that was the Valle Frances.

He approached a large, sloped rock that he knew was the perfect spectator's seat when his boots gripped the ground as he came to a halt. Someone was already sitting on his rock.

"Keep on walking," said the traveler.

"I'm sorry. I didn't know anyone else knew about this spot."

"Well, now you do." She wore rolled-up shorts, worn mid-rise hiking boots, a gray T-shirt, and a wide-brimmed hat with a neck protector over her hair wrapped into a low bun.

She seemed as determined for solitude as he was, but he wanted to behold this once-in-a-lifetime view—or in his case, twice-in-a-lifetime view.

Garence rolled his eyes. He had ditched his travel guide Marcos and hiked thirty minutes to get to this point, so he rose onto the hard plane.

"I'm afraid you're going to have to budge over. I'm doing a story on the park, so you'll have to share the view."

"Oh! You're writing about Torres del Paine? Well, I should leave and allow the great writer to work. Pardon. I'm so sorry."

A subtle shine in the texture of her enunciation gave away to few astute listeners, Garence being one of them, that Spanish was her primary language.

"Stop," he said, placing his hand upon hers. "You've proved your point."

He glanced at her. Her left wrist showcased over four inches of dark bracelets made of leather and hemp, and a three-inch leather band circled the right. Her ears were pierced several times, the first being a petite plug, but now that he was more than glancing at her, he recognized the rest were leather button earrings and that she had the tiniest diamond stub in her left nostril. Several sterling silver rings adorned her fingers...

"You might as well paint my portrait or take a photo if you're going to keep gawking at me."

His eyes rummaged the valley. "If that's what you'd like. Sure."

"I'm not suggesting we pose. I was implying that you..."

"You were being passive-aggressive. I'm over it."

He took out his camera, and then he remembered seeing her at one of the stops earlier in the day.

"I'll move over."

With her grayish brown eyes, she gave him a sideways glance.

He accepted her awkward grin as a sign he was on the right track. "Here. Turn your upper body a bit."

She obliged and removed her hat.

"Now we'll get that whole view from this angle."

Her sudden easiness made him chuckle, and he was glad he'd stayed.

"Say cheese."

"*Queso.*"

She laughed, and when Garence felt her lean toward him, he snapped the picture.

She moved over a nudge while he unzipped his binder and scribbled into the journal.

"What are you writing this time?" she asked as if they were old friends.

"This time? You've been stalking me?"

"You wish. I've seen you once or twice, nose-deep in your journal. Busy. Busy. Busy."

"They're my observations and experiences, and the hellish other travelers," he replied, closing the worn journal and zipping it up. "I'm a freelance travel writer."

Sabina's eyebrows rose from the impression he had lain upon her. "That's an alluring profession."

"It didn't start off that way," he disclosed, remembering the score of unreliable low-paying travel assignments that hadn't even covered his up-front costs. Assignments that had forced his hand to become a semi-satisfied editorial assistant at two publishing houses in London, where several years of financial stability were afforded. His path had been dusty, crooked, and as plateaued as possible, but Garence persevered; he had rappelled into unexpected caverns to scale three peaks. He'd fortified passing connections with editors at other houses and publications during meetings or social events and landed advantageous opportunities. Today, fourteen years later and with thirty-eight years of life experience in his backpack, Garence had anchored his hold on the global travel writing industry.

Removing himself from his memories, he understated his triumph: "But now it is."

Sabina identified his humility straight away and paired it with his hard-earned self-worth as a means of understanding who he was—this man who was becoming less and less of a stranger to her as the seconds ticked by. She was drawn to him. Yes, she was attracted to him—let's get that out of the way—but in all honesty, he possessed a rugged warmth that soothed her senses like the perfect nightcap to an eventful day. Peeking into his earth-colored eyes made Sabina forget herself, and when the corner of his mouth turned up at her, she blushed for the first time in her life.

"So, are you going to tell me who's publishing it so that I can keep watch and pick up a copy?"

"*Rove* magazine."

She wasn't familiar with it.

"They're an American active lifestyle periodical based out of Colorado, and they've been in publication for ten months—they're doing quite well. The next issue should be a special of sorts, and they want something pretty exclusive to mark their one-year anniversary with a six-page spread of the 'O' and 'W' Circuits of the park. I've written for them before, three or four times, so it's nice to be a part of their celebration."

Sabina gathered that he was very good at his job and well respected in his field, but she shelved her assessment of him before it marked her face. "Well, it's no wonder they're a success, having you to give them flight."

"You don't even know me," he regaled, looking at her square.

She was stunned. Garence had been forthcoming up to this point. The weight of their silence gave her more reason to reflect. She was inclined to look away, but she identified this as a challenge to let someone new in. She was never going to see him again, yet the man before her was having an influence on her. A positive one. Did she appreciate this subconscious change? Shadows had danced upon her soul for so long she wasn't certain she could ever let them go. If there was ever a reason to change her frequency, it was now.

"I'm Sabina," she said, extending her hand. "Sabina Mondragón. I am an excellent judge of character."

He swore he saw a twinkle in her eye, but he wasn't sure. Now that she had introduced herself, he couldn't say she didn't know him. She offered him a handshake to solidify their introduction.

"Garence Leitner."

"It was nice of *Rove* to take you out to celebrate their moment."

"It was."

She liked his laugh and the social roller-coaster ride their meeting was taking them on.

"Maybe next time they'll pitch in for a laptop or something," she said, dropping her eyes to his old-school writing supplies.

"I wouldn't be opposed to it," he disclosed. "But let's back up a bit. I happen to enjoy writing by hand. I write down all my thoughts before I draft a document."

Sabina resituated herself on the angular rock and extended her legs. "You enjoy writing by hand?" she repeated as her eyes trolled the sky. "As in calligraphy, or that you like doing things more than once?"

"You are spirited, aren't you?"

She covered her face with her hands, and her cheeks felt hot.

"I didn't mean anything by it. It's all right. There's no need to blush."

He placed a hand upon her arm, and goose bumps erupted.

"I don't blush," she blurted, defensive. She removed the elastic tie from her hair and then tousled it.

"But you are, and I'm your witness. What about yourself? What drew you to the towers?"

She shrugged, feeling the uncharacteristic reddening of the apples vanishing. "I am trying my hand at going with the flow."

"Care to elaborate?"

She combed through her thoughts as her fingers went through her hair. The horizon was ever changing. Unsettled. Cold. She smiled because, despite everything, her reality would be striking.

She bit her lower lip. "Well, I have a world map framed over corkboard in my living room," she began, "and I threw a dart at the map. It landed on Torres del Paine."

"Very bold. A lady cut from the same cloth as myself."

"Well, we remnants have to stick together, don't we?" she joked, leaning toward him.

"It took a while, but we've found each other." Garence met her lean and caught a whiff of her body lotion, hibiscus and coconut. He examined the river, then referred back to her. "Why did you allow a dart to choose your holiday?"

Her smile had all but extinguished. "I was having lunch with my mother at Mendi Goikoa, and I was telling her about a birthday trip my boyfriend and I were planning to Bora Bora when I realized I didn't want to go with him."

Garence's intrigue was plastered all over his face, but she went on.

"I wasn't madly into him, so there was no point in going anywhere with him. That sounds so horrible. Yes, it does—you don't have to be polite and shake your head." She covered her face, laughing at her embarrassment. "I don't know what I'm trying to say. I don't want to talk about it."

And right there, Garence knew there was always more to Sabina's story, but he wasn't going to let that be an excuse. "Can you try?"

She met his eyes and then they fell. "Well, as individuals, we were very strong. He's a great guy, but we weren't strong as a couple. In all honesty, we didn't complement each other's strengths and weaknesses, and I deserve to be in that kind of relationship. Anyway, I had money saved and I still wanted to take a holiday, but I wasn't sure where to go. So, I threw a dart. I think it's still fixed to the wall because I don't remember prying it off." She dismissed the distracting reflection with a wave, and the sterling silver rings caught the light. "Everything happens in divine timing, so allow things to unfold." She panned the landscape. "This is an unforeseen adventure. I can't believe I am here."

"You created it. I'm glad you're enjoying it. Where are you from?" he asked, enamored and wanting to know everything about her.

"Bilbao. I teach English."

"That's brilliant! And Bilbao is gorgeous."

"And yourself?" she asked, feeling as though she should have already covered this ground.

"London. I like your bracelets," he commented, his fingertips touching the wrist nearest him.

"Thanks," she replied, avoiding his eyes.

He wasn't sure if she was put off by him touching her, because it couldn't have been his complimenting her bohemian indulgences. "Are you okay?"

"Yup."

His eyes narrowed. "You can talk to me. I know we just met, but I'm a brilliant soundboard."

"*Gracias.* You can drop it now."

"Fair enough," he said with resolution. He had traveled the world and encountered all kinds of personalities and conversations, so he switched gears. "When is your birthday?"

"In three days. I'll be thirty-three," she said, warming up to him again. "I look forward to each birthday, so I'll be damned if this one was contaminated. Did you catch the repeated threes?"

Garence leaned back against his hands. "Thirty-three in three? Now I do. Are you interested in numerology?"

"A bit," she disclosed, grinning.

Pleased that her mood had lifted, he nodded as if he had figured her out. "Tell me, what do repeat threes mean?"

"That the Divine is supporting all that you aspire."

"*All* that I aspire, is that a fact?"

Sabina tilted her chin as if looking over her shoulder. "Mm-hmm."

"And what do you aspire?"

"That, my friend, remains to be seen."

"So that covers threes. What about all the other numbers?"

"Well, let's start at the beginning." Sabina leaned back against the palms of her hands to get comfortable, and her hair fell over her shoulder as she tilted her head. "I'll give you the high-level rundown."

"All right."

"First off, one is a sacred number, so when you see it repeated in a three-digit pattern, as in 111, know that it holds the vibration for new beginnings. 222 is for matters of the heart. 333 vibrates manifestation and the exploration of our potential. With 444, the universe is supporting your hopes and dreams." She sat straighter. "555 is for letting go of what no longer serves you and being open to change. 666 holds the vibration of fear, so you'll need to step out of whatever you're afraid of and zero in on the beauty that's possible."

"So, the infamous 666 is not so evil after all."

With a dip of her chin, she said, "No, it's not. 777 represents your intuition. 888 speaks to your growth, and with 999, you are being reminded to clear your mind."

"And where would I see these patterns? Especially the higher numbers?"

"Oomph, everywhere. The time and the date are big ones. You can also see repeated numbers in a telephone number, a flight number, on an odometer, stats. A page number, weight. The possibilities are endless."

"What happens when I recognize a pattern? What am I supposed to do?"

"If you ever see these patterns, take count of what is going through your mind and listen to the message that's sent to you. There's no reason to overcomplicate things."

"Got it."

"Do you?" she asked with measured amounts of amusement and skepticism. She watched him absorb what he'd learned; his eyes had a far-off appearance as he recalled each pattern.

"For the most part," he admitted. "Anything else I should know?"

She collected her thoughts. "Just 11:11. It's the most powerful of all the patterns."

"Why is that?"

"We're all cocreators of our own reality, right?"

"Of course," Garence said. "We make our own choices and decisions every moment of our lives."

"Exactly. When you see 11:11, it represents an awakening, and it carries the vibration that the Divine being is alive within you and that you should be open to the potential that exists."

"What about the phases of the moon, the position of the sun and the planets, and the zodiac signs?"

"Ooh! That's a whole other book."

Garence laughed.

"*But* I will leave you with a small tidbit on the moon, being that it's a favorite of mine. The new moon symbolizes new beginnings while the full moon represents…"

"Closure."

"*Exactamente.*"

"All right. You'll have to share the rest with me some other time. So, your thirty-third birthday is in three days," he said, leaning against her shoulder, hoping she appreciated his acknowledging the pattern in her approaching birthday.

"You know, age doesn't mean a damn thing to me."

"Cheers," he said, appreciating another one of her views. "What I'm trying to get at is that in three days you'll be near Grey Glacier."

"I guess, so then I'm hanging out a few days afterward. But this entire trip is a gift to myself, so every bit of it is special."

A single breath was all she needed to speak from a place of clarity before saying, "As every day is a gift."

He watched as his words swept her attention away from him. The corner of her mouth turned up, but it was as if she were remembering something that didn't concern him. There was more to that look, just like there was more to the woman who had stolen his rock.

Chapter Three

FIVE YEARS AGO

— OCTOBER 8TH —

Going with the flow was the path Sabina tried to follow at all costs. Inspiration was at every angle, and when it found her, she gripped it with one hand. Inspiration was a funny thing. It expanded upon her grand ideas and even compelled her to act upon what she wouldn't have otherwise done. That and intuition. Her instincts were her foundation for better or for worse, and now her instincts were telling her there was something about the Englishman she'd met. He possessed a frequency she was curious to continue to vibe with. As with any thought, wish, or curiosity, she expressed a heartfelt interest in this and let it slip away. Soon, "I bet Garence is fun to travel with" would be manifested into an invitation.

The corner of her mouth turned up once he asked her to join him and his guide for the rest of their trip. He could have continued on his way and away from the moody self she presented herself to be, but the universe presented a sweet opportunity, so she was game. The group Sabina was traveling with wasn't bothered by her decision to jump parties. They viewed the peaks of Torres del Paine's Cerro Paine mountain range and everything the park offered—even four hours of aggressive Patagonian winds.

She held the hand he offered as the winds threatened to bully her off the steep incline. The surface of his fingers looked rough, but they were smooth, and they laced around hers. Four hours of no communication, just a firm connection between two. It was an unusual sensation to follow a man she didn't know. Interesting, but unusual, nonetheless, as she was an intense independent.

She preferred things her way. Though that's not to say she was a control freak. It was the only way to curb her inclination to self-harm, which was another form of self-control she didn't want to remember. The laws of the universe were her foundation as religion was others'. The law of attraction, the law of paradoxical intent and such were what was practiced for several years.

Because I am human, she thought, *I have moments when I am out of my vortex. That inspirational and feel-good vibration within myself that exists without resistance. Ever since I was a teenager, it's been a struggle to pull myself out of those dark periods when life feels cruel and challenging. But an uncluttered mind and an open heart allow energy to flow. I do what I can, whatever I have to do to maintain balance between my ego and my emotions. Even when it doesn't seem like a gift.*

Even as she and Garence surpassed the blustery weather, she held his hand. She felt safe and relaxed with him as if she didn't need her guard up. It was refreshing—he was refreshing.

Next on their list was the spectacle that was the world's second largest continuous nonpolar ice field: The Southern Patagonian Ice Field. No one was more surprised than she when Garence announced he was taking her kayaking on Lago Grey for her birthday, then ice hiking on Grey Glacier the next. Her silence and alarmed eyes screamed "what?" followed by "I want to do all that." She voiced her concern regarding her travel plans home, but Garence assured her it wasn't in jeopardy, so he scheduled plans for them. Sabina stood in angst between their tents as she absorbed his surprise—another thing she hated because of its unpredictability. Surprises.

"I'm not sure I fully appreciate what you've done. Or that *you* grasp what you've done."

"I guess I don't." He shook his head. "No. I'm pretty sure I do. I've gone through great lengths to get us what we needed for these activities at the last minute—not to mention persuading Marcos to extend our journey by an extra day at Lago Grey."

"*And* you should have spoken with me. It's my life you're affecting. You can't keep me here because…" The morning sun caught her eye, and she shifted her body away from him.

He stepped toward her and got in her face. "Because what? I wanted to do something extraordinary on your birthday. We've only just met, and here I am…"

"What *are* you doing here?" she retorted, challenging him, but for what reason she did not know, other than to keep pushing him.

"What are you asking me? What the hell is going on? You're still going to catch your flight."

"Do you need to talk everything out?"

"I do. Don't you? You know what? Let's take a step back. I haven't changed your return trip home. You were already going to hang out in the area for a few days. I'm the one whose travels were affected. I canceled my reservations to visit Milodón Cave for the online piece I was writing. I can try to get them back. It doesn't even matter at this point. We don't have to do any of it."

"Ay yai yai," she said in a sigh, looking skyward.

"No. It's fine. We'll have a good time here." He turned and headed for his room.

"Garence, come back." Exasperation slumped her shoulders before she jogged to catch up with him. She got in front of him and made him halt. "I'm sorry. I don't like surprises, and… I freaked out."

"I wasn't thinking," he said matter-of-factly. "But you're going to have to let loose a bit."

She dipped her chin as she composed herself. *Oh, mis estrellas. This guy is relentless.* "Would you stop talking for one minute? Please? You're right. I'm not losing out on anything except for a kick-ass adventure. With you. On my birthday."

That he said nothing while eyeing her left her to wonder if he believed her. "Okay?"

"Are you sure?"

"We're doing it all," she said. "Thanks to…"

He placed his hands upon her face and dove into her lips.

"Happy Birthday."

"Thank you. You should have led with that instead."

"Just kiss me."

And just like that, Sabina let Garence in. She soaked in a hot tub with him at Refugio Los Cuernos, canoed past glaciers, trekked on Grey Glacier, and even enjoyed stiff drinks on the rocks—or, rather, glacier chips. She felt like she was living in a dream. Traveling and experiencing new things in life and expanding upon what she was already grateful for. Most importantly, she was also free from herself. The silent incessant need to influence every aspect of her life. Garence was the calm ironing the wrinkles in her personality by allowing it. He made going with the flow look easy.

She acted upon her intuition, yet being with Garence caused her to question the duration of their connection. Was he a serene fling or someone who would inspire adventure? To be honest, she wouldn't mind extending their acquaintance, friendship, or whatever the connection she had with him was. She reclaimed that dreamy influence by inviting Garence on an evening walk with the new moon before them. New moons meant new beginnings. Perhaps tonight would be a new beginning for her. She looked up at the sky and wished for a life filled with wonderful moments. Life would never be perfect, but she expressed her desire for a multitude of intensities from the things she enjoyed, joy and laughter, traveling and experiencing different cultures, and everything that transpired whilst creating those memories. After all she had been through in her short time, she yearned for a satiable life.

Sabina sensed Garence's presence behind her. While he wasn't wishing for the very thing she was, Sabina was certain he detected the energy surging through the air as much as she did. She looked over her shoulder and outstretched an arm to him.

Garence stood behind her, caressing her arms.

One of Sabina's threaded bracelets carried a bell resembling lily of the valley, and it chimed when he wriggled his thumb beneath the cord like a dog on a hunt, sniffing out her truth. She was reminded of the heavily scarred wrists concealed beneath the multitude of accessories; her smile faded. She had never taken the bracelets off, except to shower, nor had she ever shared the existence of the scars with anyone. That Garence liked to play with the bracelets wasn't lost on her, but then he wrapped his arms around her and pulled her out of her bad memories. She closed her eyes and accepted his rescue. His touch heightened the energy within her, and the butterflies in her stomach took flight.

It had been clear to Sabina for some time where the course of their relationship would lead, and she welcomed it. She welcomed him. She held the reins, and this was her night to celebrate, but this would be their moment.

The minute growl within his mute request and the tender grip of his teeth against her neck sent sparks through her body, and she knew her wish had been answered. Maybe it had been granted when she threw the dart at the map over her couch. Whatever had allowed their paths to cross was setting a course of extreme events into motion.

She reached into her back pocket, pulled out a condom, and handed it to him.

He thanked her. "I salute your preparedness."

Undressing, she looked askance at him. "Someone has to be."

"If I knew what to be prepared for, I would have been. Believe me."

Then she heard him speak, but his lips weren't moving. He was going to ask if she slept with random guys often. She didn't overthink this phenomenon and followed it like a ray of light.

"No," she answered.

"Then why…"

She ran her fingers through her mane. "We've had a lovely time getting to know each other, so I figured I would carry a condom, seeing as you are solely armed to document your travels."

His eyes shot up at her, warning her to back off, then his face became the billboard for self-control as he counted to three.

"You don't have to tell me twice." Her alarmed eyes zeroed in on him. "I'm sorry, Garence."

He looked puzzled. "I didn't say anything."

As he attempted to understand how she knew what was going on in his head, he looked at her with sharp curiosity. "Can you…"

"No, I cannot read your thoughts. But I can read your face as plain as you read your journal, which is quite charming," she said, raising an eyebrow and hoping to avoid further insult. She wrapped her arms around his waist, savoring the feel of a man against her and the weight of his arms wrapped around her. "If I read minds, I wouldn't invade your privacy."

"I appreciate that."

She unfastened his trousers and allowed them to drop to the ground, and Garence stepped out of them to avoid entanglement, then slipped off his shirt. His chest and abdomen were covered in the same fashion as his jaw, a thin layer of facial hair she thought was more like midnight fervor.

He kissed her.

Her skin pricked with sensation and she wanted to let go. Go with the flow. She wanted this moment with him. Everything felt easy, and there wasn't a shred of friction, only her mind. She pulled her lips away from his and looked into the darkness all around them, and she found his eyes. As clear as day, she saw him and felt the core of his existence upon her skin. This was the man who would love her without hesitation and to the far stretches of the universe. She wondered if he saw her for who she was. A woman with a dark past doing everything to keep her vibration as high as she could. She sensed that he didn't, but if he did know the part about her she kept hidden, would he stick around? This was her greatest fear with any man because she scared some away.

"You're quiet," he said, startling her. He held her hands and kissed them as an apology. "I can't read minds, so you're going to have to share what you're thinking with me."

She appreciated his honesty as much as she did his energy. She closed her eyes and put her hands flat on his chest and listened for something, anything. A thought or a feeling. Then it arrived with an inhale. He was falling for her. Her eyes widened. She had closed herself off for so long, she wasn't sure if she could allow herself to follow suit. But then she grinned. That wasn't true, and her cheeks warmed. The real question was, could she fully open up to him? And then the next question, if he saw her full self, would he stay?

She squeezed his hands and sent a thought out into the universe: Please stay.

"You have a firm grip on reality," he said.

She smiled at him. "I am accustomed to seeing in the dark, so I can perceive a bit more."

"All right. That does nothing to help me right now."

"You can't see me, can you?"

"Not really. It's..."

"Dark?" she said, finishing his sentence once again.

"Yes. I can feel you though. Your energy. You vibrate with intensity."

He did not see her physical form, but he saw what mattered, and that held more relevance. She pushed her lips toward his and gave into him, moaning as his hands rubbed her body.

Garence traced the curves of her body, and his imagination connected the dots. The canter at which she moved turned him on. He placed his hand between her legs and moved his fingers in a circular motion. Sabina became wetter the more he unwound her, and his fervor grew. He switched places with her and, before re-entering her, nipped her bottom lip, then kissed her before driving them to the crest of their adventure.

Sabina reached into one of the side pockets of her cargo trousers and pulled out a small rubbish bag for Garence to stow away his sheath.

"I am not surprised," he said.

They remained on the clearing, and she rested her head upon his shoulder. They gazed upon the new moon and the radiance beyond it.

Garence had enjoyed meeting her, and now it was clear to him that he would miss her when they parted ways.

She pulled his mobile phone from his trouser pocket, and he watched her enter her details into his phone.

"Now you're taking control of my phone too. I should be running from you."

"Stop," she said to his teasing. She found the picture he'd taken of them in his gallery, then texted it to herself. "And send."

Garence rolled his eyes, then kissed her. "Our holiday is almost over."

"Yeah," she replied with a heavy sigh.

"I'd like to write to you."

She sat halfway up and leaned on his chest. "Is that how we'll keep in touch?"

"It'll be a courtship. Most definitely." He followed the trail her voice left in the dark and nudged her nose with his.

"I'm in for a ride, aren't I?"

"I wouldn't raise the bar so high. I find writing relaxing, and I wanted to share that experience with you. What do you think?"

The notion of writing letters meant snail mail, which seemed like a step in the wrong direction. Forward but not as intuitive. Would Garence always hit the high road in pursuing her?

"It's different, for sure, but I like it," she said.

"A Spanish–English teacher pen-palling an Englishman does sound intriguing."

"It does, and fun, so I like it even more."

Chapter Four

FIVE YEARS AGO

It had been four days since the Chilean trip. Garence was alone in his flat in Shoreditch, the East End of London, leaning against a bank of wall-to-wall windows unmasked by curtains and the blinds pulled to the far right.

Like many street walls in the district, there were murals created from paint and paper and spray paint, like the one Garence was admiring. Roughly six meters tall, it was of an amused woman looking down the alleyway at something that piqued her interest, windblown dreadlocks swept over her shoulder. Garence recalled sitting curbside to watch the Puerto Rican artist, MazCult, create it. She'd held the spray can close to the wall and held the nozzle too long so that the paint dripped to create a beautiful blend of color for subtle depth and brilliance. Garence loved that he lived in an area akin to an urban galleria and, most of all, where he could admire some of it from his third-floor window.

Lost in thought, he didn't notice the incited couple crossing the mural. He had anticipated missing Sabina when they parted ways in Torres del Paine, but when the event occurred, the missing took on more of a pang in his chest. A piece of him was missing, and she had it. To be clear, Garence had never been whole. He'd always had an undetectable void boarded over by his worldly travels, but Sabina's steps had burned the planks when she followed him to Valle Frances and backfilled that forever-exposed void with herself. Now that he was in London and she in Spain, that crater sucked the meaning out of everything in his life.

He could call or text her. She made sure to exchange that information beforehand, not to mention their photo—that cheeky minx—and he could hear her voice or read her words. It was tempting. Garence looked into the distance before deciding to forgo the instantaneous pleasure. He walked to the living room and went to the glass coffee table where he left his leather journal. He grabbed a sheet of paper.

His first memory of letter writing came from childhood. He and his parents, Christoph and Elle Leitner, would travel during school breaks and around football tournaments from West London to visit his maternal grandparents in Marlborough, Wiltshire before heading onward to his paternal grandparents in Hallstatt, Austria. He had often watched each of his grandparents compose handwritten letters to their loved ones between the numerous occasions that called for greetings cards. This personalized form of communication stayed with him. He'd written to a few of his past girlfriends, but none of them ever took to the notion. Sabina, on the other hand, was older and he rather looked forward to this expansion of intimacy with her.

Dear Sabina,

Although it feels more like a month, it has been a few days since we departed Torres del Paine. The time we spent together was evanescent, yet your hibiscus and coconut scent perfume the air. The memory of your smile and your laughter brighten my days, and my skin still remembers your touch—heightening my senses to the point of insanity.

I must see you again. May I come to Bilbao?

Affectionately,
Garence

— OCTOBER 24TH —

Garence, mi amor,

Sí! I couldn't have agreed with another person more. A meeting under the stars. Oh, mis estrellas!

We have only met, but I feel as though I have known you for ages, and I can see you as clear as if you were beside me now. The seven diminutive scars on your face and those on your arms—quite a few! The markings of a life of adventure and from hearty laughter. Your unassuming strength is a breath of fresh air to my self-restraint. It's like being on vacation from myself.

I believe in the power of influencing my perception with 'I am' affirmations. I enjoyed my trip to Chile, but I am most grateful for meeting you. Having said that, I shouldn't be saying the following, but it's the truth. I am a bit terrified of seeing you again. Would we pick up where we left off? Would you and I still have that spark? I suppose our written words have already proven otherwise. What if we were patient and we waited to see where this path leads us?

I cannot say how we crossed paths in Valle Frances, but I am glad we did. In the back of my mind is the awareness that you travel often and have visited the places where I've been. I find myself looking for you in the crowd at the cinema or museum or around the bend on a mountainous hike. It would not surprise me to see you outside my dreams.

Then again, setting a date would save me from searching for your ghost.

Sabina

P.S. How is it that my letter is longer than yours?

— OCTOBER 31ST —

Dear Sabina,

I know what I want, and I want you. I want to see where this relationship will go.

I understand your reservation, but only partly. It is doubtful that we would experience a sophomore upset. Allow me to ease your mind. We have already proven we are suited for each other on a multitude of levels; we enjoy travel and outdoor exercises; we can talk and banter. You and I are a wonderful balance of everything that is cherished most in this world. There is only one path for us to travel, and that is together.

And don't forget that I am around the bend from where you are. Granted, that bend is over 800 miles if you sling round France or the Celtic Sea, but we are a fourteen-hour drive away from each other, or a mere two hours by air. From every angle, I am nearby. So never fear. Hold my hand and trust in me.

I will travel anywhere you wish. Name the date, throw a dart, and that is where you will find me.

Impatiently yours,
Garence

— NOVEMBER 8TH —

Sabina was curled up in bed, the perfect image of someone who'd tossed and turned at least three times in their sleep, and her right cheek had impressions from the pillowcase. As she read Garence's letter, she examined his penmanship, the graceful and fluid strokes achieved from years of practice or a stern schoolmaster. She reread it and fell in love with his desire to see her again.

She glared at her mobile phone on the nightstand. She really wanted to talk with him, hear his voice. She reached for the phone and pulled up his number, but she stared at the call button that could have connected her to Garence and granted her morning wish. The thought of hearing the reflections in his voice tickled her, and she became giddy, then self-doubt caused her pause. She tapped her forehead with her fingertips.

Should she call him?

She stared at his name, then the time. It was 9:46. There were no repeated numbers, so there was no obvious sign to follow through on this idea. He said he wanted to write to her, and he hadn't called her even though he had her number...

The waiting was gnawing at her patience! She should call him. Why was she overthinking this? She shook her head then closed her eyes. *Allow things to unfold.* She took a deep breath, and her shoulders relaxed.

She had to admit she liked their letters, his guiding their communications, and their relationship. If this was his route, then she was all for this new and unexpected ride. She wondered what else he had in store for her. Her curiosity was as strong as wanting to talk.

She tossed her phone onto the mattress and sighed, surrendering. She went to her desk near the kitchen, then returned with a pen and paper and a coffee-table book. She glanced at his letter and familiarized herself with the words even though she had memorized them, then wrote her reply on top of the book.

Garence, mi amor,

I have a hard time trusting people, yet I trust you more than most. I need time, amor... No. That doesn't feel true. There is so much light in this world that I cannot deny myself the truth. You have steadied my nerves and shown me what is possible.

It's also not easy trying to determine the best time to get away from my work, no matter how much I look forward to seeing you again. I am afraid you'll have to practice patience. Or work on your codependency issues. With that being said, I already know what your reply would be. "And you have control issues." Noted, mi amor.

I am light and you are what illuminates me.

Sabina

— THE USUAL ONE WEEK LATER —

Sabina was lying on the slate-blue couch with her gray-fuzzy-socked feet resting on the velvet armrest. A blue on white crewel-embroidered throw pillow was squashed beneath her head. Behind the couch was an exposed brick wall that backdropped a massive map of the world in a detailed ebony frame with a dart still marking Torres del Paine. Sabina was reading from *The Man from St. Petersburg* by Ken Follett, the spine and pages unmarked from careful handling, when someone rapped on her door. She had no desire to put down the book, especially as she was on the final chapter, but she was sure whoever was on the other side was there for a good reason, seeing as she wasn't expecting anyone and solicitors were uncommon.

After the second knock, she called out, *"Dame un minuto,"* while placing a paper marker in the book. She then found her next-door neighbor, Fabian, smiling back at her with a package in his burly hands.

The tall Spaniard apologized in Spanish for his intrusion, then said a parcel had been left on his doorstep by accident.

She waved his apology aside. *"No te preocupes. Gracias,"* she replied, accepting the object from his extended hand, then closed the door.

Seeing Garence's name as the sender brought a smile to Sabina's face. She went back to the sofa, forgetting all about her book, and removed the parcel's protective covering and opened the box.

The first thing she saw was an envelope with 'Sabina' scrawled on it. Beneath it was a small rectangular box wrapped in green linen. She eyed the package with suspicion while popping the corner of the sealed envelope flap.

Dear Sabina,

You've advised me to be patient, but I know too much of anything is a bad thing.
Here is a gift... in case you have misplaced your own.

Garence

Sabina scowled at the note as if it were Garence. She placed the letter on top of a stack of three art-and-photography books resting on the coffee table, then opened the box.

She released a laugh.

Inside was a brown, feathered, steel-tipped wooden dart.

— FOUR DAYS LATER —

Garence, mi amor,

I love the vintage dart. Muchas gracias, Mr. Persistente. With that being said, I will not cast it. I'll reserve my right to wield its illustrious power another time.
I have time off from school during the New Year, and Epiphany galas, and the Fiesta de Los tres Reyes Magos will be celebrated.
Come during this illuminating time of the year.

Sabina

Chapter Five

FIVE YEARS AGO

— END OF DECEMBER —

Sabina and Garence proved to be an amorous couple even outside the Chilean wilderness, and they were accustomed to each other's nuances from day one. She walked into the water closet without knocking while Garence used the urinal, to grab a comb or an elastic hair tie, and Garence had the predisposition to rise before dawn from years of frequent travel and jam-packed itineraries. One thing that Sabina was conscious of was Garence's arms around her or his fingers entwined with hers; he made walking around town and watching movies intimate with these simple embraces. She was by nature an affectionate person, so Garence's tendencies suited her like a glove. Sleeping in the same bed was a welcomed nightcap. She slept harder, and all thoughts and sounds were silenced by his presence.

On New Year's, they joined Sabina's friends and watched fireworks and wished every month of the new year their very best by eating twelve grapes. When Epiphany Eve arrived, January 5th, they baked Rosca de Reyes, a round-shaped fruit cake, and hung out in the contemporary kitchen. Sabina explained the local traditions of the season.

"On Epiphany Eve, which is tonight," she said, "it is tradition to leave glasses of cognac for the three kings who brought gifts for the baby Jesus," she showcased a brand-new bottle of Hennessy XO, "and water for their camels, on balconies or under the tree. But I think we should enjoy this delightful beverage," she added with a wink.

Sabina poured cognac into two tulip glasses and then handed one to Garence. "*¡Salud!*"

"*¡Salud!*"

They consumed the welcomed spirit in a leisurely swallow. Sabina grabbed the bottle and replenished their glasses and held up hers. "*Todo el mundo debería creer en algo,*" which translated to *everyone should believe in something.*

Garence finished the toast. "*Yo creo que debemos tomar otra copa.*" *I believe we should have another drink.*

Sabina let out a shout, "*¡Sí!*", then kissed him.

They moved to the living room and sat on the velvet couch, set their drinks on the coffee table, and gazed upon the holiday tree adorned with old-world ornaments and blue lights that made the five-foot tree glow like a glacier.

Weary from all the hustle and bustle of the past couple of days, Sabina sighed, and Garence suggested she lay her head down. She stretched her legs over the cushions, rested her head on his lap, extended an arm over her head, and then finalized her shuffle with a decompressing moan. All she required now was a massage or a tender caress and she would melt.

"Mm. Now I think *you* can read minds," she said, plunging deeper into relaxation with every stroke that slid across the anterior of her arm.

Garence strummed her bracelets every now and then.

There he goes again, she thought nervously, *blowing at my smoke screen.*

She brought that hand down, then rubbed her forehead; it bothered her to associate his touch with the pain she'd inflicted upon herself. Someone as loving as he should not caress mutilations as horrendous as these. Although it would have been a lovely way to heal her scars. Sabina's eyes fluttered at this possibility, but they remained closed, still shutting out Garence. She didn't want him mixed in with the distorted images of her lashing out her willingness to die.

"Are you all right?" he asked, noticing this was the first time she sought to escape his touch.

"Mm-hmm," was all she mustered, because she wasn't ready to combat her past and a new love all at once. If this love was as real as it felt, then she had to throw the first punch.

"We can go to bed if you're ready."

Sabina bit her lip, then spoke. "I need a moment to work it all out, is all."

Garence draped his arm across her body.

Sabina was comforted by his mute understanding, and it should have given her the strength to let him in, but she feared his reaction to her deepest and darkest secrets.

Was she ready to be that vulnerable?

Would he go running for the hills?

No, that was absurd... but it could change how he saw her. And if it did, then that would mean he wasn't the one for her. What a painful thought that was. She didn't want to lose him. The past week had proven he was ideal, so she shouldn't doubt his character... nothing would change.

Then another form of shame fell upon her; Garence deserved more credit than she was giving him.

She took a silent deep breath and released it as if she were jumping to her death.

"At sixteen, I was diagnosed with clinical depression. A severe form of depression that can be genetic or the aftershock of an event." Her anxiety climbed. She bit her lip but forged on. "In my case, it was the latter."

Chapter Six

SIXTEEN-YEAR-OLD SABINA

— BILBAO, SPAIN —

Rosalinda had a black pixie cut and wore red lip balm to embellish her thin lips, and she was Sabina's best friend for three years. They met in religion class, and they questioned the exact same things about the world they lived in. Why are human beings on Earth? What's going on in the rest of the universe? Why was sex made to be pleasurable if you're not allowed to have it? Rosalinda was the one person Sabina trusted with everything, as best friends do; they swapped opinions, asked embarrassing questions about their bodies, thoughts, and feelings they would never talk about with anyone else, and shared secret crushes. Then one day, it was all gone.

Shopping for school clothes, they had bags in their hands as they crossed the busy street when Rosalinda realized she'd left her phone in the dressing room of the last shop. She ran back to fetch it when she was hit by a car. She died. The whole thing replayed in Sabina's head. Over and over again until it drove her insane. Rosalinda jogged to the edge of the car parked along the busy street. She looked over her shoulder at Sabina, gave her a frantic, cheesy grin at the traffic, chuckled, then ran across the street as a motorcyclist buzzed past. A car had pulled around the corner and onto the street to beat the next wave of cars, and the driver never saw her until she hit his windscreen. Rosalinda had wanted to be a pediatrician when she grew up, and if everything unfolded in divine timing, then she'd never had a chance to reach for her dreams. It was a disheartening realization, and it deepened Sabina's grief.

She was prescribed an antidepressant, and it did the trick. But only for a bit. She was then switched to a stronger drug with stronger effects. She lost her appetite, and she was nauseated. She wasn't sleeping, but then again, she never felt as if she had ever woken up from her nightmares; nothing ever changed the dream world or the real one. She hated her memories, her very existence, and she wanted it all to end. She searched for a box cutter in the shed, emptied the plastic prescription bottle into her mouth, and sliced her wrists. She ended up alive, very angry, and even more depressed than before.

She underwent a psychiatric evaluation because those who slit their wrists were at a higher risk of doing it again, cutting the tendons and disabling themselves. She was prescribed another medication that left her numb. She didn't feel anything or think about anything or speak—you'd think she would have welcomed this state, but she didn't. She didn't want to live, so why would she want a stupefied existence?

Her parents raided the house for every sharp object—even glass. For weeks when they weren't looking, she scavenged the house for anything sharp, and she came across a craft knife on the floor behind a cabinet. Her eyes widened in this moment of discovery, and she stared at it for five whole seconds as tears welled. It was the best gift in the world, bright and shiny and sharp, and it was what she needed. It even had an ergonomic cushion on the handle—it was a miracle! She still couldn't believe she'd found it.

She was sleep-deprived, doped up on meds, and starved, but she knew what she wanted, and this time she would do it right by cutting herself vertically.

The only thing she hadn't planned on and should have was her parents bursting into the bathroom. She was three-quarters of the way down when they arrived. She fell to the floor, and her blood tarnished the cold white tiles. Her heart beat into her ears like a seething drum. Her mother grabbed a washcloth to stop the bleeding and clamped her hands over Sabina's wrist. She applied her entire body weight while Father rang for emergency assistance.

— FOUR YEARS AGO, EPIPHANY EVE —

She brought a hand to her brow. "I was institutionalized for a good part of a year," said Sabina to Garence.

She removed four inches of bracelets from her right wrist. Garence's eyes were fixed on her wrists, but he wasn't horrified. She handed him her left wrist. He removed the three-inch leather band and saw six horizontal mutilations. Rather than caress the brutal scars with his thumb or wrap his fingers around her wrist, he kissed the scars.

Sabina revealed a thick weld-like scar that ran down her wrist like an arrow aiming for her heart. Garence kissed the entire length of her arm and the hands that had exerted these hurtful acts. She closed her eyes, absorbing his gifts.

He pointed to the minuscule fault in the long laceration. "Is this the point when your parents arrived?"

She knew the position of the hairline distinction from memory, and she said, "Yes." She saw herself back in that moment; the knife falling onto the floor at the same time she did, hitting her head on the toilet seat. Only this time, it was Garence who leaned over her, and there was no blood.

Sabina was warmed by his touch and him cauterizing her wounds, freeing her from the shame she harbored.

He reached for a tissue and handed it to her.

Sabina wiped her face.

"I can't believe I did all of this to myself or how much I hurt my parents. It was a battle, but things unfold as they are meant to. I believe in that with all of my heart—even if I haven't been able to rationalize Rosalinda's death. I cried, and I struggled every day to understand, but I was trapped.

"During this time, I realized I was in control of my thoughts and my emotions and that I wanted to be in control again. I wanted to heal and be better. So, I set things into motion, and everything from my health and belief system shifted. I sat with a shaman and accepted the things that I could not change, like Rosalinda's death. I leaned on my parents' love and support, and before I knew it, I *was* in a better state."

"You manifested your health."

"I did."

"I wish I had been there for you, Sabina."

A smile warmed her face, and she thought, *You can't fix everything*, but she focused on gratitude instead. "You are here now, and I am in a much better place." She reached up toward Garence and kissed him. "Have you experienced anything like this?"

"I've lost friends and family, but I've never wanted to kill myself. I do understand where you were coming from."

She placed her hand upon his face, admiring his cool demeanor. "Nothing could ever bring you down. You're pretty solid."

Sabina placed a hand over her mouth, a yawn approaching.

"Come on. Let's get you to bed," he suggested, standing.

"No. It's Epiphany Eve. We have to stay up and celebrate."

Garence swept Sabina into his arms. "Let's rest, then we'll celebrate in the morning."

She wrapped her arms around his neck and surrendered; she was no match against Garence and her weariness. "I can't wait to eat Rosca de Reyes," she muttered as sleep called her to rest her head upon Garence's shoulder, claiming her for the night.

"Me too. I hope you won't mind what I brought you," he whispered apprehensively, kissing her forehead.

In the morning, they sat by the illuminated tree, surrounded by ripped and balled-up holiday paper and gifts from Sabina's parents and friends. A gray crochet cowl scarf with round buttons, an olive-green asymmetrical sweater, a sterling silver sparrow ear cuff, two novels, and a hardcover book with astonishing landscapes from around the globe. It was raining, and the windows glowed as if they were frosted. The tapping on the glass seemed to be in synchronization with the traditional Spanish carols playing from the stereo.

Sabina saved Garence's gift for last, and as soon as she saw the small gift bag, she guessed it was in the realm of accessories.

"I fell asleep regretting my gift choice," he said.

"Why?" Her hand went to her chest. "Garence!"

Within a turquoise box was a Tiffany & Co. platinum bracelet with three round diamonds.

"I acknowledged the huge possibility that you would not appreciate this. I wrestled with the idea of not giving it to you all night, but I still wanted you to have it."

Sabina's heart melted. "No, I love it. I do. It's gorgeous."

Garence sighed with relief. "That's what I thought when I saw it. It's unassuming, dazzling, and just right. You could wear it every day or not. I thought it personified you to a T."

"I wouldn't say so, but this absolutely is." She gazed upon the dainty bracelet in the box. "Would you put it on me?"

Garence placed the box on the coffee table, between their dessert plates of half-eaten Rosca de Reyes, whilst Sabina immediately removed her other bracelets, although she was only wearing half of them with Garence knowing the truth, including the leather band. She extended her right wrist, unflinching at the sight of her vertically marred skin.

Garence fastened the bracelet then kissed her hand.

"This is perfect," she said, nuzzling his nose with hers.

"Is it?"

"Yes." She bit her lower lip, reflected a moment, and then looked up at him with glistening eyes. "You have given me something that no one else in my family has dared to give me." She thought for a second on the significance of receiving the bracelet, then continued, "You knew nothing of my past, yet you chose something not only romantic and feminine but also something to replace the leather and the long-lived threads that have covered up my past. I can't describe the release I'm experiencing."

"I'm glad I didn't know beforehand. Otherwise you wouldn't have this moment."

And there it is. A moment delivered at the right time. "It unfolded as it was meant to."

Their lips were about to meet when she halted. "*Espera!* I have a gift for you too." She turned around, reached behind a tufted floor cushion, and retrieved a trunk small enough to house a textbook, hand-carved by a local artist with mountainous landscapes on all sides.

Garence ran his hand over the smooth surface and admired the fine details the master craftsman had accomplished. "It's magnificent."

"Open it."

Garence flipped the lid and discovered a new leather journal. The scent was enough to make him smile even if the hidden contents hadn't. For a full second, he was taken back to his grandfather's stable in Austria, where the horse saddles were kept. The one-inch spine was engraved to resemble an antique book with a strap to secure the entirety. The travel journal held a fountain pen and a drawing pencil within the inseam of the spine, two left pockets held a pad of paper for Garence to write about his travels and a pad of sketch paper, and on the right side was a flat clip holding several sheets of customized stationery with his monogram, GL, embossed at the top.

"Sabina," he rumbled. "This… This is staggering."

"Do you like it?"

"Like it? It's bloody perfect!"

"I'm glad. I didn't know what to expect when you said that you wanted to write to me, but I enjoy your letters; they're such an intimate gift. I always look forward to the next one."

"You don't think they're corny?" he asked, seeking her honest opinion.

"Not at all." Her warm expression transformed into an inquiring smirk. "If I did would you stop?" she asked, curious.

"No."

She laughed. "Lucky for me."

Sabina had the best smile he'd ever seen, and just knowing it was directed at him made him as happy as Larry. He wanted more moments, all moments, with Sabina, and he couldn't wait to set future plans in motion.

"I'd like nothing more than to see you again. Would you visit me in London?"

"All right. I haven't been in several years."

"I'm also flying out to Sydney in two months to meet with a publisher, Henry, about a slew of my photographs he wants to release in a three-book series."

"Your photos are going to be published?"

"Yeah. He—"

"That's marvelous! *Felicidades!*" She wrapped her arms around his neck and congratulated him.

"Thank you." He beamed. "Why don't you come with me? I only need to be there for a couple of days, but we can make a holiday of it. Stay somewhere in the Whitsunday Islands, scuba dive in the Great Barrier Reef, tour Daintree Rainforest."

Her eyes grew with anticipation as they planned to see each other twice more; she had already imagined herself submitting the time off from work. "*Perfecto.*"

Chapter Seven

FOUR YEARS AGO

— FEBRUARY —

Garence, mi amor,

I had the best time with you in lovely London! I had forgotten how busy and vivacious it is and the endless number of things to do. Such energy. I'd have to say my favorite part of these past nine days was cheering for you on the football field, shopping at the vintage shops around your block, and the days we stayed in Gloucestershire; I could have stayed in our charming cottage, complete with exposed beams and fairytale fireplace, forever.

It never ceases to amaze me how easily we slip into each other's worlds. It's as if we are an ordinary couple with two residences.

Now it is time to part, but the best part of these stopovers is looking forward to seeing you and the pent-up enthusiasm that springs out when we finally meet! I am buoyant with you to give me air.

Let's advance to Australia!

Sabina

— FOUR YEARS AGO, MARCH —

Garence and Sabina were on a departing flight from Australia, sitting in silence with their bodies turned toward each other, their foreheads butting. Their faces beamed as they scribbled on a pad of paper.

Garence: Sabina, you made Australia even more glorious and memorable. I cannot believe my luck.

Sabina: You do have the best job—lucky bugger.

Garence: I mean you. I'm lucky to have you.

Sabina: I am the lucky one. You also get the trophy for most memorable proposal.

Garence: I can't take credit for something I didn't plan—I had every intention of proposing, and I carried the ring in my pocket every single day—but it was memorable. Walking on the beach with our shoes in one hand and the other hand entwined in each other's, I wasn't thinking about the ring. Neither of us was paying attention because that pixie wave splashed us from a few feet away, and then we tumbled from the scare.

Sabina: I like how you say "we" lost our footing, because it was I who was startled and dragged you down with me.

Garence: WE lost our footing.

Sabina: I was thinking about how perfect we were. Are! Surrounded by such beauty, the soft sand below and a serene sky above, yet all I thought about was spending every day with you.

Garence: Instead of a lightning bolt, we were splashed.

Sabina: Exactamente! You didn't even have to kneel down on one knee. We were both on our bums, laughing... It was a nice moment given to us.

Garence: When do you want to get married?

Sabina: I was thinking we shouldn't wait long. You?

Garence: In the autumn. October.

Sabina turned on her phone and pulled up the October calendar. She wasn't searching for a particular date, but one that fell on the weekend. And sooner rather than later—the first Saturday.

Sabina: October 6th.

Garence: Perfecto.

Anything she suggested would have suited him. Garence thought of a few idyllic locations and then jotted them down.

Garence: Italy. France. Maldives.

Sabina smiled. His suggestions were fantastic, but she knew their wedding should reflect them. Unpretentious, pure, and with a correlation to their mutual fancies.

Bursting with anticipation, Sabina wrote: *Let's get married on Gaztelugatxe!*

Garence found the idea of exchanging vows on a Spanish island the ultimate option.

Garence: You win!

Sabina looked at her engagement ring. Each stone represented a past, present, and future together, while the ring represented their undying love for each other. She knew everything held meaning and purpose, and if you asked for something, you would receive it. She had asked for great moments, and this was a great moment—as all the ones to follow would be because she would spend them with Garence. As sure as there were stars above, Sabina knew that whatever lay ahead, she and Garence would be united for all of eternity.

— FOUR YEARS AGO, OCTOBER 6TH —

The wedding ceremony was held a stone's throw away from Bilbao in a tenth-century hermitage on Gaztelugatxe, an islet connected to Spain by a narrow man-made stone bridge with a lengthy staircase of over two hundred steps. Garence and Sabina stood across from each other at the altar with their palms up, the other's right palm cupped in their left, and they exchanged their own vows before twenty-six guests and a blooming sunset of violet and powdered slate. Garence donned black, slim-fit trousers, a collared shirt, and a black tie. Sabina's beach waves flowed down her bare back and she wore a lace V-neck midi in white, to represent her solemn commitment to her marriage. The reception was held in the church patio area with unobstructed views of the gorgeous Bay of Biscay and the rocky Spanish coast, whose surface was cloaked with moss-colored grasses and speckled with wild blossoms.

Garence and Sabina began the reception slow-dancing to their song, "To Your Shore," and the guests had disappeared. They held each other's eyes, and no one else mattered in the world except for them. She ran her fingers over his boxed beard, tapped his moles, and wondered how he'd managed to stay single all these years, but she knew they were meant for each other. This was the reason the dart had landed on Torres del Paine.

Love. One of life's greatest experiences was the reason she was never able to take her own life successfully.

Sabina looked at her wrists. They were bare, without the many thread and leather bracelets that had shrouded her maimed skin, and her past was exposed on her special day. She was without fear of persecution. Yes, people noticed the scars—it was hard not to. Their eyes widened as if they had seen a large venomous snake slithering their way, sometimes an involuntary sharp breath escaped their mouth, but their reaction rolled off Sabina's shoulders more and more. She was stronger for it, and she was proud of where she was at in her life. Trading shame for gratitude, she doffed the accessorized bandages in exchange for the freedom that delicate platinum had gifted her.

Chapter Eight

PRESENT DAY

In my travels, I have seen many beauties. Beaches made to have sex on, trees meant for climbing, and skies as passionate as our first kiss. In Sabina's face, I saw brilliant possibility. I believed it was my responsibility to make her as happy as I was and to provide a solid foundation for us. I remembered she wanted a cottage in Gloucestershire, so before the wedding, I sold my place and found a one-bedroom flat in Bourton-on-the-Water. Then I put the difference in living expenses into an account for us. Sabina earned a permanent full-time position at the private secondary in town, the Cotswold School, as Head of English, and moved in with me two weeks before the honeymoon in Norway. To help us save as much as possible, she also tutored students from nearby villages on English and Literature studies. I didn't want her to work so much, but she insisted it wasn't much extra effort. She adored being around children the most, and it would keep her busy while I traveled. After six months of living off what seemed like an endless supply of soup and potatoes offset by beans and rice, we saved enough to make a sizeable down payment on our first brick-and-mortar purchase. An eight-acre property with a holiday let. It was a new beginning that suited us fine.

Chapter Nine

THREE YEARS AGO

— APRIL —

Garence was lounging in an overstuffed chaise chair in the living room, reading *The Namesake* by Jhumpa Lahiri, when the sound of tires driving over gravel broke the silence. He peered through the picture window. Through the web of tree branches, a black Aston Martin drove by.

"The McCartneys left Cosmos Place," he announced.

The holiday let was a barn conversion surrounded by sleeping hawthorn trees and located two acres away from the Leitner residence. The rental was ideal for families, with its three bedrooms, two bathrooms, and a large kitchen that opened to a living space with a gas fireplace. Although the barn was original to the property, the modern amenities were tastefully done and regal. Anyone would have chosen this building as their primary residence, but he and Sabina had opted for the eighteenth-century house, with all its quirks and charm.

Garence continued to read as he walked down the hallway toward the study where Sabina was hanging out. The energy coursing through her mind, body, and spirit was stimulated, and her cognizance expanded beyond this physical world. He watched her extend every muscle and rotate each joint in her body through a series of stretches that made her look as though she were a mythical being. She had shared her practice with him numerous times, and her numerology beliefs. This was a time for reflection, stretching, quieting the mind, and visualizing what they desired, along with saying "I am" affirmations. The inspirations they offered oneself quieted the mind through focus and gratitude.

He listened for her to recite the ones he favored. "I am light, an eternal being," "I am getting ready to get ready for what lies ahead," and "I am allowing things to unfold." The affirmations were the stitches to her wounds, and he was glad she'd found something to maintain her well-being. She breathed through her chest and intestines to release stagnant energy and then ended her session by utilizing her mind to harness her energy into a ball and imagined it between her hands. He would never forget the first time she had him do this. A warm, calming sensation fell over him, and he imagine his energy being blue with a white center. It pulsed between his hands like the pull of magnets and the vibrations that coursed through his body. The experience was the definition of awesome.

When she opened her eyes, he mouthed "sorry" for hollering across the house during her meditation, and he received a smile in forgiveness. He leaned against the opening for the pocket door. It was noon. The sunlight skipped over the study's angled ceiling like an elegant and transient dance between light and nimble shadows.

"Did you know," she started, "that Halloween is a celebration of energy moving forward from the physical to the metaphysical?"

"That's random. Another divine message?"

She laughed at her own peculiarity. "No. I was reading before my meditation and didn't want to forget to share it with you. Pagans believed Halloween was when the line between the living and the dead was the thinnest. Where all three dimensions, the lower world and Earth and the upper world, were open."

"I prefer to believe that there is no hell, but I find it interesting nonetheless."

"Yeah," she said, almost absentmindedly, absorbing all that she had learned. "Sorry, what did you say before?" she asked.

"The McCartneys have gone. I'm going to launder the linen from the Cosmos, mop and hoover the floors."

"I'll grab the Fairy Liquid and help," she said, rising.

"I don't think that will be necessary. In general, renters are neat anyway. If I get started now, we should be able to sleep in tomorrow."

"I love the way you think," she answered, giving him a wink. "We'll have the entire day to ourselves."

"There then, do you have anything in mind?" he asked, provocative.

She beckoned with her index finger. Garence stepped forward, she rolled onto her back, and he hiked up his worn and frayed jeans to straddle her hips.

He loved the way she looked at him. Those mesmerizing eyes focused on him as if he were from another dimension. When he arrived at her side, she placed her hands at his jaw, tapped his moles with her fingers, then drew him close. His mouth called for hers, and so she answered with a bite into his lower lip; he groaned.

"You are so sexy."

Flashes of electricity ran through him as she ran her fingertips over his smooth skin and close-trimmed body hair.

She looked at her digital wristwatch, then said it was 1:11.

"All right," he said.

"And we're in the phase of the new moon."

"Cool. Remind me what that all means again. A spiritual awakening, right?"

"No, that's 11:11. 11:11 is the most powerful pattern. It means that the Divine being is alive. The new moon and repeated 'ones' each symbolize new beginnings."

"That's right," he said, remembering her saying this before.

She traced the contours of his lower waist then unbuttoned his trousers. With their clothing removed, Sabina pulled Garence close. "I want a baby," she whispered, heated.

Garence remained silent, but his response was clear. He cupped her breasts and kissed them, and when he entered her, he wanted to groan from the tight grip he experienced. With each thrust, he conducted their arousal, and he was heightened further by her responses to him. Her brow furrowed whenever she looked at him and before she closed her eyes to enjoy the pleasure he imparted. She bit the corner of her lower lip before they parted, and her breathing became more laborious. He took his time in pleasuring her, caressing her smooth legs and repositioning them so that he reached a different angle while he rocked her firm until they were both satiated.

He lay beside Sabina, panting, ignoring his sore knees. He placed his hand behind his head, his body tense from the exercise. "You were saying?"

"Um," she laughed, "I think we were planning on having the morning to ourselves, for... I don't know?"

"Making babies."

She smirked in that cute oblivious way he liked. "Yeah. I guess."

Garence bit into her shoulder with tenderness. "Then I better clean the rental." He got up and walked to the door leading into the garden.

She took a moment to admire his backside as he put on his underwear. "Don't forget your clothes," she said, tossing the articles to him.

"The guests left. I don't need them."

"You're even hotter for wanting to do chores like that. I think I am going to assist you."

Sabina got to her feet, secretly grabbing her underwear, and walked over to him, still wearing a white sleeveless tunic.

"You *are* wearing knickers," Garence said.

"Must I?"

"My refractory period is not as tight as yours. Give me a few more minutes."

"That long? I guess." They lassoed each other's hips with their arms. He absorbed her gaze, which dared him to take her now.

"Do you think we'll be parents soon?"

He kissed her forehead. "It won't be for lack of trying, will it?"

"That's good to know."

Garence reflected upon what they were asking for. A child.

A child would change their lives. A bit. They were both as solid as a monolith, and they were already in synchronization as far as morals, values, and financial and spiritual matters were concerned. And a child would be an extension of their love for each other, and that new love would live on beyond their own lives.

She met his eyes. "I love you, Garence."

His heart burned and swelled. He would gladly fulfill this woman's every request and desire, even if that meant his rightful place in the home was akin to a caboose in the long queue of carriages.

"Now unclench those knickers," he ordered with a roguish smile, revealing his knowledge that Sabina had them all along.

Her face illuminated without a crack of a smile. She extended her arm and dropped her underpants in defiance.

"You saucy minx." Garence narrowed his eyes at her, then removed his underwear.

— END OF MAY —

Sabina found Garence on his lounge chair in the living room, sketching on a large pad of thick drawing paper; he swept the point of the drawing pencil over the surface in quick and deliberate motions inaudible to her ears.

There was always a writing tool within his grasp to write or draw. He used a shiny robust fountain pen to outline his agenda and record his daily experiences, while a sleek drawing pencil captured his surroundings in detailed landscapes or quick representations of the lodgings. Garence not only logged his travels, but he also exercised his hand at sketching characters and placed them in his depictions.

Sabina peeked over his shoulder and watched his imagination spill onto the paper.

A mature dragon with an expression that exuded an almost super-natural awareness or wonder, with four smaller dragons at her side, their cast-iron legs crouched and inclining their bodies forward to obtain the elder's exact viewpoint. A diminutive light reflected in its all-knowing eyes, but it was not in the frame of the picture.

"You've been drawing this clan a lot as of late," she said, leaning against his body.

Garence shrugged. "They keep popping into my head. I figured I should release them from my mind's captivity to see what became of them."

"I see one more. There were only four dragons before, right? Or did I forget one?"

"I think this dragon ate after midnight to spawn these creatures."

She rolled her eyes. "There's a marvel in this scene that captures my curiosity. Tell me about them."

Garence pulled the drawing pad toward him. He studied the creatures and harmonized the rendering with what he knew about them.

"Is the dragon wearing a collar around her ankle?" Sabina asked, incredulous. She wanted to be keen on the drawing and had hoped she was wrong. "What an odd thing to put on a fantastical beast."

"No!" Garence shook away the implication. "Dragons don't wear collars. That's an anklet."

A smile swept across Sabina's lips. Now she was digging this fantastic cosmic realm.

Garence caressed her arm. "You can't see it, but on the other side of the anklet is a token with a full lunar phase stamped on it."

"A time for closure," she muttered, absentminded.

He smiled. "Perhaps."

The longer she looked at the dragon, the more she recognized herself in it. The eyes; the connection with her last name; the fact that the brace-let was worn on the dragon's right wrist, the same wrist Sabina's vertical scar was on. There was no denying the similarities, but she had to ask.

"Am I the dragon?"

Garence went silent for a moment, then the answer seemed to slip out. "Yeah."

"You realized that just now, didn't you?" she asked, reading his mind.

She stared at the other dragons.

"Who's she supposed to be?" she asked, pointing to the first dragon and then the next.

Garence shrugged. "I don't know. I keep seeing her." Sabina shrugged as well, then Garence flipped a couple of pages back to where he had drawn them again. "Here, they're soaring over..."

"Torres del Paine!" she exclaimed, recognizing the commanding tower of a mountain she and Garence had visited. Sabina motioned for the book and admired the fine detail of the mountains and the mature dragon that sailed over the landscape; the brisk air brushed past her ears, and she got goose pimples.

"I love it! We are framing this baby."

She flipped the page on the metal coil and through the next two renderings, each completed with the same attention.

"Garence, you should write a book." She handed the drawing pad back to him.

"No way," he said disparagingly.

"Why not? You're the perfect person!"

"Is that so?"

"It is, and not everyone has traveled the globe countless times and experienced the cool things you have."

Garence raised an eyebrow.

"Release them from your mind's captivity," she declared, echoing his earlier words. "The world should be sprinkled with bits of your imagination. You could write them for our child," she whispered into his ear, her gentle breath arousing him.

Garence froze.

She chuckled then placed her arms around him.

"You're sure?"

She responded with a hardy squeeze. "Doctor says I'm five weeks."

"What? Why didn't you tell me? I would have gone with you."

She shrugged and dropped her head. "I guess I'm nervous, but I wanted to tell you when it was confirmed."

"Nervous? You don't get nervous," he said, leaning in for a better look at her face. Sabina was self-reliant and confident, so her nerves suggested something was off. "What is it?"

"I can't say what it is. I've got a weird feeling is all, just a pinch, but I've never felt it before."

Seeing her squirm over being pregnant amused him; he loved seeing new shades of her. "You're going to be a wonderful mother. I'm not worried."

He nuzzled her hair.

"Good, because you're my rock." She smiled. "You're going to be a papa."

He grabbed Sabina and spun her around. "We're going to be parents!"

Chapter Ten

PRESENT DAY

Garence had abandoned the study, with his pen and paper in hand, and the packing he still had to do. He sat on the floor in the nursery with his back against the wall. He slid his damaged fingers along its surface and closed his eyelids. He drifted in and out of the present as if he were blocking out the existence of the baby space. His head and his heart were already in chaos. He couldn't look at the nursery in its current state, joyful and expectant, and see where he was in the timeline of the letters that approached. For just one moment, he wanted to see it for what it had been at the beginning. What it stood for and the hope and love that filled it.

Transforming the second bedroom into a nursery was a labor of love. We sold the queen bed set, the striped curtains were removed from the windows, and sheets of plastic protected the floor. There were four trays with different colors of sample paint poured into them. Let me advise you, Sabina and I had a hard time acquiring these hues because the paint shop kept mixing up the digital entries in the paint machine, but we received the correct samples, and we were eager to color the nursery.

He got to his bare feet and grabbed a box from the hallway. He removed the blankets and sheets from the crib, then folded them and placed them in boxes with the clothes from the dresser. He completed his tasks in a robotic motion. Next was the changing station that doubled as a bookcase. A vase was perched on the windowsill above, streaked with water lines that represented not just levels of evaporation but everything that had disappeared until there was nothing left to sustain. No life. No love. No existence. Tulips wilted over the glass edge, once powder pink and full of celebration for the new baby. Garence's last joy. His last reason for living.

One by one, the stuffed pig, horse, duck, dogs, and goose went into a box, then fables, nursery rhymes, picture books, and large wooden puzzles in another. He placed the crib in his car first, then fit the boxes from the living room and nursery beside it. He couldn't see out of the back glass, but he drove to a nearby daycare anyway. They had agreed the day before to accept these items for donation. The sun shone in his eyes on his drive to the community center, where he would drop off the remaining items. A gentle spotlight whispering a goodbye to two stages of his life, that he would have to relive once he arrived home to the next batch of letters.

His lip trembled at the thought of returning home to read the next bundle of letters. He knew what moments would ensue in the following chapters of their life, and rereading the letters would mean reliving them. They were difficult to experience the first time around, but a second? He was fine with packing the baby's things because the excessive grief had numbed him beyond belief, but the letters would illustrate a sharp turn into a series of vile events that had destroyed Sabina. The letters would be hers. Page by page. Word by word. Her heartbreak.

When Garence returned, the changing table stared at him like an abandoned dog: cute, well-built, and cared for with no one to love it. With one hand on the inside of a shelf, he carried it outside and placed it by the bin.

Chapter Eleven

THREE YEARS AGO

— MAY —

Garence dipped a roller into the first tray of paint and plastered a single vertical line of twlight blue across the second bedroom. He repeated the process with three other paint samples: putti, in the neutral color wheel; a beige sand; and a creamy, cozy white. Garence joined Sabina on the floor on the opposite side of the room. They both sat and watched the paint dry into what would become the defining tone of the nursery.

The samples were distinctive, and any of them would have created a tranquil nursery. Sabina couldn't make up her mind.

She sighed. "I like them all."

Garence looked away from the samples. "Well, that's why they are the final four."

"That's not very helpful."

Without any imagination, Sabina stared at the plain wall where broad streaks of light filtered through the two bedroom windows like an inching fog. This was the room their child would grow up in then return to when they were an adult. These contemplations made her grin. Their child would be the next love of her life, so the color scheme had to be calm and as natural as the light coming through the windows. She came

back into the present and wondered what paint options he had been referring to a moment ago. There was a wall with four equally fabulous colors
and one decision to make.

"Well…"

Garence curbed a smile. "We could use all the colors and paint stripes."

"No."

He beamed. "We could paint the ceiling putti and the walls white."

Sabina rather liked that idea.

"Or paint a third of the wall, or the majority, one color and the
other part another color," he suggested, raising his hand with each measured level.

Sabina plastered these options in her mind's eye. "Like wainscot wall
molding?"

"Precisely."

Sabina nodded with mild interest, although the idea grew on her the
more she considered it.

"Or we could paint blocks on the wall. Or a themed mural of some sort."

Her nose crinkled as she chewed on her options a moment longer.
These were fine ideas, but not all of them were right for their nursery.

"Well, I must say that the right person is in charge of this project."
She gave Garence a wink, grateful he was artistic in more ways than
one. "All right." She clapped her hands and then rubbed them together
as if getting ready to make a big move on a board game. "I could work
with that. We want a gender-neutral color scheme; thankfully both of
us think of blue as gender-neutral, so we can tick that box off. I like
the way the colors are drying, which is great, but it doesn't help narrow
down our choices." She looked over at Garence and wondered if he had
any contributions.

"I agree with your rationale thus far," he said, raising his eyebrows.

"Okay. We have a period home that we love for its age and all the
quirks that come with it, so we should keep that in mind. Let's avoid the
abstract techniques and keep the color combinations simplistic."

She rested her head against the wall. Her eyes glided back and forth as she imagined the various color combos. Neutral yet distinctive. Effortless and pure like her connection to Garence and their child.

"I like the white walls with the putti ceiling best," she said with finality.

"Brilliant! Let's get to work."

While Sabina taped the trim and the baseboards, Garence taped off the ceiling to paint it. They worked all afternoon and, proud of the end result, ate their next meal in the nursery.

"This is going to pair up nicely with that crib you saw on the high street."

Sabina smiled. "I had the same thought."

Garence hadn't a clue as to the exact time of day, but it was autumn and the sun was a quarter from the western horizon. "I bet that shop is still open. I could have it built before bedtime."

Her excitement demonstrated that she was caught by his cast.

"Let's go," he said.

It turned out that the lead-windowed shop with the perfect nursery furniture held bank hours and it was closed by the time they arrived, but when their doors opened for business, Garence purchased the crib and had it assembled within ninety minutes. With the addition of a rustic standing lamp resembling a tree branch and an oversized armchair in the line of sunlight, the nursery was coming into fruition.

"Run, Garence! Run dammit!"

Sabina thought she must have looked hilarious shouting from the bleachers with her fist pounding her thigh. Garence sped across the local rugby pitch, neck veins throbbing and adrenaline surging. He looked over at her but made no other response. He was the inside-center with the group of guys who got together to play. It had rained overnight, and there was hardly a speck of the blue or yellow on his jersey that wasn't covered in mud.

She watched him block an opponent, so that a teammate rushed forward with the ball while the opponent moved in and missed, kicking nothing but air. Another player rushed from behind and thrust Garence across a patch of grass. The wind was knocked out of him. Sabina dipped her chin, but she couldn't resist watching his next move. Before he got onto his feet, two players collided on top of him. Sabina winced and covered her eyes, swearing she wouldn't watch another second. She peered through her fingers.

Normally, she didn't experience sympathy pain for Garence because his team tended to be far better than their opponents, but today's opposing side bore an advanced, aggressive skill set. Their footwork was as precise as a laser, and their energy bordered alongside brutality.

A little boy from down the bench cheered, "Go, Dad!" as his eyes followed one person in particular: Wick, number 9. His chubby cheeks beamed with pride for this man, who was presumably his father, and who was giving Garence a harsh lesson in what a grueling game felt like. The boy's joy was mirrored on her face, but for a different reason.

She imagined what their child's upbringing would be like. She and Garence would enroll them in sports and music lessons, or whatever they wanted. She wondered if they would be inspired to follow in their father's footsteps and participate in artistry or rugby. Would she be exposed to another loved one being whomped to the ground? Or perhaps she would be saved from these intense moments and they would be drawn to the arts, business, science, or a trade. Her gut told her that their child would be athletic with dollops of everything else. Yes, even as she watched Garence maneuver between two players for the ball, Sabina was preparing herself for more extreme sideline moments like this one.

She winced again, only this time it was a cramp.

An unusual ache tugged at her.

She reached for her lower back, and a wet sensation crept between her legs.

Her heart raced.

Her eyes glazed over as her mind flew back to the visit with the obstetrician a few days ago when the small brown droplets had appeared on her knickers, and the physician had said spotting was natural, even at seven weeks. "Just a bit of old blood. There is nothing to worry about."

Fear emitted from her pores. She blinked.

Distinct liquid left her body.

This was not just a bit of old blood. She feared for her child. She was already frozen stiff, but the next cramp hurled her over.

A small cry expelled her mouth, and she caught the attention of a short, middle-aged Irish woman who was already dashing to her side.

"Are you all right, dear?" The pale face before her answered her question.

Sabina leaned into her, shaking her head with her lips spread wide and tight as her chin trembled.

The woman didn't have her mobile phone on her person, but her husband did. She hollered over her shoulder for him to call an ambulance. Several other concerned spectators, team wives, and family blazed toward Sabina. A few seconds later, a crescendo of footsteps pounded the stands as Garence advanced.

Chapter Twelve

THREE YEARS AGO

Dr. Han Yi, Sabina's obstetrician, sat on a rolling stool, looking up at the solemn couple sitting on the tissue-covered examination table. At thirty-nine, she was the same age as Garence and five years older than Sabina. She was not in the habit of wearing her medical coat and came across as personable, someone whom other mothers related to, dressed in white capris and a black button-down blouse, her long dark bob flipped over her right ear.

"As much as you do not want to hear this, Sabina, miscarriages are very common."

Her dialect gave away that she had been raised in Gloucestershire county. Her warm and consoling hand held Sabina's spiritless one, and she peered into the face that radiated self-blame for the inability to safeguard her unborn child.

"Fifteen to twenty percent of miscarriages occur in the first trimester. You don't have any immune disorders, and your lifestyle isn't an issue. You did not cause this miscarriage, nor did you know this was going to transpire."

A few seconds passed as the couple absorbed what was said. Garence squeezed Sabina's hands.

"Sometimes they occur before the mother even knows she is pregnant. Regardless of the knowledge, miscarrying is a natural process, and Garence and I will support you every step of the way. I mean it. I am going to call you, and I want you to call me. Any reason at all. In fact, may I see your phone?"

Garence retrieved it and handed it to the doctor.

"All right. Seeing as I indirectly have your permission, I'm going to add my personal number to your contacts."

She glanced up at the pair and received semi-humored affirmation before proceeding.

"There will be some bleeding over the next few days, but it will decrease. You shouldn't work during this time."

"I'll take a week off. It's fine."

"Good. Let me know if the bleeding or cramping increases. If there is an odor or anything else."

Sabina nodded. She appeared calm but bathed in disbelief. Her nose was red from frequent blowing, and her body hung like a storm-drenched daisy. But then, somehow, a spark of expectancy reflected through her swollen crimson eyes.

"Was it a boy or a girl?"

"It was too soon to determine."

She and Garence hadn't finalized their list of names, but now they wouldn't have to. It was too unremarkable for words. As quick as the baby had entered their lives, it was gone. Without having met their family. Without a name. The child had left this world without ever feeling the warmth of their arms.

Sabina's head slumped against Garence's chest, and he draped his left arm around her body and pressed her against him. He closed his hand tight around hers, then he kissed the top of her head. He wished he could scoop her into his arms, where they would be transported home to console each other in private. He mourned for their child, but he knew it was nothing compared to what Sabina was going through. She had experienced the physical, psychological, and emotional entrance of this being into her life and its departure. He wanted nothing more than to comfort her because that was his role. He was her husband. Her best friend and lover. He had chosen this position not knowing or caring—not fathoming—what the future held for them, but the truth was that he was useless. There was nothing he could do or say to make his other half feel even the slightest bit better.

Was he failing her?

No, and nothing would erase what happened today, but that didn't mean he wouldn't try. If he could have switched places with her so that he was going through this and not Sabina, then he would have done it. And then he remembered there was still a few more days of bleeding to pass.

He cringed, wiping away his tears.

Dr. Yi watched the couple embrace and transform each other as she scrutinized her patient. Sabina had a history of mental illness, so she was naturally concerned for her overall health. Sabina was strong, and her husband provided her with solid support, so there was no cause for concern there. The only concerning thing was the possibility of a depression relapse. She scribbled a note to herself on a piece of paper to call on her in one week—to be certain that she was coping. It was too easy to get caught up with everyday tasks and the sporadic emergencies that made even the most experienced staff member tumble helter-skelter.

She placed one hand over the couple's collapsed hands and the other hand over Sabina's, and she squeezed both of them. Her gaze was fixed onto Sabina. There was hope and possibility in their future.

"You know yourself and your body very well. I want you to know that the odds are in your favor. Ninety-eight percent of second pregnancies are carried to full term. I do not see any reason why you cannot be one of those women."

There was something within Dr. Yi's tone or her choice of words. Perhaps it was the death grip on her hands that rang the bell of hope with a message to not give up.

Sabina's eyes fluttered as she looked away, and tears streamed down her cheeks. She felt an emptiness she had not known before. It wasn't the same grief she had experienced when Rosalinda died, but it was some sort of hollowness that only her child could fill. *I will survive this*, she thought to herself. *I am love. I am light. I am getting ready to get ready. I can do this.*

Her body language shifted, but she continued to stare at the polished floor. "How long before we can attempt to conceive?"

"As early as two weeks and not sooner, but I would prefer you to wait a full cycle. We need to allow time for the cervix to close."

Garence rubbed her arm when she sniffed and wiped her nose with a tissue. In two to four weeks, the miscarriage would have run its course, and her body would be ready to move on. Unbelievable.

She looked up at him. He wanted a family as much as she did, and in the midst of grief and his own futility, Garence remained steady. If all she wanted was for him to be her rock and try again in the future, then she needn't say anything.

Chapter Thirteen

THREE YEARS AGO

— JUNE —

Sabina and Garence were on top of their unruffled bedsheets as he thrust himself inside her with minimal effort. His eyes told her he wasn't present, and she didn't like having sex with Garence's feeble clone. In fact, it was starting to bother her. She tried to think of what was missing, but she repositioned herself underneath him instead. All the while Garence kept pumping away like the weakest dog in the race.

He slipped out of her then lay beside her.

It was their first time at trying to conceive since the miscarriage, and it was also the first time he had shown so little interest in pleasuring her.

"Is there something I can do to keep you in the mood?" she asked.

"No. You're fine. Perfect, in fact."

They lay in silence for several minutes, and she felt inadequate. They had used to make love almost every day, but since the miscarriage, they had only done it a handful of times.

"Do you still find me attractive?"

"What? Of course I do." His head seemed to sink into the mattress from the weight of the situation. "I promise. I'll always find you attractive."

She nodded in disbelief. "Enough to still wanna fuck me?"

"Of course I do."

She leaned against his chest. "Then what's wrong?"

"Nothing. I'm... preoccupied."

She'd called it. He wasn't present, and she felt for him. His bare body against hers was a nice sensation. Then even better when he rubbed the side of her breasts. *He hasn't done that in some time*, she thought, and she forgot about how awful she felt. "You'll feel better later on?" she asked, grinning.

"Maybe," he said, in the same tone as the guy whose house you're leaving after having sex with says, "Let's do that again soon."

She lay back down and turned her head away from him, trying for the first time in her life to figure out what was going through his head.

— TWO WEEKS LATER —

Garence, mi amor,

Before we go into full-on baby mode, I wanted to write to you, as your wife, and not the baby-obsessed person that sometimes possesses me. It's been a while since we've made love. Actual, sensual, and passionate love as opposed to the procreation sex we've been having ("I am ovulating! Get in here"). It isn't the same going through the motions. Maybe I'm sending you the wrong signals. I still enjoy this part of the baby-making process. A lot. And I'm tired of not enjoying it. That's not how we operate. I fell in love with you, and I need to feel the sparks that transpire between us or I'm not alive. I am putting us back on track, so don't hold back. Ever.

I want every inch of you.

Always,
Sabina

Sabina,

After we lost Sol, our bright burning sun and child, and held a ceremony on Gaztelugatxe, I was afraid of us trying for another baby. I saw how fragile this tiny life was and how much you went through after the miscarriage... I was terrified. I was scared to death I would hurt you by entering your body and even more during sex. I feared my chromosomes weren't compatible with yours and that I was the reason for the destruction of our child and your suffering. I was so scared, yet I needed you badly. I went through the motions. I did it because I wanted to enable the possibility of having a child with you, but I didn't want to play a part in your heartache again. You deserve one hundred percent of me, and I wasn't giving it to you. I'm so sorry. As selfish as it makes me to think this, but I have to be honest with you, I'd rather have you whole than see you broken after another miscarriage. I will promise you this, whether you want to keep trying for children or not, I will always keep doing my part. I promise to continue to honor and love you. You are my true north. My light. Nothing could ever change that.

Your humble husband,
Garence

Sabina's entire body swirled in a numbing buzzed sensation, and she tossed her limp hand onto Garence's heaving chest. They lay on their bed, surrounded by disheveled white sheets, their bodies lathered in perspiration.

"I've missed that," said Garence.

"Me too. I am not going to move for the next thirty minutes, at least."

He caught a glimpse of her raising her eyebrows, and the corner of his mouth turned up.

Garence turned onto his side. Euro pillows and bed pillows had been thrown all over the room except for the one beneath Sabina's buttocks to allow for greater cervix stimulation. "We're not ever going back to that other kind of sex."

She removed the pillow and placed it under her head. "Agreed. So not worth it," she declared between pants.

"It's probably the reason why we're not pregnant yet."

She laughed. "Probably." She rolled onto her side to face him. "At least with this route, we'll kick erogenous goals every time."

"The league cup would be nice too."

Sabina understood what he meant. The league cup would be a baby. "Of course, but you are my number one. Even if we don't become parents… I have nothing without you."

He dropped his gaze. "I love you."

"*Te amor.*" She nuzzled his nose because she knew he liked it. "Is that what you wanted to know?"

"You are a mind reader."

"Thankfully, just yours."

"I love that you had named our babe Sol."

"Our sun." Then she buried her forehead in his shoulder and wished for sunny days.

Chapter Fourteen

THREE YEARS AGO

— MID-SEPTEMBER —

"The early nineteenth-century English Victorian pub table, or, rather, the changing table, correct?" asked Nina, the antiquity appraiser. A sly grin passed over her thin, tinted lips as she stood behind the counter, finalizing the Leitners' bid. Her heart-shaped face reflected the silvery-white glow from the monitor.

"That and the wardrobe from a century before," said Garence. "You said it would be shipped by freight in a fortnight."

"That's correct. And it won't be at your expense since you're purchasing two of their last items." Astonished, she shook her head, and her fifties-inspired glasses slid down the narrow bridge of her nose. "Your offer was gutsy. I'm pleased it was accepted." She pushed the frames up with her fingertips.

Sabina beamed at Garence.

The old furnishings were expected to coexist with the new crib stained in the same medium shade. Seeing as the wardrobe and table would outlive their position in the house, Garence and Sabina had opted to make an investment in antiques rather than children's furniture. The Queen Anne wardrobe dated back to 1732 and was the quintessence of sensibility and minimalism with its grand height and dome topping the double doors and two drawers. The 1852 Victorian table boasted medieval influences and authentic wear, scrapes, dents and gashes on all edges that made it impossible not to imagine pints of beer and bar meals being slammed onto its surface for dozens of decades.

"I appreciate you calling them to seal the deal. You've sent Sabina over the moon."

Sabina's smile displayed with pride.

"How far along are you?" asked Nina, not seeing any obvious physical signs to guide her guess.

"Ten weeks."

"Too precious!" Nina gushed. "Is this your first child?"

Sabina's smile froze, but her alarmed eyes told a different story. She released a straight "No."

The couple had promised to never cover up the loss of their first child, so Garence spoke first. "We miscarried before—no, it's okay! You couldn't have known. We named the baby Sol because he or she was the center of our universe, our celestial light," he added, "and we're very anxious to meet this little one."

Nina removed her glasses. "I am sorry to hear about Sol. Would you permit me to extend my sincerest congratulations on your upcoming pregnancy?"

"Of course. Thank you!" said Sabina.

Nina grinned; their enthusiasm melted her countenance like Irish butter over hot toast. "I am very happy for you both. Congratulations. Well, everything is settled. I'll call you if there any changes."

Garence and Sabina were all smiles when they exited the shop.

"The nursery is going to look amazing," she said.

"That it is. Perfect with the paint job we did so well with." Garence looked at his wristwatch.

"Time to fly out?" she asked.

"I should make my way to the station. I wish you were joining me. Victoria is beautiful."

She crinkled her nose. "As lovely as a fourteen-hour flight sounds, I want to stay home. Let's go in the spring sometime when everything is in bloom and we can walk outside. Besides, I need some girl time." She placed a hand over her stomach.

"You don't know we're having a girl. Can you read her mind as well?"

"No, I have an inkling we're going to have all girls."

He chuckled. "Wow. Teenaged years are gonna be fun. Ugh! I don't want to leave you. Are you sure you don't want to change your mind? You've never been to Canada."

"Still passing."

"Fine."

"If you were going to Auckland, New Zealand, you might have had me."

"I would love to live in Auckland. Maybe I'll find you there someday."

"Perhaps," she said, finishing with a kiss.

"I'll see you in eight days. I'll have my phone on silent throughout the duration of the conference, but I'll check in often."

They kissed each other goodbye, and Sabina watched him walk across the road then down toward where his car was parked. She entered a boutique shop where she purchased a giraffe jumper with brown velvet ossicones, or horns, attached to the hoodie. When she exited the honey-colored stone shop, she was struck with a sharp cramp. She stood cemented beneath one of the long white dome awnings that hung over the display windows, where faceless mannequins in children's clothing gawked at her.

It was happening. The bloody "natural process." She was sure of it.

She placed a protective hand over her stomach.

Luna!

This couldn't be happening again. She had been so careful and intentional. She hadn't lifted anything heavier than a bottle of milk from their local milkround or performed any of the more strenuous chores around the house or the rental. She had focused her thoughts on delivering a healthy baby to full term, and she had kept that image so close to her heart that she was obsessed with the idea.

Sabina grew scared, and her heartbeat raced like that of a hunted rabbit. She and the babe were in danger.

She wanted to scream, but the thought of distressing herself and harming the baby forced her to remain calm. There was no use becoming hysterical.

She took a deep breath, her heart beating erratically.

Her mind was troubled by the imminent danger her child was in. She raised a hand to her temple to block the sun, looking left and right. She closed her eyes. Where was she? Dr. Yi's office had to be close. The nearest street sign read Moore Street, and that meant the clinic was a few minutes away.

Should she drive?

No, she had walked over from the library after she and Garence had returned several books, so her car was not nearby. She had to make her way to the office safely and right this minute! There was still time to save the baby.

Her chest lifted, and her muscles prepared to burst into a run, but she stopped herself. Running was out of the question. She couldn't risk that kind of exertion.

With every millisecond that passed, her anxieties heightened, and her imagination convinced her she was contributing to the miscarriage. Was she helping gravity in its part in this by standing here? Then she started to say affirmations.

"I can do this. I am going to take care of you."

She looked around again as if she were searching for a magic portal to transport her to Dr. Yi. She had a few seconds to pull up the office's number on her phone before she acknowledged the growing wet sensation.

A terrible cramp launched, and she froze.

She was wasting valuable time.

She peered into the window of the baby clothing shop. The counter was empty. The clerk must have gone to the back of the store.

Armed with the experience of having miscarried and the knowledge of what her body was doing, Sabina's imagination was taking flight—or perhaps it wasn't just her imagination? Her cervix was dilating at an alarming rate. The bleeding was heavier than the last time, and it felt fleshy.

The cramping worsened.

She banged on the glass with more than a firm tap. No one heard her.

Sabina looked to her right where there were more shops, but nobody was outside.

She looked left. There was a man walking along the double line toward her general direction.

In fact, it looked as though he were heading straight for her, and even though it wasn't true, she was relieved. He was almost as tall as Garence, and he had short black hair, a dark complexion, and a presence that calmed her anxieties.

Sabina was too scared to cry out for his attention, so she raised a hand and waved it without seeming too unstable. He looked at her, and she saw the look of unfamiliarity blemish his face. She panicked. A flame of fury sparked within her when she feared he would keep on walking or cross the street to avoid her.

Dammit, I need your help! she screamed inwardly.

She released the breath she had been holding, then made eye contact. She came out of the gate strong but finished enfeebled. "I think I'm losing my baby. I need your help."

The man's expression morphed into concern, and her emergency spread into his consciousness.

He reached for his phone and answered with a Bengali accent. "Of course, I'll call an…"

Sabina already had the call connected on her phone and, unable to hold herself together, shoved the phone into his hand. "Tell Dr. Yi's office that we're two blocks away."

She was so close to the office, but the fear of losing her child made the distance expand exponentially.

Hyperventilation encroached, and she was desperate to keep her tears at bay.

She heard him tell someone, likely the receptionist, that he was bringing in a pregnant woman; Sabina uttered her name. The call ended, and the man slipped the phone inside her shoulder bag for safe keeping. If events happened for a reason, then people were placed in one's path for a reason as well; that was one small relief. She closed her eyes and was thankful for at least that.

She grabbed his arm and started to walk down the row. "I need you to guide me there, please," she said, pointing her feeble hand straight ahead.

There was a strange and frightening sense that someone was squeezing the baby out of her, and this time, she cried out.

Her complexion was bloodless, for it all seemed to be seeping through her trousers.

Sabina's knees shook. She was swept into his arms, then carried the entire distance to the clinic. Her body was curled into his chest, so that she almost didn't feel any of his long strides down the narrow road as he avoided passersby.

A bolt of pain struck Sabina's abdomen and her lower back as they reached the building's main entrance doors.

Dr. Yi was outside, searching for Sabina, with a wheelchair on hand. Once Sabina was placed into the chair, she was sped into an examination room. Fifteen minutes later, blood was already drawn, Garence had arrived, and everyone was waiting to learn how Sabina's pregnancy hormone levels looked. Sabina lay on a gurney in a hospital gown, half shaken, while the doctor prepared for a transvaginal ultrasound. She held up the long handle dressed in a clear, gelled sleeve and topped it with lubricant.

"This is the probe. I'm going to hand this to you, and I'd like you to insert it into your vagina and let me know when you are ready for me to take over."

Sabina did as she was instructed, then allowed the doctor control.

Whilst reviewing the ultrasound, Dr. Yi explained to Garence and Sabina what they were viewing. "Do you see this? Your cervix is already dilated. It looks to be about one centimeter… That's quite a bit. I'm so sorry, but I cannot save your baby."

Sabina sobbed.

Garence held her while staring at the monitor as if he couldn't believe the person he was looking at would not survive.

"You have options," said Dr. Yi.

Garence and Sabina had the exact same awful interpretation, and their eyes widened. How did they have options in aiding the loss of their child?

Dr. Yi was cautious yet concise. "You can allow the miscarriage to take its course naturally, which may take a few days. I can prescribe something that will progress the process and cause the uterine to contract, or we can remove the fetus with a suction curettage. The choice is yours."

Sabina fell silent for a minute that seemed to stretch into eternity. This was happening. How was it possible that this miscarriage had happened so much quicker and more painfully than the first one, even allowing them to have options?

She looked at Garence for a moment, and without saying a word, her expression said she was losing their baby. Her body burned with shame. She closed her eyes and tears spilled.

She had failed yet another child.

Now she had to choose how to remove him or her from her womb. *How can I even make such a choice?* she wondered, covering her face.

She gagged.

It was like trying to decide how best to alleviate her aggravation. None of the "options" would ever alleviate her burden. Nothing would ever bring either of her babies back.

She heard the doctor's voice in her head repeat *we cannot save this baby.* Sabina shook her head, but she kept hearing it. She was in no state to make such a decision. *Why do I have a choice? Am I supposed to be grateful?* No, she couldn't do this again. It was maddening.

She looked up at Garence as if to ask him for guidance, but instead, she said, "I don't want to be awake…"

Garence nodded, and she knew he wouldn't want her to go on another minute with the knowledge of what was out of her control. The thought of allowing her to carry on through the next few days of a failed pregnancy was no longer on the table.

Dr. Yi informed her staff that the dilation and curettage would be performed with suction and IV sedation.

"We've done our due diligence in validating that your organs are normal and that neither of your chromosomes possesses any abnormalities. Studies have shown that chances for success increase dramatically with every attempt."

"You said that last time." Sabina shook her head as if to apologize, but she didn't. *I am a survivor*, she internalized. *But my babies aren't.* "This shouldn't be happening."

No! I will be fine. Someday, I will be fine.

In the doctor's attempt to console her, she failed to realize the shadier side of what she was saying. Sabina's chances would increase as long as her failures did. The slimmest possibility of another miscarriage was sickening.

"Sabina, it's not at all as it seems. You're seeing the glass as half-empty."

"That was before two of my children died in my body, wasn't it?"

"You're forgetting the fact that you carried further this time around."

As a rule, Sabina wasn't one to dwell on the negative, but this moment was a challenge to climb even for her. She hadn't realized it until Dr. Yi had said it, but she had carried two weeks longer than before. She grabbed that hope as if it were a cane, then forced a weak smile.

Dr. Yi heard the smidgeon of pessimism underlining Sabina's voice. The cogs of her heart turned for Sabina whilst she attempted to read her thoughts, but she came up with nothing.

Sabina was emotionally and physically exhausted, and she hadn't the strength to say anything other than "I know the drill."

Chapter Fifteen

PRESENT DAY

You and I—

Garence winced. He didn't like to talk about Sabina as if she were right beside him; it was too painful. *Strange*, he thought, *it was once the opposite.* Perhaps it was the fact that he had come to terms with her absence.

> *Sabina and I always traveled the same path hand in hand. That magical connection between us was as strong as tungsten, even over troubled water. Life could be brilliant one moment, a complete wreck the next, and then the insanity cycled back. It's hard to watch someone you love go through heartbreak, particularly a heartache you share, yet possess no clue as to what the other person is going through. The second miscarriage was harder than the first. She took a week off from work, and I canceled my travel plans, and we pulled from our savings account like we had last time. We grieved together, but the faith we shared that we would someday have a child, and our love for each other, kept us going.*
>
> *Because of this, we were perfect.*

We believed our chances of sustaining a pregnancy toward full gestation were increasing, and, even though we had faced significant hardships, the ups and downs we faced together only made us stronger. Sabina was so in tune with her body that she noticed the slightest differences from the previous pregnancies and believed that our chances were the best they could ever be. There was no better person to know this, so I believed her.

After the second miscarriage, it was five weeks before Sabina's period returned, and she was eager for another go, like before, then before we knew it, we were pregnant.

One afternoon, we were taking advantage of the sunlight where the bubbly clouds danced their way around the warm rays as if they were another couple on the ballroom floor. I suppose it would be more accurate to say it was partly sunny, but that leaves the impression the day was dreary when it was not. Sabina and I were lying on the dormant grass, holding hands by the hawthorn trees. We watched the clouds drift over us and spoke of the images we saw in them. It was humorous yet insightful to learn what the other saw. For me, it felt like a portal into her subconscious, a place I was never able to read or predict. I saw people, their faces, and innate objects that held sentimental meaning, whilst Sabina saw rattles and baby animals. I wondered, and still wonder, if her thoughts were ever on anything else during that time. It was lovely to see this shade of vibrancy emitting from her.

We were laughing at a cloud that resembled a bumblebee whizzing toward a cub. Her laughter made me smile broader than my mouth was capable of doing, and then she grew silent.

You and I know that I couldn't read Sabina's mind like she could mine, but I knew she was thinking of the pregnancy and whether we would make it to a successful delivery. Her eyes were fixed in a reflective trance, and her skin mirrored the clouds above. Then she said out loud that her period was late. I was afraid to say anything, so I clenched her hand, but I couldn't allow another moment to pass without a greater acknowledgment, so I kissed her. With a bonny smile, she said, "I have a good feeling about this one. I've been focusing on our desire to have a family and sending it out into the universe." To which I admitted, "I've been doing the same," and squeezed her hand again.

She not only felt the life growing within her, but she also sensed a driving force in her core that told her she was connecting to a greater purpose. In her mind, that meant becoming a mother. She endured the typical symptoms of pregnancy, swollen and tender breasts and nipples, mild nausea, and frequent trips to the loo, but the majority of her experience was pleasant. The pregnancy heightened her senses, and she said everything tasted better—so much so that she demanded I take the food away at certain portions because she refused to turn herself into a garbage disposal. As her body prepared for the pregnancy, more progesterone was created, and, in her case, resulted in more restful sleep and not the opposite as Dr. Yi had warned us about. The universe seemed to send outward signs she was on the right path. Even children and animals flocked to her as if she were an enchanting princess singing in a forest.

Sabina often shared her dreams with me, especially when they were about the baby. She would wake up with a broad grin, her fresh face framed by her perfect mess of disheveled hair, skin glowing like the moon, her eyes as clear as a crystal ball. She'd say that my presence in her dreams was not known to her, not at first. She couldn't explain any further why I wasn't present, but dreams are funny like that, aren't they? She said it was like the world they inhabited was for her and the baby, but then, sometime later, I joined them. Sometimes I wondered what that meant, my not being in my family's life. Were we separated? Did I die? No, she said I joined them at a later time.

Sabina had experienced so much grief in her life; perhaps she was dreaming of a life where she had reconciled with it? I tried not to dwell on the somber fact that I wasn't in those dreams, even if it was hurtful, because I loved seeing her ecstatic about what she had seen.

But now I understand what she was seeing.

She always had a connection with the universe, and she had such unbelievable intuition. There was no way she was from this world.

She was a spirit.

Damn, I was lucky.

He cleared his throat.

Sabina said she would carry to full term. I wouldn't ever dare doubt her, and she was proving to be correct. The days puddled into pools that became weeks and the weeks cascaded into months. We dove into our shared faith that we would deliver a child, and we swam in our joy as the pregnancy progressed.

All the way to the finish, Sabina was always right, even if I can't see the very end yet.

PART TWO
CORPOREAL

Chapter Sixteen

TWO YEARS AGO

— MARCH —

The logs in the fireplace cracked as combustion spewed embers up the chimney while a hint of eucalyptus fragranced the living room. Garence sat on the sofa while Sabina lay with her feet on his lap. It was a quarter past three. A coffee table constructed out of three-inch-thick reclaimed floorboards from a ruinous building near Loch Lomond sat before them, and plates with half-eaten shepherd's pie sat on it, alongside glass vases with floating candles and cranberries. Sabina had simmered hot chocolate on the hob earlier, and now she had the opportunity to take her first sip. With the smallest hairline of a chocolate mustache, she leaned back, then placed her hand under her stomach.

"I know it's too soon to feel our baby girl move and kick, but she's so quiet," said Sabina.

"Probably listening to you talk. I know I would love to experience life through you." Garence placed his broad hand over her small belly.

"Perhaps." She caressed her stomach. "She is going to be such a good baby. I can't imagine her being fussy. A perfect lady. Thoughtful and adventurous like you. Open-minded. She'll have your wavy hair and talent too."

Sabina was one to appreciate the inside of a person above the physical traits. Since she had those qualities ticked off, he continued to add to the list. "She has your full smile, your eyes, and your spirit."

Sabina displayed her pearly whites. Her gaze drifted through the window over Garence's shoulder and into the distant snowy countryside; a rabbit scurried out of their property whilst a deer strode out of the trees some four hectares away.

"We should finalize our list of names," he said, not liking the idea of their not having one. They had come so close to picking one out many times, then they'd decide they had time.

"I know… I do have an overwhelming liking toward one…"

With his favorite name in mind, he asked, "Which?"

"The same one you have chosen, Estrella."

The hairs on his neck should have stood on end at her inextricable ability to read his mind, but they didn't. He was used to Sabina interpreting him, and he wasn't surprised that they'd both picked Star for a name.

"I can't wait until the day we can bring her home." Sabina bit her lip.

Garence pressed his thumbs into the base of her foot and rubbed it. "Are you nervous?"

"Mm… A little, but not really. I am more anxious to meet her. It's unreal. I'm so damn tired of being pregnant, but it's going to be worth it." She rubbed her stomach and grinned at their unborn child.

"Has it been?" he asked.

She gazed into his eyes, where the bittersweet memories burned. He wondered if their heartache and her suffering would amount to anything.

"Yes."

"Can you believe we only met a little over three years ago?"

"That is so bizarre!" she said with a laugh.

"I know."

"A lot has happened, I will admit that. Most of it was wonderful, but I am grateful that every second of it has been spent with you by my side. Oh yeah, right there."

Garence's hands had moved from her feet to her ankles.

His fingers were like kisses on her skin as they soothed her aching muscles. She rested her head on the arm of the sofa and closed her eyes. "At the end of the day, we will always have each other."

Three days later, Garence held the door open for Sabina as they strolled through Dr. Yi's office for their first appointment in the third trimester. The delicate aroma of cranberries with a hint of mandarin oranges filled the air. Garence knew this was the work of nurse Maureen. The Irish woman valued the scents of the seasons as he did. The office was almost like a second home to them, having frequented it so often, and Garence was glad of this. They were familiar with the staff, and so he greeted them. He and Sabina received bright eyes, genuine smiles, and pleasantries.

Garence stood beside Sabina as she rested on the examination table with two pillows beneath her back and neck. The staff talked with Sabina whilst her vitals were checked.

They were spot-on.

Garence released a sigh of relief, the first box ticked off.

The nerves in his stomach spiraled into each other. He cleared his throat and took a deep breath.

Why was he so nervous?

Perhaps it had something to do with overstepping every gestational period they'd encountered. He feared his happiness was too good to be true and would end up rooted from his very soul, like the other occasions.

He observed Dr. Yi move the wand over Sabina's gelled belly as she located the baby. She stared at the mute monitor positioned for her eyes. She pursed her lips, and her skin became taut as fear stripped away her hopefulness. Her attempt to maintain a neutral demeanor was mostly a success, but Garence stretched his neck to capture a glimpse of what the obstetrician was too eager not to share with them.

She noticed his slight movement and moved the wand away, and the baby was gone.

Dr. Yi turned her body around and looked at Maureen, her all too knowing nurse. In the unnatural silence, they exchanged concerns and instructions before they completed their wordless conversation with a nod.

Spine-wrenching dread crippled Garence.

The obstetrician turned to them and forced a small unnatural smile. Seconds had passed, but he could tell she was wrestling with her method of delivery. The silence in the room was deafening, unbearable, and then it hit him.

There was no heartbeat.

He watched Dr. Yi look intently at the monitor. Her eyes went stir-crazy as they searched for the slightest movement. Once he saw her lips tighten and her brow furrow, his eyes darted for Sabina. Any second now, the sunny mother-to-be would notice the approaching storm, and her raw wounds would be slashed open again.

Whether she felt the mood in the room shift for the worse or she read their body language, Sabina looked up at Garence and found that, for once, he was a step ahead of her.

The horror in her eyes tore him apart, and he couldn't prevent the tears from welling up.

He squeezed her hand.

He watched the staff move urgently without erupting a single warning sound, oblivious that their hush was the alarm.

"What's wrong?" Sabina asked.

Dr. Yi stared at the blank monitor, her face as still as the babe's heart inside Sabina's womb.

"What…" She strained to lift her upper body off the bed. "What aren't you saying?" she demanded with what Garence knew was the last of her strength.

He was already eyeing her when she looked at him, her terror mirroring his own.

Dr. Yi watched this exchange and wondered how the most deserving couple was so unlucky in delivering a child to full term. She didn't say the words out loud, at least not yet.

The doctor cleared her throat. She willed her tears to dry as quickly as possible. Sabina's body would go into delivery soon, but she couldn't let the Leitners go home with this news. She should allow the natural birth to develop, but she couldn't. Not this time. Dr. Yi wiped her nose with the back of her hand. Thank goodness Maureen understood her unspoken instructions.

She walked to the head of the bed and pushed Sabina into a room around the corner. "I'm taking you to the surgery theatre."

Without calling any attention to herself, Nurse Maureen moved in and out of the operating room whilst preparing for the obstetrician's mute plan to proceed with an unexpected cesarean.

The anesthetist, a tall man with untroubled gray scrubs, entered the room, rubbing his hand through his brown hair.

Dr. Yi acknowledged him, then turned to Sabina and Garence. "Dr. Nevez is the country's leading anesthetist, and it is his duty to ensure you are as comfortable as possible."

"Hello, Sabina," he started, his arms akimbo. A small, genial smile displayed his genuine balance of responsiveness and empathy.

He placed a hand upon hers. "I'm going to administer general anesthesia through your IV. Don't worry. I'll smooth things over for you. Give me a few seconds."

Maureen jumped in and took Dr. Nevez's place at Sabina's side. "Our number one concern is you and your baby," she said. "That means putting you under so you do not feel a thing, and Dr. Yi needs every second she can to deliver your daughter... That's it. You're drifting off now... We'll take good care of you." For Sabina to breathe during the procedure, a respiratory tube was inserted into her esophagus.

Garence watched Dr. Yi make a lateral incision above the short pubic hairline into the skin, then the muscles and the fat, until the uterus was cut open. With her hands in Sabina's pelvis, Dr. Yi ascertained the baby was frank breech in her mother's right anterior, which meant she was facing Sabina's back with her head down and her legs and knees pressed against her own body. This position would have made it difficult for a lesser-experienced obstetrician to deliver the baby, but not Dr. Yi. Her skill set afforded her the ability to remove the baby and hand her over to the pediatrician in one seamless motion before she dove in to remove the placenta.

Garence saw the crimson body, cursed with desquamation. The precious skin bubbled and peeled from her face, head, back, and legs whilst Dr. Yi sewed his wife's abdomen together.

"Is she all right? Can you resuscitate her?"

Garence lost all focus from the shock, and events blurred over each other and dubbed over the staff's hushed words. Everything was absorbed as half mumbled and incoherent.

"Why isn't Estrella crying?" Garence asked, doing his best to control the emotions that would burst through his tone.

He glared at Dr. Yi. She had known something was wrong this whole time, but she wasn't telling him anything.

Dammit, he deserved to know what was happening to their child. Then it slammed Garence in the chest like a blast from a bomb.

Estrella was dead.

His jaw dropped as his cheeks wetted with mourning. "Estrella," his feeble voice called out. "Where's our child?" he asked at last.

The second nurse assisting Dr. Yi approached him. She was a mere five feet with hair as black as a raven. Her hawk eyes pierced his and unsettled him. "Mr. Leitner, you'll have to stay calm. Yes, I understand, but you'll have to remain calm, or we'll have to ask you to leave."

"You can't make me leave," he growled.

"I am asking you to remain calm, but if you can't do that, then we'll have you escorted to the lobby. Is that what you want?"

"Don't patronize me. Yes, you are. I deserve to know what happened to my daughter. Are you going to drug me too?"

Dr. Yi composed herself, then approached him. "Mr. Leitner, please wait for me outside this room. I cannot attend to your wife under these conditions."

Garence was slapped in the face by her request. Whirling in the events had made him dizzy, and he had forgotten himself. He took two steps toward Sabina, kissed her forehead, then walked out. Thirty minutes later, Dr. Yi exited the room and ushered him into another room, where Sabina would later be admitted for the evening.

"Mr. Leitner, would you please sit down?"

Garence did not comply with her request, but he waited for the door to close before he asked, "How did Estrella die?"

Dr. Yi was caught off guard. "The umbilical cord had a knot in it, cutting off oxygen and food from the baby. There was no heartbeat, and that's why we proceeded with the C-section earlier than scheduled. I know how much both of you have been through, and I didn't want to alarm either of you until I knew for certain whether I could save her or not. I'm sorry I didn't tell you sooner."

Garence gestured for her to stop. His voice broke with emotion before he turned his face away from her. "You didn't betray us."

"After years of practicing, no other couple has affected me like you two have. So much grief has befallen you that it makes me nauseous." She brought a hand to her temple. "With her medical history, I know Sabina's trigger is grief. I've checked on her a few times. She's been doing well, but I'll continue to call."

"She's a much stronger person than she was then. And I'll..."

"Yes, of course she is. And she has you. I'm concerned for her. For both of you." The human side of Dr. Yi broke through her professionalism. "I am so sorry, Garence."

"Would Sabina have felt the baby...?" His large hands concealed his sobs. It was too ghastly an image to verbalize; that his child had struggled to live.

She went to place her arms around him, but her structured manner made her pause. She placed a light hand upon his shoulder instead. "There's no way Sabina would have known. Despite her keen instincts and insight-fulness." Without meaning to, her forehead rested upon his bent head, making it look as if they were both weeping. "I wish things were different."

Garence nodded.

Dr. Yi removed her hand once his emotions had subsided. "I'd like to have Sabina stay the night. Is that all right? Okay. You're more than welcome to stay with her. I'll be sure to send extra blankets and several pillows for both of you. Hopefully they will help make that ole brown chair as comfortable for you as possible."

"It's fine. It doesn't matter. I appreciate your consideration, I do. Thank you."

A tech opened the door and another pushed Sabina's rollaway bed into the room. She was waking up from the sedative when she laid eyes on the rooms' occupants. As soon as she saw the same grave look on Dr. Yi's and Garence's faces and his swollen eyes, she didn't need to know what they were discussing. She had always read Garence, and right now, she wished she couldn't. She wished she needed to ask them why she hadn't seen or heard about her little girl. If only it meant that Estrella was alive and being cared for somewhere in the hospital and not dead like the pair of eyes gawking at her now.

She closed her eyes, slumped over, and buried her head in the pillow. "No. No. Not Estrella."

Chapter Seventeen

PRESENT DAY

Garence was in the hallway between the main bedroom and the nursery. His back leaned against the dividing wall between both rooms. His bare feet pressed against the opposite wall with a window. It was past eleven o'clock, and Garence identified the sky as a sheet of ebony with silver fire emitting through holes created by the universe's needlepoint. The moon wasn't in frame but it was a few degrees from full. A time for letting go. If he let go of all that had transpired, then he could transcend to the next phase of his life as well. But the moon was on the cusp of its next phase, as he was. Thankfully it illuminated the hallway so he could see what he was writing.

They say if these walls could talk that they could tell stories. I can testify to this and extend that narration to the ones I am leaning against in this very corridor. The wall within the main bedroom and baby's room served as a dam preventing my and Sabina's surging grief from drowning us. As with every dam, you can peer over the edge and witness the great volume behind it. That was me checking in on Sabina from the hallway but from the bottom edge of the door. She was barmy with grief—

and rightfully so. Her isolation clawed at my sanity, but I was a useless prat. All I could do was be here for her. Even if she didn't want to be near me.

She took a leave of absence from work, and since I wanted to be here for her, I didn't travel, just as I didn't after each tragedy. We got by on our savings and accepted a select few rental reservations. She slept most of the time, and even when she wasn't asleep, she was crying until she drifted off again. She turned away everyone who came into town to see her, her friends and her parents, except for Dr. Yi, whose calls she accepted, which I was very grateful for. It seemed she wanted no one in the house except for me, even if she kept me at bay.

I turned down all impending writing offers and removed the availability of our rental from the website to keep an eye on her full-time. Thankfully, we didn't have to worry about cash flow for at least six months with our emergency fund and low living expenses.

I had prepared three meals for Sabina throughout the day and left them at the door to find the previous one untouched and cold, though it was encouraging that she emptied her glass of water each time. I didn't have much of an appetite myself, but I had to maintain my health if I was going to be of any service to Sabina. I forced myself to consume whatever she didn't eat, at least half when I was without an appetite.

Whenever I moved from one room to the other or went outside to check the post, Sabina would grab her glass and use the loo, then proceed to lock herself in the bedroom. As she kept to the bedroom, I remained within a few feet of her. I stayed in the next room or lay on the floor outside the bedroom. There wasn't any light coming from beneath the door, and I knew she was truly in the dark. A shadow within the shadows.

Chapter Eighteen

TWO YEARS AGO

— MARCH —

Sabina shoved a sheet of letter paper into the drawer of a nightstand beside her marital bed, where there was a box of razor blades. After a second thought, she turned the page over so the handwritten words were upside down and even further concealed from her mind. She slammed the drawer shut, and the nightstand rocked. She was then ashamed of mistreating such a fine possession. Garence had purchased it and its twin while on assignment four years prior. The timber nightstand boasted charming, unpainted Scandinavian details and was old, with deep gashes and worn edges; it was as beaten up as the Leitners, but it was all the lovelier for it. She thought it would be better suited as a table of sorts, at least for the time being, to set the writing paper and pen upon. It also seemed better situated in the middle of the room so she could access it from every corner. She dragged the nightstand from beside the headboard to the foot of the bed. One of the bun feet was missing, the padding that allowed it to glide over the floor, so it limped over the hardwood and grunted when Sabina applied too much force. She retrieved the bottle of Scotch from around the bed and found it empty. She grabbed the glass of water that Garence had set outside the door for her several hours ago, sipping enough to wet her gums, and then set the glass down; the only evidence she had taken a few occasional sips was the near-invisible impressions that her saliva-moistened lips had left on the rim.

She settled her back on the floor. Her bum was on the washed-out jute rug that crept out from beneath the bed while her bare legs and feet were sprawled over the hardwood. Her arms were outstretched at forty-five-degree angles, her left palm faced the ceiling and the exposed beams while the fingers of her right hand strummed the grooves in the floorboard as if she were picking at a scab. The longer her thoughts skulked in the trenches of her misery, the deeper her nails dug into the cracks of the wood.

She had a writing pen in her hand and a sheet of paper under her fist.

> I want to scream and feel a different kind of pain
>   anything but this hell that keeps threatening me
> Sometimes I experience bouts of numbness in my chest
>   and in my mind
> It's nice

Her fingertips caressed the smooth floor as if they were gliding over piano keys.

> ... like I am high without ever having inhaled or
>   injecting anything into my veins
> It's a lovely break...
> That is, until my mind takes me for a whirl and I'm drowning again.

She clawed at the wood again.

If Sabina hated herself for their tragedies, Garence tormented himself for never being capable of making her feel as if their miscarriages weren't her fault. He didn't know how to convince her she wasn't to blame. He never said or did anything to even hint he was disappointed in her, in any shape or form. She could never disappoint him. He accepted their infertility… It wasn't in their cards to have more than each other. As long as he had her by his side, he could live without children.

Garence held a sheet of his embossed letter paper and folded it into thirds, more out of habit rather than to slip it into an envelope and deliver it to Sabina. Within the creases was written:

Why aren't we seeing this tragedy through together? I hate that we're not talking or even sleeping in the same room. It is beyond unnatural, and it's something I never thought we would ever do. We didn't separate from each other with the miscarriages, so why are we doing it now? I guess, allow me to correct myself, I know I can't understand what you are going through… I need someone to talk to… and I don't want to talk to just anyone. I want to talk to you. I need you. We've always supported each other. Why is this any different?

I feel like you're slipping away, but I have to give you room, if that's what you want. I hope I'm not giving you too much room. I don't know when I'm supposed to step in and be your husband. I don't mean I want to swoop in like some knight in shining armor because that's not what I am, and that's not real. I want to be your rock and solace, but I don't know when you'll want me back. I hope you will call me when you are ready. I'll wait forever if I have to…

In the safety of her seclusion, Sabina unstitched healed wounds and those that were never meant to mend. The moon visited her and lulled her into a few hours of hellish sleep. Now the sun had come around to take its turn at her side on the floor. She sat against the wall on the opposite side of her bed with a sheet of paper in a clipboard on her lap and a pen in her hand.

I can't stand the fact that I...

She stopped writing and looked upward. Her head hit the wall with a thump. Ouch! She closed her inflamed eyes and wondered what she was trying to say in these letters that she couldn't and wouldn't share with Garence. She hadn't the faintest clue about anything anymore. A tear streamed down her cheek; she was so lost.

I can't stand the fact that I am a failure as a mother and a wife. Why can't I deliver a single baby? Why do they all keep dying?

Weeping, she stopped writing to catch her breath, her eyes in saccades over the page as if the answer would appear and somehow make her feel better.

I am so angry! I don't understand why this keeps happening. What's wrong with me?

Tears stained the page.

I've done everything right. I ate the right foods and supplements. I never overexerted myself. My organs are healthy and normal. It doesn't make any sense. I've placed every bit of my soul into my and my child's well-being.

She tossed the pen to the side as if her best attempts meant nothing, then she wiped her nose with the back of her hand. Her weary hand wavered from her nose to her forehead, and she rubbed it absentmindedly.

Her eyes fluttered as her thoughts sailed from one misunderstanding to the other. She supposed she could jot them down. The pen had skidded a meter from her person, but when she reached for it, she tumbled over herself. Her elbow and ribs hit the floor hard, but she recovered with minimal effort to resume her letter.

> I keep thinking about Rosalinda and the day she died. The way her lifeless body was bent on the street; it was unsettling, and it haunted my dreams for months. I was gobsmacked and distraught. I didn't understand her death just as I don't understand the deaths of my children.
>
> It is the most dreadful feeling in the world to see a person, a loved one, sprawled on the ground dead, to experience death from within you, and then there is the horrid knowledge that there is nothing you can do about any of it.

Sabina's fingernails were broken and cracked from clawing the floorboards during the first few days; they couldn't get in worse shape, but she picked at the cuticles on her right hand. She needed something to do, something to focus on, even if it was self-destructive.

She crumpled the letter paper with a mighty fist, then threw it toward the corner of the bedroom, imagining it disintegrating into nothing from the force. The ball of paper hit the wall, bounced off the floor, then slid underneath the bed and out of her view, which was as good as it disintegrating. For now.

Garence folded a sheet of his embossed paper into thirds and slipped it into an envelope as he had before. His mind was tired of worrying over Sabina. Although his heart was broken and weak and as heavy as the day he and Sabina had lost Estrella, it still contained an unforeseen hope that his wife would someday return to him.

The next room is silent. So silent that I wonder if you are still in there. Although you could have slipped out of the house through the windows like a teenager desperate to break loose from the confines of the four walls that provide you with shelter, I know you are there. I've checked numerous times by lying flat on my stomach and peeking underneath the door, and I can see your shadow on the floor when you sit against the chest of blankets. Or I'll listen to you sob into the pillows or mumble disjointed sentences in your sleep. You have no idea how difficult it is to be a bystander in all of this. It is cocking hell, and I'm spitting feathers. All I want to do is curl you into my arms and console you, but you've shut me out, and I know I have to allow you every inch of room possible—that and the fact that the door is locked.

I would do whatever it took to keep you healthy and safe and buzzing with joy, but we cannot bear children. I don't know how to fix that. I don't know how to fix us. I am so helpless, and I'm a failure for this.

I'm afraid to admit this, but I am forgetting what it feels like to have your body pressed against mine. I never thought we would be separated as we are. Again.

All I can think about is you. Not work or taking care of the holiday let, the cottage or the crazy world whirling around us. I long for your skin, how I long to slide my hands and lips over it. I can't feel my heart beat without you or air filling my lungs. Am I even alive? I can't be. It is an atrocity to feel this way *when you are a few meters away from me. I can't imagine what it would feel like if I were dead and away from you, my love.*

What are you going through? I know this time is different, but we've experienced hardship together before.

This separation is showing me what it's like to be with someone who isn't present, and this isn't a lesson I want to learn. There is nothing and no one who could ever replace or destroy my love for you.

I'm here,
Garence

Sabina heard the letter slide under the door, and she rolled her eyes. She read it, threw it in a nightstand drawer, opened the door, and stared Garence down. It was midday, and her bedroom windows flooded him and the floor he was sitting on with light. His long curls fell back from his face when he looked up, and she saw her own weariness reflecting back. The light caught his eyes, while hers were shadowed.

"What do you want from me?"

His brow furrowed. "I want to help us through this."

"I don't need any help. I've been talking with Dr. Yi."

"I know, and I'm grateful, but why won't you let *me* in?"

Silence.

"It's my job…"

"It's not your job to do anything. You have no idea what's going on."

"Then tell me."

"You're camping at my door. I can feel your goddamn presence every second of the day. It's maddening."

"I'm making sure you're okay."

"No, it's your fucking codependence. I'm fine, Garence. You need to work this out in your own way because this is mine."

She turned around and threw the door behind her, but it didn't close.

"You don't get to slam the door in my face. Tell me what to do because I'm at a loss." He waited a moment before placing his hands around her arms.

Sabina's eyes searched his for an answer, but then she erupted. "I don't want anything from you. I don't want you to hold me." She broke free from his hands. "I don't want you to try and console me and tell me that we can try again or not to try again. I don't want anything from you ever again. I'm so sick of you telling me this is no one's fault. I'm sick of you telling me not to blame myself and how to feel. I'm angry. I'm mad. I'm hurt. I'm clawing at myself for my babies. This is all I know. This is all I feel! This is all I want to feel! You can't help me! You can't do anything because I don't need you, so stop trying!"

"You don't get to tell me what to do, Sabina. If you want to feel all of this, that's your right, but you have no right to lash out at me. But, hey, if you want to, go right ahead. I'm hurting too, but I can take it. I would go to hell and back for you."

"That's bullshit. You don't believe in hell. Get out!" She pushed her weight against his chest, but she was no match for his stature. "Give me this one thing," she sputtered as she pushed harder.

Then she no longer felt him resist her, and he was out of the bedroom, and she slammed the door.

Sabina had fallen asleep. It was now dark, and she was curled up in the fetal position. Somehow, the bedsheet had got wrapped around her so tightly that she looked like the crescent moon. Her hair hung off the side of the bed, and the ends skirted the floor and the letters she had written but shredded into a dozen pieces. From an awakened state, she felt a sense of calm move over her. Sprinkled on the surface of those bits of paper were hopelessness and uncertainty.

I don't see the point…
in trying…
in anything…
Not anymore.
I'm afraid.
I don't know what's going to happen next. I'm terrified, and
I'm all alone. I have no one I can talk to about this.
~~Garence couldn't understand.~~

She had taken a moment to reflect upon her husband—the man who loved her and supported her and had changed her life for the better because he loved her. And that's when she'd crossed out the bit about Garence not being capable of understanding.

He might…
If I let him in.
Could I let him in?
Yes.

Should I?

It was troublesome for Garence to think of how long she hadn't showered or exercised. After the eighth day, he tapped on the bedroom door.

"Sabina? Darling?"

Her voice was hoarse. "The door isn't locked."

It felt as though his head jerked up toward the doorknob, but he was so tired it drifted upward. How long had it been unlocked? He sat up and turned the knob.

The door swung open in a gentle sway and without a squeak, as if a ghost were guiding it. Garence peered into the room. Pillows were scattered all over the bed, and the sheets were half falling off the mattress. Sabina was sitting on the bed with her arms wrapped around her legs as if she were a bird huddled beneath a dying tree on a stormy afternoon. She was wearing one of his dress shirts, one of a gray tone that was as fragrant as natural body oils tinged with vinegar and now rumpled beyond the repair of a hot iron, long socks, and black lace knickers. Her filthy hair was ripe and tangled from the constant rustling in her sleep, and her complexion was pallid.

He walked over to the foot of the bed and sat on it. He didn't dare touch her or say anything for fear of distressing her. He crawled toward her, sat behind her, and pulled her against his warm body, then swathed a leg over hers.

Sabina didn't flinch or push him away but welcomed his touch. They grieved for their daughter, Estrella, but he was comforted by having Sabina in his arms once again. For the first time since arriving home from hospital, they united in their sorrow. Their bodies shook with expression as their loneliness evaporated; all the while, a realization was sinking in that things between them would never be as they had been before. His body radiated heat, yet within seconds, his temperature dropped to her level.

It was some time before either of them ventured to break free of their pain. Sabina sat up and stared out the window, planning her next move, then left the bed.

"Would you like some help…"

"No. I can do this myself," she said flat out. Sabina didn't need to avoid his eyes when she left the bedroom.

Garence watched her round the doorway toward the nursery. He had spent significant time in there himself and found that the love and care they had put into it had comforted him during this dark time; perhaps she would find solace in it too. He had often leaned against her crib and imagined Estrella sleeping in it or giggling at his silly faces. He had perused the books on the shelves, nursery rhymes and folklore and such, that he had so often planned on reading to his daughter while he held her in his arms within the snug embrace of the armchair that Sabina had picked out. He was frightened by the thought of how she would react to being in Estrella's room, but he wouldn't keep her out of it for any reason.

Bang!

Crack!

Smash!

Garence's head jerked. He sprinted out of the bedroom and slid into the corridor wall with a thud as he attempted to make an immediate turn into the baby's room.

His face deteriorated as he saw she had destroyed everything they had worked for. The gash in the wall was evidence that Sabina had shoved the bookcase into it. Books were scattered across the floor, as well as ceramic shards from the fallen statue of a mother holding a baby.

Sabina held the standing lamp in her grasp, broken glass from the lightbulb and cover around her bare feet, and she wielded the stand against the crib with all her might once more.

"Sabina! Stop! You're going to hurt yourself. Give me that."

"I don't care!"

"Well, I do." He ripped the lamp from her hands.

Garence turned around and saw Sabina lunge for the framed map of the globe, the one from her Bilbao apartment, that hung over the baby's bookcase. She grabbed her dart from the point that was Torres del Paine.

He went to grab it out of her hand, but she threw it at the window, and it flew into a distant bush.

He drew her into his arms.

She wailed, "I don't want to keep bringing death into this world."

"You're not."

Sabina didn't hear him, nor was she listening. It was as if her auditory senses were turned off and she was broadcasting her thoughts. "I don't deserve this? How many times do I have to repent?"

Garence was stunned and angered to realize she was implying that she was being punished with death for wanting her own.

"This has nothing to do with that. Absolutely nothing."

She still wasn't listening.

She cursed the night of her thirty-third birthday in Torres del Paine when she had wished for intense moments, the night she and Garence had made love for the first time under a billion stars. She said she had wanted favorable moments, passionate and intense ones filled with heart-bursting love, joy, and laughter, not deep bouts of misery and loss.

"I've said I was sorry for trying to take my own life." Then her voice dropped to a whisper. "And I am. I am sorry for wanting it so bad."

How much more pain and suffering was she going to endure?

Sabina raised her trembling hands; pulsing veins further exposed her state. "I am so fucking sorry!" she screeched.

If the room were missing walls, her voice would have echoed through the rolling hills for several minutes, and the birds would have fallen to their deaths.

Her entire body shook with such ferocity that Garence could not contain her, and he thought she would never calm down.

She kept whispering, "I am sorry. I am sorry."

"You've already been forgiven. I love you." Garence knew she wasn't listening to him, but he repeated these words six more times. She kept muttering her apologies, and, as he rocked her, she succumbed to her weariness and fell asleep.

Hours passed with Garence still holding her in his arms. The sun had set, and the room was as cold as their torn hearts, but he would not budge. He would hold Sabina and share his body warmth with her for as long as she needed him to.

He was drifting in and out of sleep himself when she spoke. Unaware she was awake, he drew a sharp inhale.

"I don't want to try to have another baby."

The fact that she had been referring to herself as "I" rather than "us" wasn't lost on him. "That's fine."

"Is it?"

He couldn't decipher if she was being sarcastic or inciting.

He rubbed his face.

He was tired of the emotional roller coaster they had been riding, but he loved Sabina too much to participate in anything other than support.

"I can't believe I didn't see it before... I was manifesting my own limitations by focusing on the outcome, but I won't keep getting pregnant to have death hovering over my shoulder."

"You're still creating your own restriction in doing so."

"Don't you think I know that? I can't help it."

"May I pose a question?"

She stared at him.

"Should we look into surrogacy?"

She pondered this for several minutes. She wanted to bear her own children and experience him or her growing inside her, every kick, every heartburn, every opportunity to pee every couple of minutes, the swollen ankles and everything, but it wasn't in her stars. No, she shouldn't be so selfish and proud. She wanted a child, and she should be grateful to be blessed with one by any means possible. With her eyes closed, Sabina focused on her desire to have a child and sent this final thought into the universe with a kiss.

"That may be our only avenue," she began, rolling her eyes, "but not in this lifetime. To be honest, I am tired of all of this. I'm knackered."

"I'm also tired of this and the heartache—and I'm not the one completely experiencing this. You have the final say."

"Fine."

Was it? he wondered, but he dared not ask this out loud.

She got up and muttered something indistinct under her breath, but he thought she said that nothing mattered.

Chapter Nineteen

TWO YEARS AGO

— APRIL —

Just before dawn, Sabina exited the bedroom to shower and dried off in her bedroom. It was a quiet, murky morning, unfit for a stroll, but she needed air. She donned light-gray leggings and an oversized, black wool sweater and combed her dark hair with her fingers.

She tiptoed down the hallway, then stopped at the front room when she saw Garence sleeping in an armchair. His body was slumped as if he had been trying to sleep reclined, his head rested on the arm at an awkward angle; his white T-shirt had ridden up his back a bit after the weight of his body slid down the chair, and a book was tucked in the cushions. He looked uncomfortable, but he was at least sleeping; the corner of her mouth turned up with this relief. She tiptoed to the doorframe and right through the sound of a floorboard creaking like it didn't happen. There was a thump, and she was certain it was his bare feet jolting. She reached the door, looked over her shoulder, and waited for him to speak. He said nothing, nor did he stir.

She was going out for a solitary stroll, and she didn't care if he followed her. Fresh air would do them both some good. As long as he recognized that "stay back" glare, she would enjoy her walk.

She opened the front door, and her eyes had a difficult time adjusting to the overcast luster. The increased spectrum of light she was now exposed to, whether it was overcast or misty or partly sunny, was particularly bright when compared to the dimly lit bedroom she had enclosed herself in. She leaned back inside the house, grabbed her large, black-framed sunglasses from the side table, and put them on.

The English air wafted through the naked chestnut trees and filtered the stagnant energy out of her body, not to mention frosted the surface of her skin. They walked barefoot on the nutrient-rich path, meandering through the forest that sutured their property with the neighbors'. The cushionesque soil was cold under their feet, but they did not notice. This was their first walk together, and they weren't about to complain about anything. The edges of the trail were fringed with leaves cast aside from the previous season, their color resembling aged leather. Forever-reaching ivy slivered over exposed tree roots and scaled the trunks of every other tree, like serpents wanting to reach the sky. The minutes flew off the clock, and their hearts worked toward pulsing as one again, and every time their surreptitious glances intersected, they were encouraged to remain in each other's hold.

Sabina tugged at her sleeves for warmth, and Garence responded by withdrawing his hands from his trouser pockets. Now that they were out of their personal imprisonment, he rubbed the back of one of his hands against Sabina's to test whether she would welcome holding it.

Her fingers flickered with recognition.

She reacquainted herself with the smoothness of his skin and the sensations he used to bring. Sparks erupted within her, and her nipples jutted while her flesh pricked with goose bumps. Her fingertips stroked down his arm before greeting his fingers with a tap.

He took her hand, and another flicker warmed her. It was a tantalizing gesture, one they would have experienced on any normal day, but today it altered their course. He stepped on a dead branch, and it cracked. A raven thrust itself from the chestnuts and fled the developing scene.

Their hearts were thawing just as the ground beneath their feet was expecting spring, a season of new beginnings. The morning dew moistened their perception of what was the present reality and wet their senses with revival. The air was sweet with the scent of wet bark and moss clinging to north-facing surfaces. The dismal sky glowed with fits of pluming white clouds as the distant outstretched clouds laid shadows over the months that had separated them, annihilating their loneliness.

Their path was hidden beyond the thickening forest, where it was sure to be boggy. Garence tugged at her arm. She flinched, but neither of them said anything. He propelled her to him, and for the first time in days, they stood facing each other. She knew he couldn't stand their way of life any longer. When he removed her sunglasses, she wanted to turn away and hide her face, but she didn't. He rubbed his thumb across her cheek and wiped away the tears. She leaned into his hand. Her lips were as crimson as a rose, and they parted as her chest expanded with each deepening breath.

He placed his hand behind her neck and drew her close. He kissed her without applying any pressure, and she breathed him in like inhalant.

Grabbing her wrists, he led her off the path and pinned her against a dormant tree; her back scraped against the bark with each impact.

"Is it too rough?"

She shook her head; she welcomed every thrust and the extra pressure that being pinned offered. Lost in his spell, Sabina closed her eyes and willed him to possess her, and mold her, and transform her into someone pristine.

His lips swept over her ears and jawline, and he trailed dozens of kisses down her neck.

Their connection proved that the wintry land was not dead yet. She saw their separation had dulled his brilliant features, and she was taken aback by the subtle changes; his brow was arched heavy over his eyes and dark circles, whilst new fine lines blemished his skin.

She put her hand to his jaw, almost absorbing his pain. "I'm here," she whispered before pressing her lips against his.

That night, they shared the same bed and remained there into the following afternoon, talking and caressing each other's skin. They worked through their pain and misery until, at times, neither of them could remember why they had been apart.

Garence's face softened with a glow because their love was rekindled.

Their entrails had been gutted not once but several times, and although they drifted apart after despair, they always came together and illuminated the other's darkness.

Chapter Twenty

PRESENT DAY

I'm glad I packed the nursery. I can't imagine boxing everything whilst reading Sabina's letters about our babies. I have to move on to Sabina's things, but I can't bring myself to do it. She's gone, but she's not really gone. You saw her earlier, didn't you? She guided me to the luggage of letters. I know you saw her.

I need to do something. A distraction of sorts.

Plop!

Garence looked down at this letter. There was something dark and round on it. Upon closer examination, it was blood. Another drop fell, and the dome burst.

"Oh, fuck!"

He covered his nose and hustled to the kitchen, where he grabbed a paper towel. He bled through the paper towel, so he grabbed another. Then it too was replaced. If he wasn't under enough pressure, this was not helping matters.

When the bleeding stopped, he blew out the blood clot into several tissues and threw them and the blood-soaked towels into the bin with the magazines. Garence dropped a paper towel onto his letter. Some of the blood was absorbed, but a significant amount had soaked through it. He eyed the letter with mild disgust and wondered if he should rewrite the page and throw this one in the bin, or if he should keep it. It was his own letter and his own blood. It's not like anyone would read the letter. Nor did he have a profusion of stationery on hand.

"Fuck it." He tossed the pen onto the table and told himself he would return to it.

The study needed a few things packed, but when he entered it, he discovered there was more to do than he remembered. He still had six rows of books in three shelves to pack, including his own published works, framed photographs, and global memorabilia. A stack of magazines from two, three, four, and five years ago was filed on the shelf, which made him pause. He had packed those already. He had found them on the end table by the armchair and then thrown them away one by one before tossing the lot in the bin. *But the end table and the armchair weren't in the study*, he thought. *Were they? There and unpacked.* His eyes rummaged the room as if they would appear out of thin air, until the room spun. He fumbled through the magazines he thought he had packed earlier. The covers were different. The dates were the same, but the covers were different. Horror pricked at his skin as he wondered how they were altered, and moved into a different room.

He stormed into the living room and grabbed the rubbish bin with his right hand. It was heavy, and the unexpected load fell through his grasp. Inside it were the magazines he had thought were in the study. His memory straightened itself out, and he remembered these magazines were different from the others. He rubbed his head, wondering how he had got himself mixed up. His stomach growled, but he ignored it, then took a drink of wine.

He returned to the study and filled nineteen boxes with books. The rest would fit in another ten boxes, which he didn't have, but he moved the existing ones into his car and dropped them off at the local library with a promise to return with more before closing. He got in his car and stopped at the village center café.

A bell rang as he opened the door.

"Garence. You're a sight for sore eyes," said the man behind the ordering counter, who appeared to want to take back his comment.

"It's nice to see you too, Dan." He rubbed his eye, then ran his hand through his hair. "I'm rather crunched for time. Would you make me a half of a turkey sandwich while I go next door to pick up some packing supplies?"

The man's face dropped at the mention of packing. "Of course. I'm sure you're almost done packing your beautiful estate."

Garence's eyebrows shot up. Almost done? He had so much to clear before he considered his progress at such a lofty state. He offered the man a forced, thin smile as he slid several bills across the counter. "No change."

Almost done. Fuck, he'd have to keep telling himself that until it was true.

He turned to leave when he heard the man say his order would be ready when he returned, so he waved his appreciation. He received the same heartbreaking greeting from the lady at the hardware shop, and she offered to help him locate items.

"I have boxes by the pallet and in different sizes. Standard, large, and extra-large. What do you need?"

"Ten of your standards."

"That's it? You should have more on hand, just in case. Wouldn't want to run out, say at seven o'clock and kill your momentum. Are you on the last of it all?"

"No." He reconsidered the amount he would need for the study, and his eyebrow shot up when he remembered the main bedroom. He had a closet and a dresser with both of their belongings to pack, the nightstands were already sold, but he had the bed linen as well. "I'll take twenty of the large ones. And packing tape."

"I'm glad I asked." She grabbed her walkie-talkie from her belt loop. "Jess, can you load ten standard boxes and twenty of the large ones into Garence's car, please? Thank you. As for the tape, I'm afraid we're out of packing tape. We have everything else though. Let me walk you down that aisle. Oops. I'm a liar. We have a boatload of packing tape."

"I'll take four of those and a roll of duct tape."

The woman grabbed a carrying basket at the end of the aisle and relieved Garence of the stash in his arms. "I'll ring this up for you."

"Thanks for your help," he said, clearing his throat. He hadn't spoken this much in succession in a whole week, and the sudden use of his vocal cords was escaping him.

"Of course. If you need any help packing or hauling, Harry and I can stop by at the click of a horse's hoof."

"Thank you, but that won't be necessary. I'm almost done." His voice mirrored the neighboring shop owner, drizzled with the right facetiousness to fool her and make his hollow abdomen jump.

"Oh, good. So, did you purchase another place?"

A young girl came from behind with boxes in her arms, and Garence disarmed his car, and it auto unlocked.

"I haven't planned anything beyond this weekend."

"Really? That's unusual. Then again, you're like a nomad. Traveling all over the world. You'll figure it out. I hope I'll see you soon."

All he said was "thank you" when he took the shopping bag. He met her eyes, but nothing else came out. He walked next door, and the café owner was on the phone. Garence picked up his sandwich and was allowed to slip out with a single wave.

He drove home down a narrow road while going over his to-pack list. Overall, there was still so much to do: wrap up the study, drop off the next load back in town in a few short hours, pack their bedroom, and read through one year and seven months of letters. He felt his scalp tense at this thought. There was nothing he could do about any of the letters right now, so he let it go.

The road would have been shaded, but it was November, and the trees were barren. The towering trunks varied in thickness, and they reminded him of barcodes. Tall streaks of black on all sides of him, with the sunlight behind them, blinding him in erratic patterns. A sudden dizzy spell caught him, and the lines closed in on him. Exhaustion and lack of sleep seized him, and he veered into the next lane. His head bobbed as if it weren't attached, but he didn't catch himself. An oncoming car's horn sounded, and the siren didn't stop. The noise resounded in Garence's ears even after the impact.

The accident was an opportunity. The answer to his never-ending request to leave this world. This was the perfect way. The same way Sabina had.

Garence didn't move. His curls obscured his face, and there was no way of knowing if he was dead or alive.

The other car didn't have any passengers, and the driver exited, slamming the door.

He surveyed the damage to his car, which was limited to the front driver's-side fender and headlight.

Garence got out of his car. His movements were slow, but he understood all that had transpired.

"What are you trying to do?" said the man. "Kill us? I have a family, bastard."

Garence looked puzzled. "I'm..." Scrambled words and thoughts were off-kilter even as he shook them. "I'm sorry. I..."

"Sorry isn't good enough. Look at my new car. The fender is crumbled. Good thing I hit the brakes. Otherwise the damage would have been substantial. We could have died."

The passing cars drove around them.

Garence's vision blurred in and out of focus. "I think my foot let off the gas. It would have had to if I... I'm sorry."

"Hey, are you high? Were you driving while fucking high?"

"No. I'm a little disoriented. I was in the accident too. A little compassion here?"

"You want what? How dare you. You know what? I'm done. There's something wrong with you. Give me your insurance information—you have insurance, correct?"

Garence's voice and his vision had steadied. "Of course I do."

"Perfect. Fetch your info. I'll file a report and a claim myself when I get home. You do the same on your end."

Garence retrieved everything he didn't know by heart from his phone, and within minutes, the driver was off. With no traffic on either side of him, Garence had his first opportunity to assess the damage to his car. It was the same as the driver's but on the opposite side. It could have been so much worse if they were both traveling at faster speeds.

It was strange to have been so close to death. The very stage of life he sought had been within his grasp, but it hadn't come to pass. It was unexpected and unsuccessful, and he couldn't determine if he was happy or sad about it. He remained in a state of bewilderment, but his blood sugar was low. With no cars coming, he reached for the sandwich in the passenger seat, ripped off a mouthful, and tossed the rest back in the bag. He then donned his sunglasses and drove. There was so much to pack, and he would get it all done, even if it killed him.

Garence finished packing the books and trinkets in the study, then filled his car. He had eighteen minutes to get back into town for the next drop-off. It would have been smooth sailing if he hadn't lost time in the accident.

He called the family center to say he was on his way and asked if they would still accept his donation even if he was five minutes late. They said they didn't mind waiting for him, so he got in his car and saw there was room for two more boxes. He ran back inside, thinking he would have two fewer boxes to load in the morning. The sun had set and the house was dark. He reached for the light switch as he ran into the living room toward the study, but his fingers missed. He kicked a table.

Chapter Twenty-One

PRESENT DAY

Garence was on the living room floor when his shivering woke him. He raised his head, and he knew he had been asleep for some time because it was dark.

The boxes. The delivery.

"Fuck!"

Frozen stiff, he reached for anything in the darkness when his hand hit the underside of the coffee table. He used it to support himself, then sat up, released the kink in his neck, and rubbed his biceps. There was a draft. The throbbing from his forehead felt damp, which told him he was close to the source. He took count of what had happened, then realized he was by the fireplace and that the draft was coming from the open flue pipe. The house was cold, but it was filled with the ghosts of his past. As much as he wanted to shut them out, he needed the warmth. A new log went aflame, and he wished the emptiness he lived with would burn as well as all of the memories.

He brought a bottle of wine from the kitchen and refilled his glass. He hadn't drunk anything since before he'd left for the shops, so he drank two whole glasses before pouring himself a third. The fire lifted the temperature in the room and the atmosphere. Flames capered on his eyes and the letter. He had missed the drop-off for this last donation, and that meant he would be crunched for time tomorrow. He still had to finish packing the study, read the rest of the letters, and pack Sabina's belongings; he wished he had more time. He chuckled, then irony threw him into hysterics. He had been wishing to die for over a year, and now he was asking for more time. Wonders never ceased.

Garence drove to the donation center and emptied his car at the designated stop. He wasn't supposed to leave donations after hours, but he didn't care. He was technically littering, but they were expecting him, and the weather was supposed to be fine, so he wasn't worried. He returned home, packed the rest of the study, wrote the center a note of apology and appreciation of service. He dropped off the next load at their back doors with his note underneath one of the boxes for them to find. He had so much to read and to get off his chest in his letter that all he wanted was to get back on track.

When he arrived home, he started a fire, then passed out for what seemed like a blink. It was still dark outside, but the fire was low. Garence rested his head against the back of the chair. He was settled with where he was in his tasks, but something was rubbing at him. He closed his eyes and allowed himself to be open and receptive.

His leather binder and the letter were on the table and warm from being near the flames. The blood that had fallen from his nose and onto the page had dried too. He ripped the page from the pad's adhesive and inserted it into the left pocket where the other written pages were stowed.

Saturday has left me, and I am greeted with a solemn Sunday. As I look outside, I am reminded of that April morning two years ago. I don't know what today will bring me, but it will not be the same as that blood-pumping woodland rendezvous. The mist will climb this dreadful sky, and I hope that the ghostly clouds will cloak the land with darkness as I will be forced to relive what has sent me spiraling deep into the abyss.

After Estrella's death, Sabina took three months' leave from her post at the school. We survived on our savings. I tried not to think about our depleting resources when Sabina was my number one priority, but I'm glad we had it. We should have clung to each other for life support, but we didn't. I don't know if that is peculiar or if others in our situation had experienced this type of separation, but sometimes I wonder why Sabina isolated herself after we lost a child. Maybe I shouldn't. Maybe I'm arrogant or selfish in thinking I could have helped her cope like I needed her.

Have you ever tried balancing on one leg? Have you ever tried it with your eyes closed? Didn't think so. Here, try it with me. Stand up straight and lift one leg off the ground. It doesn't have to be high. An inch or two will do. Keep your eyes open and count to ten.

Now, switch legs and count to ten again.

Chances are one leg is stronger than the other, but I want you to repeat the whole process, only this time, close your eyes. Keep them shut, no peeking. Suddenly, it doesn't matter which leg was weaker, you're trying to avoid toppling over. When your eyes are open, you can focus on something and can better locate your center of gravity, at least I can. When your eyes are closed, you can't focus, and you have to rely on your mind.

That's how grieving was for me. It was a dark place to be, as dark as a train tunnel, and it was difficult to maintain my balance. For this reason, I never liked following the tracks in the pitch-black alone... I guess Sabina did. She could focus in the dark. She had done it before as an adolescent. I would have preferred to have had Sabina console me, to be my focal point, rather than to go on each day in my own wretched head, failing to come to terms with reality For myself, the journey wasn't always easy, but Sabina was the light at the end of my tunnel, and I know I was hers too because she always turned a corner when our tracks converged.

Sabina had become a shell of herself, with her spiritless body walking the earth as if she didn't want to anymore. She was almost recognizable to those who knew her, but I saw the minute differences. Sabina was a beautiful woman. Her heart was generous, her soul was angelic, and her face was unforgettable. I know I've said this already, but it's true. Don't even think that I am romanticizing. When you love and adore someone, you can't help but sing their praises, and if you knew Sabina, you would join the choir.

Garence gave his weary eyes a stretch and took a long, long swig of Bordeaux straight from the bottle.

Hmm.

Every five years, that region got a rub, and the terroir was heaven. He liked the tannins in this bottle of Cabernet Sauvignon and wished he had another one to look forward to, but there wasn't one. He and Sabina had purchased two bottles when they had visited Médoc and Graves, on the Left Bank of Bordeaux, France, and had drunk the first upon arriving home. A passing moment of regret consumed him as he realized he'd never had the opportunity to take her to Saône to taste any of her favorite Burgundies, but before this enmeshed him, he took to pen and paper.

As I look at Sabina's next letter, I am reminded of her kind spirit because even in her darkest days, that part of her was burning.

There was never another woman for me, there never will be, and I'm glad to share more facets of her with you.

Garence,

I've handed the neighbors a gift basket I put together for them in honor of their fifty-second anniversary, and even though their faces expressed their concern for my well-being (I must have looked a fright), they were grateful. I was blessed to learn of the instant they fell in love with each other.

Millie was working in her father's coffee shop serving a guest a cup of her famous hot custard, along with her killer spotted dick pudding (I had to add in the word "pudding," otherwise, you'd never stop rolling, as that dessert's name always does… Okay, I might be smirking) when William strolled in and they clapped eyes on each other, and it was love at first sight. I knew that kind of love existed, but I saw their scene unfold in my mind's eye with every passing word. It was a sensational experience, and inspirational, to witness the beginning of their story.

Garence, I have loved you for a very long time. I can't say when I first knew it. Although every woman doubtless remembers the instant her heart called out to another, if I'm being honest, I do not. I have never felt as though you and I were like other couples, for sure none I was familiar with. I can't explain our connection other than you and I were entwined with each other, like a vigorous vine growing around a post, only we continued to grow all year long. We have maintained that connection through such stormy weather and cheery skies that I never felt we were ever not in love.

In my heart of hearts, I believe we were under a spell before we met. We were going through life without encountering its fullest capacity. But the universe brought us together, and then the spell was broken once we both set foot in Torres del Paine. We had always drunk from such a reservoir, with other people and by experiencing the world. Our spirits had always known we were out there for each other, and *when we met, we were swimming in the sea of love. For that reason, I can say that I always loved you. I knew you were my twin flame and that you were the one man I would love and desire for the rest of my life.*

Even though I cannot carry your children into this world, I know that we will all meet in another life. I hate that we can't grow old together with our children visiting us, and I hate that a piece of you won't survive because of me. This world deserves to have a piece of you in it at all times. I don't know what else to say or write, but... I'm sorry.

I am grateful to have experienced true love. To have had the pleasure of loving you and to be loved by a man as attentive as you are. For this reason, I will always be grateful for the gift of life.

She hadn't signed her name—that knocked the wind out of Garence.

In his initial interpretation of this letter, she had given up on them, maybe herself, but he didn't believe that, so he disregarded the omitted signature. Her story, the good and the bad and everything between, was also his story.

This was the first time he had ever read the letters that Sabina had written while she kept to their room. It was saddening but enlightening. Funny how he hadn't seen them before. He supposed he wasn't ready for that information until now. All he ever wanted was to understand, and now he did.

Underneath the next letter was an envelope with an unbroken seal. An odd feeling came over him at an unsettling rate. The others weren't sealed. It was overstuffed, and there was a huge crinkle at the top.

He should have been elated to read more new letters, but he wasn't. He stared at this one. Terrified. She had never sealed a letter written for him once they were married. What more did she have to say to him? Was it a secret? He reached for it, then paused in midair.

In the timeline of the letters, Garence and Sabina hadn't spoken in ages. When folded, legal documents were thick and bowing. What sort of papers would these be? They had been having marital trouble, very distant, but nothing threatening. Right? The thought of Sabina asking for a divorce was breaking him. But that was preposterous. She couldn't have met with a solicitor. She never left the house.

His heart beat into his throat.

He picked the envelope up and placed his hands along the top. Yes, it was as if she'd tried to rip the whole thing, but it was too thick. He turned it over. *Garence* was scrawled across the center.

He grabbed his envelope opener from his set, and his erratic heartbeat seemed to slice through the closing flap. Inside were three envelopes. Each unsealed. Nothing was written on any of them. No date. No numbering. No indication of which one to read first. Perhaps it didn't matter? They were in the same envelope, so everything would be out in the open in the end. This wasn't good. Was he supposed to be reading this?

His hands shook. Something was wrong with this discovery.

Garence,

I've been thinking about my life and everything that has happened for me. I didn't want to finish that sentence, but it's what I believe. If I allow things to unfold, I am learning my life's lesson in accepting all that I can't change. But I am failing.

It's like it was before, and there is nothing anyone can do except allow it.

So, allow me this.

Please forgive me, Garence.

I can't stop seeing blood from between my legs, and I can't stop feeling a lifeless being in my own. It's insufferable. I can't live like this anymore. Even for you.

You've been my best friend, husband, and lover. I could not have asked for a better partner to travel through life's most difficult *challenges with than you. You've been my champion, in good times and bad, and I am forever grateful. What a life we have had.*

I love you,
Sabina

The letter was crumbling within Garence's fingers. What had he just read? Was this a suicide letter?

"Fuck. No. No. No. No. No. No. No. No!"

He ripped open the other letter and found a short list of dates and brief descriptions.

March 19th. Scratching at my arms.
March 24th. Scratches are healing. Ripped them open.
March 27th. Box of 50 razor blades, a bottle of Scotch, dressings,
hydrogen peroxide.
March 28th. It's like it was before.
March 29th. Each blade is equally sharp. I was wrong.
I do deserve this.

"She left me a fucking log?"

He couldn't process her self-mutilation or what he was supposed to do with this information.

There was one other sealed envelope, but he threw it across the house, then rammed the others into the luggage underneath all the letters he had read.

Chapter Twenty-Two

TWO YEARS AGO

— JUNE —

The supermarket trolley contained bits and bobs, like deodorant and shampoo; a box of Frosties; the ingredients required to bake puff pastry mince pies: flour, eggs, salt, and a jar of mincemeat. Garence and Sabina planned on spending the evening eating and drinking and listening to a stack of new albums they had purchased from a thrift shop earlier in the day. With a bit of luck, they would be inspired to join and sway together.

That hope was looking even more prosperous during a moment when Sabina displayed the tiniest bit of delight and laughed at something Garence had said. Her face brightened, and she placed her hand upon his cheek, as if she were remembering this beloved side of Garence from a past life or awaking up from a deep sleep and her foggy brain was trying to retrieve a vague memory. The queue moved forward, and Sabina instructed Garence to budge up.

An eerie buzz was in the air. Sabina identified it and turned her head to the source, another shopper in the next checkout lane. A woman in her sixties with shimmering salt-and-pepper hair and sharp eyes. She was gawking at Sabina. It took Sabina a moment to realize why the woman was staring at her with such unsettling disdain. The scars on her marred wrists. The woman must have seen them when she had her hand upon Garence's cheek. *Ignore her*, Sabina said to herself.

Her waist was clutched within Garence's arm as he kissed her cheek, but Sabina dared to look back at the woman. The shopper still stared. She dropped her chin and raised a disapproving eyebrow.

Sabina sensed an old friend, shame, resurface. She didn't like how the woman's eyes bore into her like a heated iron poker, jabbing at her with judgment over and over and over again.

She wanted to tell the fiend she had no right to judge her. She hadn't the faintest idea how hard it was to see her best friend die right before her eyes—for no explicable reason at all. The woman had no idea of the pain she bore, but there was no point in sharing this background with someone who lacked empathy and compassion for her fellow man. Just because the fiend would never come to the point of attempting suicide didn't mean everyone else was supposed to follow her beliefs and her moral code. Not everyone had the same capabilities and limitations as the next person. It was almost inhumane not to put herself in someone else's shoes, even for one minute. Sabina was not legitimizing her suicide attempts, but she was infuriated she'd allowed a stranger to back her into a corner with a single judgment.

Sabina's indignation erupted like hives.

Why was she allowing this brute to make her feel this way?

Determination shifted into gear as she decided not to let this ridiculous stranger bedevil her further.

Sabina looked straight at the woman and shot her voice like a swishing arrow toward a bullseye, "Ma'am, I don't deserve your judgment."

Disgusted by Sabina's opposition, the woman sneered and hissed, "Tis a sin to take ye own life."

Sabina narrowed her eyes, and they retorted, *you are the sin*.

Having never seen this side of Sabina before, Garence would have never thought she was capable of clawing at another person even if she was standing up for herself. He had to admit he was more than taken aback by her confrontation.

"Not that it is any of your business," Sabina began, not caring a fiddler's fart who overheard, "but since you brought it up, I must remind you that God is forgiving."

As much as Sabina didn't want to justify this callous woman's wicked judgment, she was too fired up to remain silent. After everything Sabina had been through, all she wanted to do was pound this unsympathetic snake into the ground.

She thrust a frustrated fist over her head.

Despite what this woman's ethics and morals and values were, she was not exercising any of them.

Sabina wondered where they were when she managed to regain her composure. "I suggest you follow His lead."

"I don't have to listen to this!"

Garence had stitched their conversation together before he stole the baton from his wife. "Ma'am. You are out of line." His hawk eyes motioned toward the moving checkout lane.

The woman's stiff chest rose in defeat, and her narrow nose lashed into the air as quick as a cracked whip. She took three steps forward and unloaded the items from her trolley.

The couple exited the shop, her hand in his. Sabina's thoughts were back on her out-of-body experience. Garence's thumb caressed her hand, but it didn't draw her out. She was barely holding on to the shopping bags as she relived the situation in her mind. They were only twenty minutes away. Twenty short minutes from food, wine, and gala. He took the shopping bags from her.

As they approached their car, Sabina stopped at the boot. "Hey."

"Yes." Garence came back around to meet her and placed the shopping bags on the floor.

"Thank you for tooling up in the market. I was about to crumble before you jumped in."

"Of course."

She closed the gap between them. "As of right now, I'm releasing all of my sadness; I'm no longer looking in the rearview mirror. I deserve to be happy, and I deserve to be with you. That's what I'm going to focus on. Again. Are you good with that?"

He hoisted her into his arms, applied intense pressure to her mouth with his lips, then whirled her around.

"Thank you. I love how you show me your answer," she said.

"Actions speak louder than words."

"That they do."

She slapped his bum. "Now, let's go home and listen to our albums."

Sabina started the car and fastened her seatbelt as Garence loaded the groceries and got into the passenger seat.

Something in the air shifted, and an energy alignment occurred. She smiled, sensing Garence's thoughts. At long last, he had his wife back, and they were moving forward. Together. She leaned toward him, placed his hands upon her face, and pressed his lips against hers; an electric current shot down their spines.

"Ready?"

"Definitely."

Sabina looked for traffic. It was clear. She looked back at Garence with a smile, then turned onto the main road.

CRASH!

The car was thrust backward from the impact.

Metal twisted and groaned as the driver's side imploded into the cabin.

Shattered glass from the windscreen and side window flew into the cab, pelting Garence and Sabina like machine-gun fire.

Their limp bodies swooped parallel to the angle of the attack, then jolted back into the seats.

Garence sat inside the ambulance with Sabina. She was strapped to a spinal board and barely coherent to those around her. Having experienced the brunt of the impact, her surface wounds were more severe than his almost nonexistent ones. The right side of her face was scarlet and swelling, and her ear bled beneath the gauze protecting it, but the paramedics feared more for the extent of her internal injuries and her back than her superficial wounds.

With every breath, Garence saw Sabina's chest rise and fall, pinched as it was within the limitations of the straps.

"She can't breathe," he said. "She can't breathe! Loosen the straps."

The paramedic did one better and unbuckled the head and chest straps.

Her breathing calmed, and her head oscillated with every bump in the road.

Garence leaped forward and gripped her hands. "Sabina. Sabina. Wake up. Look at me, darling."

She was silent, unable to do as she was told.

"Stay with me, love."

She opened her eyes and stared at him, leaving Garence to fear the worst.

"I can't."

What is she on about? She never says she "can't."

"Yes, you can. I should have driven."

"Don't," she winced, "blame. Please, Garence... don't."

A piercing ring swelled into her ears, and she had a premonition. A terrifying one that sucked all the color from her face, but it softened when she saw the silver lining within her vision; something beautiful would arise from the ashes. The vision vanished and she was left with the dark aspect of what she was privy to see.

She stared daggers at Garence.

"Don't do it," she whispered.

"What's that?" He believed she was in a daze, and it sounded as if she were talking in her sleep.

"Garence," she said, tears welling in her eyes. "Promise me you'll remain strong."

Garence kissed her hands. "Not without you."

She gritted her teeth, thinking how unfair everything was, but she zeroed in on him.

"If I am grateful for anything in this reality, it's you. Promise me you won't do it. For us," she finished, breathless.

He tightened his grip on her hands. "I love you."

Her heartbeat dropped.

The paramedics did their best to tend to her while working around Garence. Her hold on him relaxed.

Chapter Twenty-Three

TWO YEARS AGO

— JUNE —

It was an outdoor celebration to honor Sabina Leitner at sunset. Glowing candles on tabletops and dangling from giant tree limbs. A waiter served hors d'oeuvres while an array of Sabina's favorite artists streamed the airwaves: Marc Antoine, Eliane Elias, the Beatles, Friendly Fires, Amy Macdonald. Guests from as far away as Australia, Spain, and Brazil, including their Chilean tour guide, Marcos, were present, wearing hues other than black. Sabina's parents donned her favorite color, green. Garence wore the same gray shirt Sabina had worn the week after Estrella died, when she'd locked herself in their bedroom.

He stalked away from the party and leaned against a hawthorn tree at the far edge of their land, listening to their song from his phone in his back pocket.

He thought he had nodded off because his vision was clouded by a sheer curtain that was Sabina in the carnation-white, halter shift dress she'd worn when they'd visited the Great Barrier Reef. He blinked. The iridescence disappeared, and she was there.

He was frozen solid whilst she stood not three meters away from him, enjoying the sunset, humming to the melody of the instrumental.

He whispered her name.

She looked over her shoulder, smiled, and then she was gone.

"Come back," he whispered, emotions consuming him. "Come back."

The sun sank into the rolling hills as Sabina's father, Gael, approached.

"There you are," he said. "I'm sorry, I didn't mean to startle you."

He was as tall as Garence and broader in the shoulders.

"She would have loved this."

"Yeah. I still needed to get away from it all."

Gael smirked. "Wanna fly and have a glass or two in town?"

Garence shook his head.

"Why not? We'll catch up over some cognac and raise our glasses to the angel who has returned to her maker."

"It won't bring her back."

"Nothing will, son. Clara and I are going to head back to the hotel."

"You guys should have stayed at the house," said Garence. "It's your home too."

"*Sí.* We know, but you don't need to worry about guests. And… your *madre* and I aren't…"

"Too soon?"

"I'm sorry, son."

"Me too. I have to live in it."

"Come here." He embraced Garence with both arms.

"We should meet up before Clara and I head back in a couple of days. We were in Bali last month, and I wondered if you had been to a few of the spots we visited."

"Gael, I love you, but I can't be arsed right now."

"I understand."

Garence pressed his forefinger and thumb into his eyes, regretting his remark. "I'm sorry. Fuck… I can't… I can't forget myself. I don't want to."

"I accept that. I'll leave you then. It's a beautiful scene. If you ever need anything, ring us."

"Thanks. Oi! Sabina would have relished a drink of cognac."

A twinkle appeared in Gael's eye when Garence spoke her name. "Then we won't be drinking alone after all."

Chapter Twenty-Four

PRESENT DAY

Following Sabina's life celebration, friends and family strolled in like sprinklings on a withered white rose. It seemed as though everyone was worried about me. I can't imagine why. I wanted to die every single day, but they didn't know that. Each morning, I bathed and dressed in clean clothes as if I were looking forward to the day. I was pleasant enough. That is, I put half of my best foot forward for their sake, but they were least likely to call upon me again if they weren't scared for me. A large part of me didn't mind whatever emotions, sympathy, pity, or others, encouraged their visits. They were all a constant reminder of Sabina. I welcomed her parents the most, and they were far better at conversing with me than anyone else. I suppose it had something to do with the fact that they had lost their only child. They had each other to console, and I felt their deep need to reach out to me. To comfort the man she loved, and perhaps they wanted to be near the things she cherished. The way they asked me how I was "that day" was much more appreciated than "how are you?" What would they have said if I told them how I was? In general,

I was an utter mess and as dead as Sabina was (I had wanted to thank them for the reminder so many times, but I bit my tongue off long ago). Let's dismiss whatever benevolent tone their voice took on and focus on the question. Being asked how I was on a day-to-day basis, now that was a different conversation. On any given day, I was numb, fine, shitty, okay, or just breathing, and being asked this by these two good-hearted people would perk me up enough to drizzle on some well-meant superficial charm and say that I was getting by.

I saw Sabina's features in Clara's and Gael's faces now more than ever. The cheekbones were all her mother's. Her big smile came from her papa, and even though her laugh was all her own, I heard it mixed in with theirs, more out of memory than anything else. The rare instances when her temper flared, I recognized as being her mother's, whereas the timing of those instances was, thankfully, learned from her father. I shared countless memories of Sabina with them, and I looked forward to hearing theirs. It was a blessing, a beautiful gift, to discover something new about the woman I thought I knew everything about. It was almost as if she were alive and out fetching gelato, and upon her return, I would dangle the new information in front of her to procure a reaction. For that reason, I steadily learned to despise being reminded of her absence.

I grew angry, and I eventually stopped seeing them. I told them I had a lot to do with the house or that I was out far away. I didn't want to lie to them, but I couldn't stay in their realm of remembering what I was missing. I didn't want to see her in them anymore. I wanted her, not intangible flashes.

As I sit by the fire, I can see Sabina on the sofa, reading and tapping her foot to an inaudible beat that only she is privy to. She isn't on the sofa, of course, so I suppose I should have written the word "imagine" rather than "see." I can't conjure her up with the snap of my fingers any more than I can predict when she will arrive... but I can utilize my imagination and summon a memory of her that will cloud my vision.

To my great disappointment, whenever I spoke, she vanished as if I had broken the spell. It took the breath from my very lungs to see her gone. After the third manifestation, I identified the pattern. Then, I discovered her apparition was telepathic, so I communicated with her via that route, and the next visit felt more intimate; our bond grew. I would walk or sit close to her, hoping beyond hope to hold her in my arms. Wishing that it would be different and that perhaps she would stay with me this time, but she wouldn't, and my chest caved in at the sight of her.

During one of the more painful moments, I inadvertently tested my newfound hypothesis when I asked her, "You are never going to come back, are you?" I hated myself for making her sad and seeing her disappear.

After all the rubbish we were dragged through, Sabina and I were on our way up from the depths of the abyss, and then she was taken from me. That wasn't in the cards. That wasn't how our story was supposed to end. We were supposed to continue traveling the globe, dance in the living room together or at a concert, make love, gaze at the stars, and grow old together. Was that too much to ask for?

Apparently, it was.

She appeared in the supermarket before the apple stand, in the bed beside me, or on a flight if the seat next to me was empty. With each occurrence, she was as real as before, and her presence sang with the same energy as it had when she was breathing. As always, and to my great delight, she was unchanged. She wore the carnation-white, halter shift dress that she wore on our proposal trip to Australia. If the temperature was fresh, she sported a jean jacket or a shawl around her shoulders as she would have done if she were uncomfortable in this reality, but always in the same dress and barefoot. I cannot explain how she covered her shoulders but not her feet. What do I care? I loved her feet, and it worked for her. Actually, I'm lying. There were those very few instances during the winter when she wore... Gosh, I can't remember. What was she wearing?

Garence closed his eyes, and he was taken back to one year ago. They were crossing Oxford Street, and Sabina jogged ahead of him and onto the sidewalk.

That's it! Nude flats.

No wonder he didn't remember, they blended with her skin. On second thought, what an odd thing to wear in the English winter.

Anyway, that's enough chatter on her feet.

Chapter Twenty-Five

TWO YEARS AGO

— JUNE —

After all the physician bills from the miscarriages, the stillbirth, and Sabina's cremation and memorial service, there were three weeks of savings in the bank. Garence had been monitoring this depleting asset since Estrella's stillbirth when neither of them had worked for three months, so he had advertised the holiday let six weeks prior. It was summer, and the demand for a quiet spot in the English countryside was never low. The first guests were expected within a few days, which was a relief, but he would have to perform routine maintenance on both houses and replace some yard tools he needed in order to clean up around the grounds, leaving him a bit skint. Moreover, Garence wasn't in the mood to be as hospitable with the guests as he would have liked, but at least his superficial charm was already practiced on friends and family. He received glowing reviews, which encouraged other lodgers to book with him.

The thought of living off Sabina's forthcoming life insurance disgusted him, so that he became even more financially conservative than he already was. He never left the house or encouraged anyone to visit. He pushed for travel assignments, but the earliest wasn't for another two months. Which, in the end, was optimal because the summer bookings would slow down. He would stay afloat with the busy rental season, working as a farmhand for one neighbor and a handyman for another while he had the opportunity to assimilate into whatever his new life was.

What was once a quintessential cottage filled with cherished mementos had become a tomb encompassing Sabina's prized possessions like an Egyptian pyramid. A tomb existing for others to question the reasoning behind the sanity of those who wanted the items stowed, or in Garence's case, why he left everything as she had left it. Despite the steady flow of renters, Garence almost never saw anyone. He was deprived of human interaction and the preoccupations of travel, sport, and sketching, all of which he gave up when Estrella died. When the life insurance was deposited into Garence's account, he vomited. Rage drove him to tear the dragon renderings and burn them in the fire. Emotional and somber, he didn't eat for two days, and he slept very little. Sabina emerged, and she suggested he use the funds to pay off the mortgage. It took several more days to pass before clarity bathed him and he followed her advice. Upon leaving the bank, Garence waned into the shadows of the cozy cottage he now thought of as a burrow. A curtain-drawn and fireless hideaway where Sabina's visits were the highlight of his consciousness.

"Remember the Lake District?" Garence asked Sabina in his mind, a fitting means of communication, seeing as she'd always read his mind when she was alive.

Garence sat with his arms draped over his bent knees on the brick patio outside the study. It was sprinkling on this summer day, where the gray clouds served as a watering can. He had arrived home from an assignment, and he was still wearing the same clothes he'd had on before his fourteen-hour flight from Singapore.

Worn navy-blue sleeves were pushed up above the elbows; Sabina wore a denim jacket whilst holding the wooden handle to a red umbrella with black polka dots over them—she was always the prepared one. "Yes. Such beautiful country. You decided it was best to take the long way to the B&B after a long day of hiking and got us lost."

Garence scoffed. "*I* didn't get us lost?" he internalized.

"Yeah, *you* did."

"Why are you directing the blame at me? Both of us were in the car."

"I seem to recall you driving and attempting to pacify me with some sort of 'I know where we got off track' bullshit."

"I took a wrong turn! Anyone could have done it. Anyway, we found our way back to the B&B in no time, and we made up for lost time if I remember correctly."

"In no time! Oh, *sí!*" she exclaimed over him, reading his mind. "How can you be so delusional? Three hours off course, one of which was spent on the side of the road in thick, gray sheets of rain."

She was laughing and about to bump his shoulder in play when she caught herself; she didn't want to break her manifestation and leave his side. "I had never seen it pour so much in my entire life. I thought we were at sea and the car was going to float away. We did find our way. Didn't we?"

Garence nodded. He met her eyes, and his heart ached for her so much that he almost turned away. Sabina was correct; they always found their way back to each other—this moment was the perfect example. She was dead, yet here she was visiting him from the great beyond. He still couldn't stand to look at her. It was too painful, not to mention too soon, for Garence to reminisce upon how great they had been together, so he severed the connection as easily as pressing a remote control.

He spoke "yes" out loud, and she vanished.

Her visits were a bid to aid Garence through his lonesomeness, but her disappearance often left him feeling worse than he'd felt before her arrival. Whatever memory they had revived was intended to linger after her departure as a subtle reminder of all that was possible when living life. But these memories weren't something Garence wanted to remember; they reminded him of what he was missing.

The night after closing Sabina out, he found himself in an unfamiliar place. It was pitch-black, and he couldn't see the end of his nose. The dark space possessed a pull on his already low spirit, and he wanted to scream. Then he did, and his echoes died in the silence. If anyone was around, there was no chance of being heard. That is if there was anyone to hear him. He should've yelled for help, but then he paused. If he were trapped somewhere like a mountain cave, he didn't want to wake a sleeping predator.

Where the bloody hell was he?

He was so focused on trying to figure out where he was that he failed to register his chest was heaving, and the rhythm of his breathing had intensified to an alarming rate. The echo of his frantic pants trailed the undefined distance like smokestacks rioting out of a rushing train, and he couldn't contain his senses long enough to process this new information. Was that his heart beating in his ears, or was there a train approaching?

Wait a minute, he was in a tunnel.

The surface of his skin burned with panic.

This was *exactly* how he'd felt when Sabina shut him out after Estrella died, like he was in a tunnel without a light at the end. He was desperate to get out of here, but he didn't know which way the nearest exit was.

He felt lightheaded as his stomach clenched the bile that sloshed within it. This was too bizarre. He must be dreaming.

Wake up, mate! Wake up!

Garence awoke and vomited over the side of the bed.

All of his previous symptoms of distress disappeared as he fell back against the bed to separate himself from the clear liquid. He panted as his eyes roamed the room, as if making sure it was real and not a set his imagination had created to wedge him into a false sense of security.

It was a dream.

He closed his eyes and sighed. His entire body sank into the mattress a little bit deeper. The dream had been so real. Too real. He was lonely and scared, and those emotions had manifested in his dreams.

Garence lay in bed before recognizing an offensive scent. He lifted his arm, sniffed the pit, then jerked away. He looked at the state of the bed and figured it was likely as foul as he, and this was too disgusting even for his state of mind. He rose from the bed and put the linen in the wash while he showered.

The days disseminated like fog skulking onto the coast, defiant and strangulating. Garence was looking up at the stars from the flat of his back on the study's patio, wondering why he hadn't seen Sabina as of late, when he returned to the infernal dark.

The silence was identical to that which had haunted him a fortnight ago. He tried to tell himself to wake up, but it didn't work.

Cripes!

Why the bloody hell was he in a tunnel again? How was he going to get out of this?

No, he knew why. Grieving in the dark and all that. Hell, even in his dreams, life was taking the piss.

Focus on getting out, he told himself.

The stale air thickened with dread and drove him to look for an exit. The gravel crunched sharply beneath his first intentional step, and Garence became aware of how square his shoulders were and every muscle movement. His toes went from being pressed against the roof of his boot to clenching the insole as he struggled to find strength in each ankle and leg as the other lifted high enough to avoid any unseen obstacle. He needed a bit of help, a bit of light. He heard Sabina's name escape his lips. He was about to raise his arms to feel for his way around when he wavered and hit his right knee and chin on a track.

Garence woke up in a pool of perspiration that vibrated with his terror. He hated being alone in the dark. Why was he dreaming of an even worse situation than the one he lived in? He rubbed his chin as if to scuff the harsh impact away, but it wasn't sore. It was just a dream. The blue light emitting from the digital alarm clock seemed to illuminate brighter than usual, and it caught his attention. As well as the time: 6:66.

What the hell? There was no such possible time. The damn clock must be going out. Garence paused. 666. A pattern. But what did it represent? He wracked his brain for something Sabina had said about that message not meaning anything malicious. It meant something opposite of what people feared in this number. That was it! He had to let go of his fear and... What was it? Trust that all was going to end well or some bloody hornswoggle? He gave the clock a pound, and the digits sorted themselves out. It was 6:06. That was better.

He sat at the edge of the bed, immobilized, when Sabina appeared beside him. His elbows dug into his knees from the weight of his body being hurled over them, and his head hung as if waiting for the executioner's sword. She went to run her fingers through his hair, but she stopped in midair. She wasn't ready to leave him.

"You need to seek help, *mi amor*."

Help? He hated the notion of talking to a therapist, or worse, joining a support group and listening to everyone else share experiences that mirrored his own. If what he was feeling was the same as every other widower, then he didn't want to hear the echoes. He would rather treat himself and whatever peculiarities he had.

"You're not peculiar, stubborn," she said.

"Thank you, darling," he internalized.

"That wasn't a compliment."

"I took it as such," he thought.

His glance reached her, but she saw his attempted wink. "When was the last time you had a solid night's rest?"

"The one before we were struck."

He remembered her last day and the entire week in great detail. It was the first time since losing Estrella she had felt like herself. They'd been sleeping side by side, and he'd made her breakfast in bed. Confit tomatoes, venison sausage, and toast.

He saw her blink away the tears, mourning what was and what could have been.

"You need to talk to someone."

He stretched his stiff neck. "I'm going to see the physician."

"That's good news. When is your appointment?"

"I don't have one yet," he said through sealed lips.

"But you said you were going to see your physician."

"I am. I'm going to call him tomorrow."

Sabina turned around. Dawn was approaching. The yellow sun bled into the atmosphere with a warmth that wasn't powerful enough to penetrate his gloom.

"Why not today?"

Garence followed her gaze and rolled his eyes at the new day approaching all too quickly. "Fine. Today." He rubbed his face with his whole hand.

"What are you going to say?"

"I dunno… All I know is that I don't want to go on," he raised his hand and gestured at himself and at the bed marked with disgust, "like this. I just want to feel again; yet another part of me wants to be anesthetized. I don't want to keep feeling what it's like to be without you. When you're not here."

She studied her husband. She'd known he was struggling with his reality even before he said it. Sabina had seen his expected outcome as she lay in the ambulance on his last restful day, but she wouldn't allow it to happen. A nightmarish image of Garence covered her third eye. He was at the police station in the middle of the cold night, surrounded by a pool of blood brought upon him by his own hand. She shut the image out and wiped away the tears before they fell. She wasn't always able to visit him, but she was not going to allow him to suffer alone.

"So, what's the plan, doc?"

A plan? he asked himself. No, he didn't have a plan. He'd never planned to lose her, so why would he have a plan to live without her?

"I will phone the office as soon as it opens. I'm going to ask for an antidepressant."

She cringed. "Are you sure?" She didn't have the best experience with antidepressants, so she didn't champion their benefits, but his next thought gave her pause.

"I have nothing, Sabina."

Most people had a reason to hang on. Someone or something to keep them grounded and sane, forging onward. What did he have? Family he had no burning desire to see. His work. Maybe another woman? That would enable his codependency issues. There had to be another way for him to cope with her death other than drugs. Perhaps he did need a little support.

Garence was true to his word, and he happened to replace a cancelation for the next hour. The physician performed a thorough assessment on him and agreed that Garence was a great candidate for a selective serotonin reuptake inhibitor, a drug that would balance the serotonin and its reabsorption, and that a three-month prescription would be a good start. It helped him through this difficult time and enabled his transition into work life. As for side effects, Garence was warned that with any SSRI, there was a potential for sexual dysfunction, suicidal ideation, and coronary heart disease, to name a few, but that his chances of experiencing any of these was low.

As eager as Garence was about taking a medication to alter his natural state, he wanted to learn more about the negative effects of the quick fix that antidepressants had become, especially knowing how they'd adversely altered Sabina as a teenager. He inquired about the possibility of his becoming dependent on the drug after he stopped taking them. He was advised that it was also not probable to experience any dependencies after a short period of time and that he could be weaned off the drug if he wished before the three-month period ended rather than quitting cold turkey. Armed with this information, Garence had his serotonin levels checked, and he picked up his prescription the next day. As the weeks leaked by, his appetite increased, and he did sleep through the night, but his emotions were still heavy—even without the incarcerating black to exacerbate them. His inclination to greet each day with confrontation had not diminished, and the effort it took him to be pleasant around people was arduous enough to be classified as lethal.

Was this the extent of his medicinal saving grace? Sleep and an urge to eat? What about addressing the most prominent symptom? Hopelessness. He could do with little sleep as long as he didn't feel miserable. He could also do without an appetite and eat to sustain his health, but above all else, he wanted to feel more like himself!

Garence fell onto the sofa, bawled as if the last of his sanity depended upon it, and wished he were dead.

Chapter Twenty-Six

TWO YEARS AGO

— NOVEMBER —

The bedroom window shades shunned the sunlight from Garence. He pulled the sheets away from him, slothed out of bed, removed his underwear, and tossed it into the hamper by the wardrobe, then walked to the bathroom. The tile was as cool as fresh snow and always welcomed after a warm night. He slipped his hand through the shower curtain to turn on the faucet. The rain showerhead exploded with thousands of droplets and whispered a promise to cleanse the preceding nightmarish day and its crown jewels that were his dark dreams down the drain. Temperate showers were welcomed even on discouraging days, and as he waited for the water to heat up, his thoughts in the depths of that doomed tunnel, his spirit plummeted. It was harrowing to combat each dreadful day after these dreams. The SSRI allowed his body to rest, but his mind and his emotions never relaxed, not in the real meaning of the word.

The water had heated to his liking. He entered the shower, and the warm rain sprinkled overhead. What had he used to feel? Happiness. Relaxation. Calm. What did any of that feel like? He couldn't remember, so how would he know if the drugs were working? What if some sort of accident occurred, and he died? He hated everything about his existence;

he hoped for a near and quick death—not to mention painless. Garence rinsed the shampoo, then applied conditioner.

The next morning, he missed an opportunity to wallow through his morning routine as he rushed to meet the Cosmos Place renters, a Norwegian family of five, who requested a personal tour of the surrounding area—cripes, he'd rather someone wallop him to death. They knew nothing of his life, so he was afforded a morning distraction. They had their three children with them, all girls, and he grappled with the family life dangled before him like a carrot in front of a donkey. Was he to imagine this would have been his life if Sabina and their three children had lived? Was he supposed to be happy for this family? No, this was bullshit. These people had what he and Sabina had wanted. A family. A shot at life and love. But then again, if he had driven, Sabina would be alive.

Who's to say he could have sustained the trauma better or perhaps seen the speeding car approaching? If he had been driving, they would have left a few seconds earlier or later than the car crossing their path, and everything would be different. Either way, he should have driven. He ought to have allowed her to rest in the passenger seat from her ordeal at the market. It was his job to take care of her, and he'd failed her, and in that, he'd failed himself. Dammit, this was all his blunder. He'd killed his wife. Now Garence was forced to parade this family around his town and say what? This, here, is where my children would have gone to school if they lived. This is where my wife worked before I murdered her. Yes, she's dead; now get the fuck out of our home.

Tight-lipped, Garence gripped the steering wheel, took deep breaths, then counted to three. Before the chatty couple hushed their children away from a scuffle, he drew their attention by pointing out a landmark and reciting a few anecdotal stories about the area. It worked. Stories about mischief managed always worked and received laughs from all ages, and soon they asked him to drop them off at a restaurant, where they insisted upon hiring a car for the ride home.

The following day, his glum schedule resumed like clockwork. He underwent the ritual of a long, dismal snooze to awaken and shower, where his ideations would flourish like gnarled roots tightening around his neck. He stepped into the tub, all the while imagining himself slipping on the slick surface, hitting his head on the rim, and getting knocked unconscious, where he would bleed profusely. He wouldn't feel the cold or the wooziness that occurred after he lost the second pint of blood and then the third. He wouldn't even be conscious to fight his own death. Garence rolled his eyes—that would be too easy. It was a good way to die. Semi-painless, and the desired result would be accomplished.

"It isn't," said a reverberating voice that wafted into his thoughts like a gas, invisible and polluting his fantasy.

Garence jumped, and his foot skidded upon landing on the slick surface, granting his own wish upon this fortuitous moment. The voice was unfamiliar and reminiscent of one with a forked tongue, and it echoed off the walls and simmered in his mind so he couldn't forget its presence. He didn't know where to look to see who had spoken. He tried to make sense of what he'd heard, but nothing added up. There wasn't a chance it was the renters. No one would have dared to enter his bathroom to hiss at him like a committed patient. He pulled the shower curtain, water droplets spraying the tile like holy water, and searched frantically for the owner of the reptile-like voice. He turned off the water and heard no movement. Not a sound was made except for the water draining. Garence waited a good minute before accepting relief.

A fistful of days sauntered past with a zeal that matched Garence's enthusiasm for another pill. He was sitting on the bathroom floor in lounge pants, barefoot, back against the wall, and his arms draped over his knees. He stared at the plastic bottle of empty wishes perched on top of the pedestal sink. It seemed to stare at him like the witch who had judged Sabina in the market. The light fixture above cast an inviting glow, and in that moment, his eyes widened with possibility.

What if he took a handful of pills, or rather, all thirty? That was a brand-new bottle glaring at him. How long would it take for his body to shut down? Would thirty pills be enough to kill him? He closed his eyelids, breathed in this magnificent possibility, and imagined how wonderful a permanent rest would be. No more regret. No more tears. No more emptiness.

"Don't think it."

Garence was shaken into a state of rigidity. Fear seethed through his veins and extracted his body temperature as quickly as those three words were spoken. He tried to be brave and wondered what the hell that voice was on about. His back was up against the wall, and there was no one in the room with him. He stepped over his fright and returned to his ideation.

What if his attempt failed? He would be sick as hell, or worse, supervised by professionals who would become a ball and chain.

"Stop!"

His heartbeat went into a rage as his head shot left then right. Again, nothing or no one was there.

No! He had heard someone. Someone had commanded him to stop.

Stop what? he wondered, holding his breath.

There was no one there.

Why was he hearing someone who wasn't there? Or was the voice from within his head?

He lifted his juddering hands and rubbed his throbbing head. *I heard someone. I did*, he internalized.

Garence was on edge from this point on. Fantasies about his death also took flight throughout the day and every day. Sometimes he directed these scenes, causing the resonating hiss to revisit him and unnerve him further. Other times, he stumbled into the fantasies by happenstance, and those were more dangerous.

Driving to the market to pick up sausage for his breakfast, he stopped at a traffic light. What if a great big delivery truck slammed into him? He surveyed the traffic. Yeah, that one to his right coming through the roundabout. Or better yet, what if a train hit him? He'd want to be rammed hard so he wouldn't have time to notice what was happening.

A couple of young adults to his left were laughing and shouting in Turkish. His foot let off the brake pedal as he looked over at them and pondered if he would ever be as carefree. He didn't notice his car rolling forward into crossing traffic, but the delivery truck's blaring horn knocked him into the present.

It wasn't until Garence heard the resonating voice during his travel assignments that he believed he was schizophrenic. He was standing in his swimming trunks above Devil's Pool at Victoria Falls, Zimbabwe. A dense mist billowed from the gorge and the cascades, and two rainbows glistened. He thought about jumping into nature's ultimate infinity pool when he panicked. He was a yard above the pool, but the horizon was broad, not as wide as Trolltunga because of his vantage point, but it triggered an out-of-body urge to make a different kind of leap.

"Don't even think it!"

The cascading water roared like an angry storm, but the voice was as clear as birdsong in a meadow. Garence leaped to escape the resonating voice. He swam a few meters to the edge of the Devil's Pool, where the rocks were smooth and ultraslick.

Garence lay on his stomach, eyes closed. The sun warmed his drenched dark curls, and he took delight in the water that scuttled over his bare skin, silently pressing him over the cliff. His eyes opened, and they gradually peered over the edge. His viscera nearly disintegrated at the sight of the three-hundred-plus-foot fall, but the urge to push himself over was greater.

"No."

There was that harrowing voice again. Harassing him.

The bottom of the gorge was rocky. The fall alone would kill someone. How long would it take to reach the bottom? Two seconds or so for every one hundred feet?

What a dream it would be to fall into the mist and disappear forever.

"Don't."

Perhaps he'd stand and jump to escape the voice that echoed against his inclination.

"I said no!" it raged.

Garence's flesh surprised him with spikes of terror, and his eyes became as unsettled as a tumultuous sea. Rising, he peered over the ledge long enough to overcome his fear of the fall and its irrepressible allure.

"Excuse me, monsieur," a young boy called out and repeated when Garence didn't acknowledge him.

Garence turned his head. Having convinced himself that the voice wasn't real, he was surprised to find the boy standing on the ledge with a teenaged boy who looked to be his brother. Garence raised an arm.

"Monsieur. My family is coming, and I considered, if you're done, whether you would take our photo."

If I'm done, reflected Garence, repeating the boy's words. Was he done? Thinking about jumping, that is, or was he done thinking about killing himself? He didn't have an inclination toward either, so he supposed he'd oblige the boy.

"Or do you speak French?" the boy asked in his natural dialect, growing impatient and uneasy about not receiving an answer from a man who looked like he was harboring the weight of the world on his shoulders.

"Yes," he answered. "I speak both, and I will take your family's photo."

Approaching their sons from behind, the parents were already professing the urgency of being careful on the slick rocks and that they didn't want to see either of them fall from the cliff.

Garence made his way to the top ledge, and then the young boys jumped into the infinite pool and soon after were followed by their parents. They all hailed and smiled for the camera before Garence took his leave, clutching his shaken nerves that were no longer repressed by a distraction. He had contemplated jumping over Victoria Falls before that boy appeared. Garence was scared, and he trembled so much that he thought he was someplace cold like Greenland or Antarctica.

What the hell was happening to him? Where was Sabina when he needed her?

When Garence arrived home, the setting sun put on a display that kept Sabina longer, and he grinned like the Cheshire Cat at the sight of her standing by the front door, pressing her dress with her hands. It had been several weeks since he'd last seen her, their longest run yet, but all of that dissolved when she spoke.

"Welcome home," she said with warmth that made up for not rushing into his arms.

"I've missed you." The longing in his voice was too thick to disregard.

"I've missed you too. I knew you'd be back safe and sound and that I had to be here to greet you."

"I couldn't ask for a better homecoming." He resisted the urge to draw her into his arms.

"What is it? Let's sit down here. Something is wrong."

Internally, he caught her up on everything he'd been up to. "I've been trying to keep my mind busy. Minding the maintenance on the entire property somehow and traveling—though not as much as when you were alive." This admission made him feel ashamed of working less now that she was dead, when it should have been the other way around. He trudged through his mud-thick guilt. "But… I don't think my efforts are any good. I still feel dead inside… Sometimes, I can't tell what's real and what's not. Now I'm hearing things. A voice. It's uncanny. I don't know if I should stop taking my meds." He escaped into his hands, then established eye contact. "I'm afraid I'm mad as a gibbon."

Sabina studied him. His shoulders were bowed, and although his skin was tanned, the rays hadn't seeped into his soul. "You're not doing enough to take care of yourself. Talk to someone."

Feeling low after Sabina's disappearance, Garence knew she was right. He didn't relish the thought of being vulnerable, but if talking to someone would help him cope and get rid of this voice, then he would do it. He researched therapists and psychiatrists in the area and decided upon a professional with vast experience in dealing with depression and altering the behaviors that came after depression—and being licensed to prescribe, she could change his medication as required. Granted, this chosen psychiatrist was in the next major city over, Gloucester, but he supposed the drive would do him some good. One never knew what they'd discover until they took a different path.

Chapter Twenty-Seven

PRESENT DAY

Garence shuffled through a stack of his letters and perused some to gauge where he should begin.

He held one of his own letters and read, "Weeping every morning at first light." *Can't say I've made much progress*, he said inwardly, but his eyes were already on the next page.

"I want to die." *Had the right idea even way back then*, he discerned. He went back to writing the last letter he would ever compose.

> *I fell upon blackness with anger and bitter resentment to keep me company. I've been forsaken. Why am I trapped in this oubliette? You know what? I honestly don't care.*
>
> *I. No. Longer. Care.*
>
> *In fact, you shouldn't care either. Why are you still reading this? I have to expel everything from my being so I can move on with a thin heart, but you have no reason to listen to this rubbish.*

Garence swallowed his wretchedness as easily as he would consume cardboard.

I am so committed to my own demise that I cannot begin to apologize for everything I uttered; I am sorry you and I have met under these circumstances. I hope you recognize that I was not always like this. A helpless feck, that is. Wait, I'm not leaving this letter for anyone; therefore, no one is reading it—I have no reason to apologize. No matter.

Sabina's death was the serrated blade that exposed my entrails, but everything I faced afterward was the fire that scorched my putrefying flesh—which was thrashed against a crumbling graffitied brick wall as if the bits of me were snowballs.

You may be wondering, if I wanted my own demise so badly, why hadn't I done it before? Dependent upon your tone and your approach, I may participate in a small discussion with you or turn about-face because you weren't worth my time, but I will go with the former and say that my previous suicidal ideations were thoughts. I don't mean to diminish the severity of them, but compared to my current state of being, they were toward the weak end of alarm. Did I or do I want someone to pity me? No, I haven't ever wanted any of that. If you think back, I haven't shared the thoughts of popping my own clogs with anyone; therefore, I have asked no one to feel for me. To be clear, having suicidal thoughts is not the same as attempting or planning suicide. These considerations can be small and fleeting, or not, but most people don't act on them. Yes, they are all undeniable risk factors and should all be taken seriously. Many people discover the light at the end of their tunnel, but let's magnify my situation. I have been a suicide risk, and I have made no attempts for thirty months, but my light died a year and a half ago. There was a flare within that dark tunnel, for an instant, but it also died. This weekend is my suicide planning, and my life will end at the end of it.

Chapter Twenty-Eight

PRESENT DAY

The wine bottle was as low as his inhibitions, and he emptied the bottle into the glass, then emptied the glass. Now seemed to be as fine a time to pack as any. He dropped the bottle into the bin, grabbed a box, and went down the hallway. He wondered how they'd accumulated so much stuff in the short time they were together. Then again, they'd traveled to so many places; filling their home with mementos, books, and local artists was part of the fun. Now it was time to see them to a new home.

The hallway was partially lit by the sun at its highest hour. His steps shortened, and he wondered where he was because the hallway to the study didn't have a window, so where the hell was he? Before he could formulate a cohesive answer, horror rose to his chest. His breathing quickened, but he couldn't stop himself from approaching the bedroom. It was as if he were possessed.

There was no way he could touch her things or cart them off. Not now. Not this afternoon. He couldn't distinguish what made him travel down this hallway and not the one leading to the study like he'd intended. He had been out of sorts all morning, but he didn't want to pack the main bedroom now. He wasn't ready for this. He had one more day and that was his deadline. He would pack her things tomorrow. It was better to leave the most distressing one for last.

He opened his eyes, and Sabina's memory greeted him with a twitch of agony.

"Read my letters," she ordered.

Garence ran out of the bedroom, through the kitchen, and into the bin in the living room. The wine bottles rolled on the floor. One broke right before he landed on it, hands first. Blood emitted. He kicked the bin out of his way and stumbled to the kitchen, gripping his wrist. He left his hand under the faucet and discovered it was his wrist bleeding, not his hand. His eyelids swayed closed and opened. He couldn't tell if it was the sight of blood on his drained system drowning him or if it was the alcohol. The sink was red and his grip was loosening.

He wondered if he should let it all go. Give up the fight and bleed out. He couldn't feel anything, so what more could he ask for?

He watched the water as it came out of the faucet, and he lost himself in it. When he looked at his wrist, there wasn't as much blood coming out. He released a few fingers. The blood under his hand mixed with the water, but nothing more flowed. He turned off the water, then reached for the emergency kit underneath the sink and dressed his wound.

He couldn't pack anything now. He put another log on the fire and pulled out another bundle of letters and settled into the armchair.

Chapter Twenty-Nine

TWO YEARS AGO

— DECEMBER —

Garence buried his fists into his eye sockets, but nothing eradicated his weariness. He sucked in a gust of air and was reminded of a session with his Dutch therapist, Dr. Henrietta Visser.

Dr. Visser preferred her patients to call her Henrietta, and that's what Garence did, with the negotiation that she never called him Mr. Leitner. She was twenty years his senior, with straight blonde hair that swung past her ears whenever she tilted her head, as if it helped her to better understand whatever Garence was expressing. She'd studied in her home country before earning her PhD in psychology from the University of Birmingham, an hour north of Gloucester.

Today was his first step on his growth toward recovery, a personal journey of sorts, if that was even possible. Garence looked away from Henrietta as he acknowledged the tiny truth that fumigated the back of his mind like a gas chamber. This was his first session toward recovery from depression, meaning in the general direction of a recovered state and not to the expected and fully fledged state of being recovered. In addition, beyond the poisoned gas mentality, Garence didn't know where in the point of his life he should start.

Was he not here to release the grief that was suffocating him?

He surveyed Henrietta. She sat in a black armchair with white chalk stripes, wide enough to seat two people, with her legs pulled up on the cushion. She waited for him to speak, or rather, she sat there surveying him as if she couldn't put her finger on something and had all the time in the world to figure it out, regardless of whether he was paying her by the hour or not. She had suggested he start whenever he felt like it, so the ball was in his court.

Her office was located south of Gloucester Cathedral near the Fountain Inn, where he had drunk a pint of locally brewed ale before the meeting. The room was a refuge that included an area rug beneath a dark coffee table. The table was topped with a box of tissues and a burnt lavender candle. A lamp stood in one corner, and a large plant was at the opposite end of the room. Garence sat on a love seat that supported the entirety of his backside near a small fireplace, and it absorbed any trace of anxiety he had entered with. The three side-by-side windows across from him overlooked Stroud Road and its multitude of shops. The middle pane was open three inches, and a delicate breeze stirred the scent from the candle. Garence took a deep breath.

Now it seemed clearer to him to start at the beginning.

He rubbed his face with a hand, then ran it through his curls. "I've had three different lives. I was single the majority of it, enjoying myself as I traveled the globe and experienced different cultures. During one of my assignments, I met Sabina and fell head over heels in love with her; we were married soon after. We had a wonderful life. She made me happy, more than I ever thought was possible. We miscarried three times. Those were the worst times for us. She retreated into herself each time, at which point I was shut out and left in the dark; I hated it. I was grieving for our children too, and I needed her to comfort me. I have come to realize, or admit, that she wasn't there for me. She wasn't capable of it in those situations until she healed herself, but that's what you're supposed to do, right? Take care of yourself before you can help others. I don't know; that's what I'm going to stick by because I could never resent her. When she was ready, I knew she'd find me. I would wait forever in a world of torment for her if I knew that she would return."

He cleared his throat, and his shoulders curled. "Sabina died six months ago. We were struck by a car. She had experienced the brunt of the impact, and she died within the hour. For six months, I've been living in misery, which isn't living—it's fucking suffering. I had never experienced that kind of love before—respect, trust, and passion all rolled into one glorious energy. Our relationship was fun and intense from day one, and I wouldn't have changed any part of it for any reason. I'm trying not to look in the rearview mirror, but I cannot accept her death. I feel strangled in this life. I can't remember when I've taken a full breath; my lung capacity has shrunk, I know it. I cannot see beyond losing Sabina. I have no idea how I am still alive if I am so broken."

Garence's fidgeting was now visible, and his clawed hands went to his chest. "When she died, so did everything else. I know I don't have a heart or a bloody soul anymore, but I can't find the scars... I can't find them."

Henrietta had seen this anguished state before. This was natural, she discerned, and so were the other responses that occurred after losing a spouse. She noted the change in his body language; erect upper body, and his knees were spreading open as if he were at home, with calm enough breathing patterns. Then it occurred to her how much Garence resembled her second son, Michiel.

"Have you thought of killing yourself?"

Garence wasn't going to answer her question. That would lead to further investigation and observation. That wasn't something he was interested in, but he would receive the full extent of Henrietta's treatment.

Did he want that?

"I don't want to live like this."

Henrietta read into his answer and recognized what he didn't release. Michiel had been the same way at first. Garence and Michiel shared the same body structure, tall and lean, with dark curls, although Michiel maintained his hair shorter than Garence, and they both had the same forlorn manner, but the most prominent commonality between them was their unfortunate loss.

Michiel's wife of fifteen years had died while on holiday. Michiel had never been the same after she passed, and he wished he had died instead more than often.

"I don't want you to live like this either," Henrietta said. "You don't deserve it. So why don't you stop feeling sorry for yourself?"

Garence stared daggers at her. "Excuse me?"

"You're the only thing standing in your own way. If you want to live a different life, you have to create it."

Garence was failing to hear what Henrietta was saying. He knew it was true, but it wasn't possible.

"Are you on anything?"

"What? Like drugs? No. Why would I show up here high?" Given the tone of her counsel, Garence couldn't help being defensive.

Henrietta chuckled. "No. I can see that you're not high. Perhaps on your own self-righteous misery, but not drugs." She shook her head. "Garence, I'm asking if you are taking any medications. I need to know what you've been prescribed since your wife's death in order to help you."

"Oh! Citalopram, which I've elected to be weaned off from about a month ago. I wrote it on my medical history there."

Henrietta ignored his tone. "So you did. Congratulations."

He glared at her.

"Well, I think that's all I can absorb for today. Feel free to…"

"Excuse me. I don't think we're done."

"Garence, that's why you have more sessions to attend. Your time is up, and my next client is waiting outside."

Garence cocked his head, then searched for a clock. Well, fuck. His time was up. He rose and asked if his automatic payment arrangement was accepted.

"Oh, yes. I've received your payment. Otherwise, I wouldn't have allowed you to cross my threshold. Relax," she patted his shoulder, "it processes within the hour of your appointment, so if you ever feel the urge to cancel on me, you're not charged for the appointment so long as you call up to one hour beforehand. Which leads me to impart your one and only appointment reminder, because I don't pay a receptionist to keep you on track."

"Goes hand in hand with your one-hour cancelation policy, doesn't it?"

"I resent that comment. I am not a swindler. I run a tight ship, and I expect you to be an adult and show up when you say you will."

"Goodness, you're a ball buster."

"Why, have you wet yourself?" She sighed. "Garence, would you please leave? My day doesn't revolve around you. I have another client waiting, and I cannot pay him for your intrusion."

Garence looked at her askance with a smirk growing on his face. He shook his head and exited her office.

This is going to work out fine.

— FEBRUARY —

Henrietta was big on deep-breathing exercises to calm the nerves, but she also liked how it enabled the inhaler to center their attention. "Take a deep breath through your nostrils. Now hold it in your chest and expel it. Imagine that someday you will experience a release."

"That's cruel," he said.

Henrietta scowled at him. "You will experience a release someday."

"I will never be free."

"Not with an attitude like that you won't."

Most therapists didn't speak much, but this one was unconventional; that's why Garence had chosen her. He liked unconventional. Weren't the Dutch known for it? Wait, that was tolerance. Henrietta pushed his buttons, and he needed someone to kick him in the arse every once in a while.

"Fair enough. You are allowed to feel everything that comes your way."

He surveyed her. Was she going to let him off the hook that easy? "You're being gracious today. Are you losing your touch?"

"It's fine, for now, but it won't be for long," she said.

"Then let's ride the wave while we can."

Henrietta snickered. "You've been off the citalopram for some time. You were weaned. Is that correct?"

"Yes."

"Did you experience any adverse side effects as your brain returned to homeostasis? Depreciation for life, reduced or little appetite, or anything of that sort?"

"Mood swings and erratic sleep." He had preferred these bumps in the road in lieu of a lifetime of drug dependencies, and the chance to eradicate the resonant voice—which Henrietta knew nothing about—was appealing.

She noted this. "When did you last have your serotonin levels checked?"

"A few weeks back. I'm normal."

"I'm glad to hear it. I don't know if I would classify you as normal."

The corner of his mouth turned up.

"But I cannot discount the improvement you've made since you first arrived at my doorstep four months ago." She watched Garence stare at his hands, or perhaps he was off in reflection and his eyes had fixated on his hands by chance. "Same time in two weeks, Mr. Globe-Trekker."

"Yes. I'll be back in town by then, at which point I'll have nothing else to do."

She ignored his jab. "Where are you off to?"

"Peru, for nine days."

She was keen to notice the mild change in his disposition. She interjected, "Sounds as though you are looking forward to it?"

When she'd first met Garence, he was shattered. He spoke about his lack of desire to live without Sabina, but he didn't exhibit any signs of following through on these thoughts, and her instincts were always on point, so she monitored him. On occasion, such as now, he illustrated some signs of appreciating bits of his life.

Garence took count of himself. "I guess, a little." He shrugged. "I'll be on the Inca Trail, and if I remember to do so, I'll leave a bit of my demeanor on the Altar of the Condor," he quipped.

The Altar of the Condor was a low stone platform carved to depict the head of a vulture with a scarf of feathers around the neck. Behind the altar were two megaliths situated and chiseled to replicate the expansive wings. Garence could envision the scene now. He would sit before the altar and meditate for a bit, exhaling whatever was ready to be freed, if anything. Below the stone wings was a small cave where animals were sacrificed and burned. Perhaps a portion of his despair would corrode in the cave or evaporate behind the wings of the condor and he could find a grain of peace.

Henrietta disbelieved him. "I'm not sure the gods would accept that as a sacrifice."

He knew she would have preferred it if he weren't so grim, but at least he was working and getting far out of the cottage. That was progress. Anyone would have believed that he was coping well enough or doing a good job of preoccupying himself when in actuality, Garence just didn't want to live off the funds that were only possible because Sabina was dead.

He figured he would save Henrietta the trouble of speaking to this and point the finger at himself. "I'll do my best to work on my outlook, but I want you in top form next time. All right? None of this bloody negativity."

She looked up at him over the top of her bifocals, the corner of her mouth stretching as she saw him turn the tables. "Cheers, and you owe me a box of gevulde koeken."

Garence smiled as best as he could, for his smiles these days were mere shadows of what they once were.

"Whatever for?"

He knew what Henrietta would say. He would have purchased the paste-filled butter cookies for her even if he didn't owe them to her, but he didn't want his social engagement to end yet.

"You promised to buy me a box of gevulde koeken if you didn't get out of the house before we met again. You didn't mention anything today, not one word. I'm sure it couldn't have slipped your mind if you had, but I can tell that you have not left your cottage but for work since I last saw you. Your silence speaks volumes," she added, disappointed.

He wanted to banter, but he was running dry. "How about I get you a box of empanadas instead?" Those were some of Sabina's favorite pastries, flakey goodness that resembled a mini calzone filled with fruit or meat.

"Mm. Pineapple are my favorite," she said with a far-off look in her eye that took her back to Spain when she'd been visiting her college beau, Tomás, the man she was seeing before she married her husband. His mother made the most delicious empanadas. To say Henrietta was too distracted to notice Garence's silence was an underestimation. She could almost smell the sweetie when Garence snapped her back into the present.

"Sabina was crazy about the pineapple ones as well."

Momentary sadness fell upon Henrietta. "She had good taste, and I am not referring to you." She rose from her worn leather chair as if to see him off. "As tempting as empanadas are, I must decline. The deal was a box of gevulde koeken—though I'd prefer to hear about your social escapades."

Social escapades. He could have taken the chance presented to him to josh her about why she would want to hear about whether he got his leg over someone or not, but Garence left it. He should bugger off.

He sighed. "I'll try to work on it."

She laid a hand upon his shoulder. "Don't try. Do."

PART THREE
MILDLY NICE

Chapter Thirty

ONE YEAR AGO

— MAY —

After leaving Henrietta's office, Garence remained in the city of Gloucester. He took a stroll along the Victorian docks and watched cruisers and
narrowboats sail in and out of port as the brisk air made him burrow into
his pullover until he decided upon touring Gloucester Cathedral. The
cathedral had been built in the latter part of the first century as a place
for monks to reside, worship in, and reflect, with thousands of windows,
including decorative stained glass, and it was the final resting spot for
King Edward II in 1327. Romanesque in its manner, its cloister walkways
ran everlasting lengths, with dozens of web-like fans spanning the ceiling,
a majestic kaleidoscope in a pure buttercream hue as stunning as it was
unbelievable. Garence fancied the fans could have been the webbed cre-
ation of Spider-Man, if he were more of a comic book fan, but he wasn't,
so he decided he'd rather appreciate the building for its spirit, history,
and the eminent corridors featured in the Harry Potter films.

Garence left the cathedral's gift shop empty-handed, the interior bell
ringing of his departure, when his stomach rumbled. He could indulge
himself and have an impromptu dinner, something local as opposed to
traveling forty minutes home and not eating for another one and a half
hours from now. But what type of cuisine? Seafood. French. Thai. Sushi.

He couldn't think of what sounded the most appetizing even though it shouldn't have been hard so near an array of restaurants and cafés. He preferred not to rely on his phone and Google to present him with the most popular contemporary establishment, or the latest sensation in vegan food guaranteed to make even the hardiest carnivore salivate.

He stood at a traffic intersection and waited to cross the street. The steady sound of easy, organized traffic filtered his contemplations when he overheard a couple conversing about their fire-seared meal of lamb and steak at Gloucester Studio. He smacked his lips; a fine dinner sounded sumptuous. After following the couple's directions, Garence was greeted with a rude awakening when he was informed that reservations were booked seventy-two hours in advance. Had he checked his phone, he would have learned this before he trekked thirty minutes out here. He was fixed on calling it a fish-and-chips night when he was told there was a partial cancelation for the very meal the couple on the street corner was talking about and that he wouldn't have to pay the two-hundred-and-fifty-pound deposit. With a sizeable reduction in price, he enjoyed the dough-wrapped lamb, bonfire steak, and Crêpes Suzette, all while sipping a Middle-Eastern-inspired cocktail for the individuals who couldn't make it. Dinner proved to be the start of an enchanting evening when he learned that the Pyromaniac Chef Kathryn Minchew had been inspired to open this restaurant after visiting Barcelona. Garence expressed his love for all things Spanish—mainly thinking of Sabina—and talked with her as warmly as his saddened heart could assemble about the great capital of Catalonia and other places in which they had holidayed.

Dinner should have encouraged Garence to tick off the "get out" checkbox that Henrietta had tasked him with and head home, but he felt an indistinct calling to stick around town. The night was young and booming with verve. He proceeded down the elongated Stroud Road and arrived at a building shaking from the music erupting from within it. The weather-beaten sign hanging above the peeling, green entrance doors was engraved with "The Raucous Pint" in gold with a jolly depiction of an eighth note holding up a glass of beer.

This place ought to do the trick, Garence thought as he crossed its threshold and dodged a couple of fellows in a heated debate. The topic of concern must have been a disagreement between the two; on second thought, with the speakers blaring overhead, perhaps they had just been tired of shouting and having to repeat themselves when one thing led to another. The inside of the Raucous Pint was larger than the exterior let on. The center was lined with a sweeping mahogany bar and a series of occupied tables and chairs. The audience standing against the stage was far too great, well over the fire code occupancy limit. The audience in the back was forced into the gaps between the tables. The stage was at the opposite end of the entrance, some twenty meters away, with a four-man band upon it. The lead singer interacted with the audience in English, and from his accent, Garence discerned that the band was from Germany. The music was a harmonious marriage of rock and electronics gliding on a sweet high.

Chalise Bonner saw Garence the moment he broke out of the crowd at the entrance. She was amongst the standing audience with two of her friends. She went to the bar to order another mixed drink when he caught her attention. She had stopped in her tracks and caused the person behind to bump into her. To say Chalise was caught in a dream was an understatement; she had fallen in love at first sight. Time slowed as she watched him approach the bar. Her heartbeat quickened while her breath stuck in her throat. She was embarrassed to think of the possibility of him being aware of her watching him, so she turned away. It took her a moment to convince herself that no one was watching her watch the guy who'd entered. She gave her embarrassment a hard kick to the curb, reclaimed her self-assurance, and dared to look his way.

Garence pushed the sleeves of his dark button-down shirt to his elbows, raised one arm, and signaled to the bartender that he'd have a pint. The hairs on the back of his neck stood on end, and he had the strange feeling that someone was watching him. He looked toward the other end of the bar, and a young woman with a vibrant puff of dark, luxurious curls caught his attention, but she wasn't paying him any mind. In fact, no one was. Strange. There had been an undeniable presence following him a minute ago. He glanced at the woman again. She wore a couple of chain necklaces draped over a white T-shirt, skinny jeans, and black heels. Her eyes passed over his, but his humility persuaded him that her stare wasn't the one he had felt. Their glances happened to cross, then moved on. He dismissed her and made his way into the crowd with his beer in hand. Garence was as tall as most men in the bar, but half of the audience were women shorter than him, so he could see the entire band fine. The song had ended, and someone approached his left side, applauding and cheering.

Garence looked down and saw a billow of curls at least nine or ten inches shorter than him—in heels. She peered up and acknowledged him with a nod.

Chalise wasn't sure if she intended to pursue him, because he wasn't her type. Who was she kidding? It never mattered to her if a guy didn't look like any of her previous boyfriends. The men she dated, who sometimes turned out to be boys, all came from a broad range of physical characteristics. To say Chalise had a type was a lie. She didn't have one. She was protecting her heart, again. She tried not to think about coming out of the biggest breakup in her history and pondered moving on rather than hanging out with this man who took her breath away. She could shift her way past him and scoot toward the stage. He wouldn't even realize that she was there. So… why wasn't she leaving?

She dared to steal a glance. She smiled and allowed her hair to conceal her flush. He returned the gesture. She guessed she could stick around for a little while.

"I'm Chalise."

With the combination of not being underneath a speaker box and his ears getting used to the high volume, Garence noticed she was American, and judging by her appearance, she looked around twenty-seven.

"Garence."

She raised her arms, and her shoulders and hair and hips swayed with the idle beat. "They're great, aren't they?"

"This is the first I've heard of them, but yeah. I like what I hear so far." Why was he being so chatty?

"They're one of my favorites."

Chalise's two English friends joined her side, and the one on the right, Emma, called out, "There you are. You said you were getting another drink but didn't return."

They both looked over at Garence, who was trying not to eavesdrop. They were both taller than Chalise but smaller in their frames. The one on the left, Pauline, had shoulder-length beach waves and wore a pencil skirt and a white-collar blouse, while Emma had straight blonde hair and was decked out in boots, tights, a dress, and a leather jacket, all in black.

Pauline gave him the once-over, as if unable to decide if Garence was up to some par, but then seemed to lean toward a possible yes. "Never mind. We should have known."

Emma was more secretive—or rather, polite—in her scrutiny by locking her eyes on Garence, then using her peripherals to check him out. "We wanted to find you to tell you that a few friends are saving a table for us."

Chalise turned around to the table by the entrance with three "friends," two guys and one woman, apparently one for each, which gave her the impression they were vampires in a supernatural film and Emma and Pauline had rounded up their next meal.

Instead of declining the invitation to join them, Chalise made introductions. Pauline grinned while Emma and Garence verbalized their greetings.

"I wanted you to know where to find us," said Emma. She turned Pauline around and encouraged her to move on by pressing her hands against her back. "Enjoy the show!" she called over her shoulder.

Garence felt a moment of awkwardness with the knowledge of Chalise's preference to hang with him in lieu of her friends. To be honest, he was glad she'd stayed with him. He leaned toward her, closer than he had before. "What's the band's name?"

"Milky Chance."

Chalise caught him checking her out, and she winked at him. She went out a lot with her friends, and on dates, say four or five times a month on average. She wasn't sure if that was a lot or a little, but she wasn't one to compare herself to other people. She liked to enjoy herself and she attracted attention. Perhaps it had something to do with her deep need to love another and the self-love vibe she expelled by playing along with the law of attraction. Her friends would have never guessed in a million years that she was lonesome, and she preferred to keep it that way.

When the set ended, the audience roared and clapped. The crowd thinned, but Chalise and Garence remained as the band talked with fans and signed CDs and albums.

"Are you going to stick around?" Garence asked, motioning toward the stage.

"I was."

"Was? Does that mean you've changed your mind?" His blood boiled with guilt. What was he doing encouraging her company? He had a wife. A solemn vow to love and cherish her for the rest of his life. He changed his mind. He didn't want Chalise to hang around anymore. He should tell her it was getting late and that he ought to head home.

Chalise released a mischievous, elvish grin, and she grabbed his hand. "Come with me."

She had the band sign her empty glass with a black marker she had stowed in her trouser pocket, and asked for a picture. She would have asked Garence to take it, but the souvenir would be a double whammy having the band and the hot guy from the bar in it.

"Won't the bartender want the glass back?"

"Probably, but I want it more. I'm kidding. I gave him some cash earlier, so this is legit."

"Good. I'd hate to see you carted off to jail for nicking it."

She laughed as the scene played out in her mind. "You would have been an accomplice, so I suppose I would have been in good company."

Chalise asked another fan to snap the photo, and she and Garence shuffled between the band against the stage. She tilted her head and posed, knowing the true secret behind her gleam.

Looking back at her friend's table, Chalise saw that the guys they had met had gone, as had most of the crowd. Emma and Pauline would head back to the flat they shared three streets away. Pauline was standing contrapposto while she checked her phone, and her head angled toward the doors, which meant she wanted to go home now. Neither guy they'd talked to was interesting, and she was bored out of her mind. First off, Pauline was an open book and she didn't care who read it, although she wasn't rude about the delivery—most of the time. Emma and Chalise were more alike because they didn't gravitate toward communicating with their entire body like Pauline did. Their series of individual cues were more centralized. Raised eyebrows meant "I'm leaving this" and that they would either excuse themselves or that they didn't want to be left behind from the group, whereas fluffing one's hair implied they were interested in the guy they were talking to. To avoid mixing signals with their natural meanings, the other person had to repeat the pose and wait for a single nod of approval. This method was well-practiced and effective every time.

Chalise was having a great evening, but whether it ended now or in an hour from now, she wouldn't have been disappointed either way.

"Would you like to stay awhile and have a drink with me?"

"I would, but I have a forty-minute drive home to Bourton. I should get going." He was reserved, but he wasn't inconsiderate. "I'd offer to drive you all home if my car wasn't parked about a mile away. I can walk with you?"

"No, don't trouble yourself. We'll be all right." She drove the conversation back to their shared experience before she left him. "I'm glad you enjoyed the band."

"I am too. That was a nice surprise."

"If you're ever in the mood to catch another concert or want to meet up, you should call me."

Garence rolled with the seconds without hesitation. "Sure."

She reached for the coaster on the table, crossed Emma's glance and raised an eyebrow, and wrote her number on it with the same marker the band had used to autograph her glass.

"Did you pay for the coaster ahead of time as well?"

Her dimples made an appearance. "I won't tell if you don't."

Garence grinned, but the alteration Chalise's charms had on his permanently somber mood was so inextricable that he couldn't deny himself the indulgence. "Looks like we're in this together."

"Then let us seal the pact." She leaned forward and hugged him farewell.

Chapter Thirty-One

ONE YEAR AGO

— MAY —

The eminent Incan stone citadel that was Machu Picchu was as breath-taking as when Garence had first taken this holiday at university with a group of friends. In all honesty, it was more memorable than the last visit, even if he was traveling by himself. He had opted for the less crowded tourist route through Salkantay, the Savage Mountain, where the trail was twice as long and more strenuous. From the lush rainforest to the snowcapped Salkantay to the awe-striking cloud forest, Garence was at peace in this land that seemed to possess the very essence of magic, that never made him feel as if he were alone. The front and back elevations of the roofless shelters were pointed, resembling the forever peaks of the Andes surrounding them. From afar, the stone city and its terraces were arranged in a way that reminded him of a surreal labyrinth, where stairwells should have jutted toward the sky. Then, at certain angles, it could almost resemble a curious pattern on a tortoise's shell.

Garence did not want to live a life without Sabina, but he wasn't opposed to shaking off whatever bits of anguish he could in order to return home safely. He was true to his word, and he sat in the altar, some distance away from the condor, and managed to tune out visitors. Rather than clear his mind, Garence meditated on the peace he'd had with Sabina. He had wished to be reunited with her so many times that the notion flew from his mind like a breath of air. There were no visitors in the vicinity or birds flying in the sky and all was removed and silenced. This unexpected release calmed him, and no thoughts fired from then on for several minutes. Garence sat in the altar as if he were waiting for an expected reply from the universe.

Although Garence and Sabina hadn't visited Peru together, she did appear in Machu Picchu. She was sitting on a rock cliff that overlooked the citadel, where her gaze overshot the site. She was staring out into the never-ending sea of tropical peaks jutting from a bottomless ground many leagues below her. Garence wished he could take a photograph of her, but he knew that wasn't possible, so he did the next best thing. He closed his eyes and committed the image to his memory. When he opened them, he was grateful to see she was still there. In her white dress, with hair swaying in the breeze, and her bare feet dangling off the edge. She turned back and watched him for what seemed like several moments. He wished he could read her mind right now. Perhaps in the next life it would be possible.

She smiled, having read his mind again, and walked over to him. She brought the palms of her hands millimeters from his cheeks. The air between them served as a velvet connection as her thumb caressed his flat moles, inciting memories of what her touch felt like. He had once told her he would go to hell and back for her, but he sensed she would wait an eternity for him. She reached for his lips with hers until she was gone.

After nine solid days in Peru, Garence arrived at the Kingham station from London as weary as a sparrow who had flown the same distance in one stretch. If his eyes had been closed, he would have known summer was approaching. There was a shift in the atmosphere, and the energy sizzled with a new beginning. As he drove his black Škoda Octavia through Bourton-on-the-Water, the setting sun shot bands of gold like arrows through the rosy sky and cast a brilliant luster beneath the arches of the stone bridges that ran over the troubled waters of his disconsolate life. He forgot everything he didn't like about his solitary existence without Sabina, and his return home was more of a welcomed homecoming than anything else. Perhaps Sabina's spirit was reading him and replaced his despondency with little reminders of her.

It was twilight when he pulled onto the gravel driveway. The programmable lighting system he had installed throughout the property resembled faint breadcrumbs guiding him back home. The slate-roofed cottage appeared at the end of the drive, and the front porch and the living room illuminated as if someone or something was waiting for him inside. It was a sight akin to seeing a beacon perched atop a jagged cliff or the light at the end of a tunnel he dreaded walking through alone. He supposed he should have been used to the shifting limbo existence he'd been living since Sabina's death almost a year ago, and he had got this far with Henrietta to help him balance his return to the void, as he called his home life. He parked the car several meters away as he always did and inhaled, the exhale stripping the last of the stagnant energy from him. He exited and closed the car door with his duffle bag over his shoulder. The diminishing sun cast the last of its glow upon his back while his face flickered with promise. He closed the front door behind him.

He laid the duffle bag beside the slate-gray, velvet couch Sabina had brought with her from Spain. He tossed his keys onto the living room side table, where they bumped a circular piece of cardboard onto the floor. He bent over to pick it up. It was the coaster Chalise had written her telephone number on. Then, as if on cue, his phone vibrated. Garence retrieved it from his back pocket and saw there were no messages or notifications. His phone had pulsed for no reason. He placed the coaster and the phone down on the side table and walked toward the kitchen as the phone vibrated again. He stopped mid-step. Goose pimples flared his body as if someone had run their invisible finger down his spine. He went back to his phone and turned on the display. The time was 8:13... 813. Garence searched his memory. That number held no meaning, but his phone was going off for a certain reason. He had to figure out what the connection was before whatever opportunity being offered was removed. He looked at the numbers on the coaster. The ending digits were 813.

That was it. He was supposed to call Chalise, and he would, at some point... but that point was right now. He tried to gather what he would say to her. What had they talked about doing the last time they were together? Seeing a concert or something? But he didn't know of any shows to invite her to. He wasn't in the mood to call to talk, plus he imagined her being out with friends.

It was less awkward to text her, but Garence wasn't into texting. In fact, his infrequent replies were one of the few things that had irritated Sabina. He supposed he could call her and let it roll at will. Garence dialed her number. The phone rang four times, and he was about to hang up when she answered.

"This is Chalise."

"Hi, Chalise. This is Garence." Would she remember him? "We met at the concert in Gloucester."

Her smile could be heard over the airwaves. "Yeah, I remember you, Garence." She was surprised to hear from him after two weeks, but she would never say that out loud. "What are you up to?"

"I just arrived home from Peru."

"That sounds amazing."

Garence wasn't in the mood for chatting, instead wanting to cut straight to the point, but he didn't know what that was. He hadn't even thought of Chalise this whole time, so he wasn't sure if he still wanted to see her again.

"It was. Have you been?"

"No, but it's on my bucket list."

He bit back the urge to say "um" and instead said, "I'll be in Gloucester on Saturday. Would you like to meet for lunch?"

"Sure. It's perfect timing. I'm flat-sitting for Pauline and Emma."

He wondered why it mattered that she was flat-sitting, but he dismissed it. "Shannon's Pub at one?"

"That sounds great. I love that place."

"Brilliant. I'll see you there."

Chapter Thirty-Two

ONE YEAR AGO

— MAY —

Garence didn't invite the butterflies that fluttered in his belly into the local, but they followed him nonetheless. Then he recognized the person a few meters ahead.

"Garence, you have perfect timing, my friend," Chalise said with all the charm of a Southern belle. She placed a hand upon his shoulder and reached to kiss each of his cheeks.

"Likewise. You look magnificent."

Chalise looked down at herself as if disbelieving the flattering of her black leggings and gray T-shirt beneath a black blazer. She looked him over and found that his monochromatic attire, black sweater, dark trousers and boots, paired well with his frame.

"As do you," she said, nudging his elbow. "You know how to rock casual, don't you?"

"Well, I'm glad you noticed. I changed four times."

"Is that all? You get five stars for effort."

He winked at her. "Shall we?" he asked, holding the door open for her.

"Let's."

The bartender, a burly and red-whiskered man in his late fifties, welcomed them to his pub as he cleared two glasses from a booth to their left.

They went up to the bar and looked over the double-sided menu. Chalise glanced at the specials, nodded at a few selections, then returned the menu.

"That was quick," he said, questioning her enthusiasm.

"I was curious as to what was new on the menu, but I love their rib eye and chips."

"An ole favorite?"

"Yes, sir. What are you getting?"

"Mm. The chicken, leek, and mushroom pie."

"Mm, indeed."

"Was that a dig?" Garence looked askance at her.

"No," she said with a smile. "That's genuine agreement, my friend. I'm gonna want a bite of that."

With that being said, the bartender placed their order with the cook and said that he would take their red wines to their table in two ticks. They walked toward the front of Shannon's Pub and decided upon one of the few tables designated for two, although it was small and intended for drinking at rather than eating. Garence held the chair for Chalise as she sat. Ample light shined through the diamond-patterned paned windows, allowing the pair to see each other clearly for the first time.

"I take it from your accent that you are not from around here."

"That's right, Sherlock. I was born and raised in Austin, Texas. Ever since I was young, I've wanted to study abroad. I think I watched too much PBS with my folks. Anyway, the cost just to go to college accumulates quick, so I grabbed the bull by the horns and decided that I would move here instead."

"You dared to dream bigger. That's remarkable."

"Well, my parents thought I was nuts," she laughed at the remembrance of their stunned faces, "but they supported me. To help save for my big move, I took my core classes at the community college, saved a bunch, and then I transferred to the University of Texas at Austin and earned a degree in international business. Throughout my schooling, I worked and saved more to live my dream."

"I bet you started working and saving as soon as you were able?"

"Hell yeah. The last two years of high school and into college, I was a hotel receptionist, where I was able to do a lot of my homework at work; that was awesome. My last year of college, I was an assistant to a marketing coordinator at an agency that my uncle worked for, and here I am." She took a sip of wine.

"Have you lived in Gloucester the whole time?"

"No. I first moved to Edinburgh. That's where I met Pauline and Emma. They were in town for the Royal Edinburgh Military Tattoo. We became fast friends, and I ended up moving in with them here in Gloucester when I got an advertising job that allowed me to work from home—though I traveled quite a bit at the time. And then, two months ago, I got a job as a digital marketing associate for an online shopping site in London called Lucky Piece. When you and I first met, that was my first visit since I had moved out."

Garence looked back at her with alarm. "I'm sorry. I didn't realize you didn't live here. Otherwise, I wouldn't have asked you to travel all this way just for lunch." He wondered why she'd agreed to meet him when she was more than two hours' drive away.

"It's fine. I really am flat-sitting for my friends while they're away in Spain. Have you been to Spain?"

"I have." He raised his eyes and offered Chalise a small smile that left her relieved. "A digital marketing associate? That sounds stimulating."

"It is. Entirely. So far, I've managed to keep in step with our amazing editorial team on the final touches for the upcoming holiday campaign, and next week I'll start revamping our accessories landscape, which will include connecting with new suppliers for the spring season. I'm enjoying it." The owner dropped off their meals, and Chalise took a bite of her rib eye, but not before transitioning the conversation. "What do you do in Bourton-on-the-Water, is it?"

"I have a house and a rental there by the Whitmore Estate, but I'm a travel writer."

"So, the world is your office. Now that is the ultimate stimulation."

He hadn't been keen on sharing the intricacies of his travels, so he failed to elaborate.

She wanted to hear more about his career and his travels, though. He must have had remarkable stories. Astounding experiences. All she wanted was to hear one or two. "All right," she said, accepting his reticence. "You live in Bourton and come to Gloucester to hang out?" she asked with light-hearted hesitation.

"In a nutshell." He didn't want to delve into his personal life either, but she did make a point. He reached for his glass and leaked that he was seeing a therapist here before taking a drink.

"I apologize. I don't mean to pry." She raised her hand to motion that she was backing off the subject. *Good job, Chalise,* she thought with a cringe. *You're hitting all the right buttons.* "Your personal life is personal—"

"You need to tell her," whispered a reverberating voice so small that Garence almost missed it.

He stared at Chalise. Had she heard that? No. Judging from the fluidity of her words, she had not. The air quivered with a waning hum, and his spine was thunderstruck. Upon second thought, he hadn't seen Sabina since Peru. She hadn't appeared on the return flight or his drive home. Then again, her appearances weren't an exact science, and they weren't very frequent either. Still, this voice was new. Why did it sound so strange and distorted, yet familiar? He swept his brain for its owner, but there was no need. He should know who it belonged to, but he was afraid to admit it. Should he attempt to search for other possibilities? He swallowed. No. It was Sabina. Beads of sweat formed on his brow. He couldn't deal with this right now.

Garence zeroed in on the present. "No, it's fine. I've got some stuff to sort through."

She searched for something to say, and the best thing that came to mind was empathy. "That's great. If you don't manage it, it will manage you. I've seen a therapist whenever I needed some help throughout my life, and it was the best thing I could do for myself. In fact, the most recent occurrence was a journey, or at least it was after I found the right person to help me. The first therapist said nothing and provided me with nothing of value, but the third one was just right."

With Chalise's admission, Garence relaxed. "Goldilocks tried out three, did she? What was wrong with the second one?"

His devil-may-care grin teased her dimples. "I was too attracted to the second one to be vulnerable in the way I needed to be in order to heal."

He laughed. "Smart move."

Chalise agreed. His laughter was music to her ears, and she thought, *We're both revealing things, but not too much. This is good.*

They talked about everything except anything that revolved around relationships while they tucked into their meals, which they shared a bite of with each other. They both discovered they were skilled binge-watchers and their favorite shows were *The Hour* and *Sherlock*. Football, or soccer, as Chalise liked to call the sport, if only to be cheeky, was a must throughout the year, whether they were playing it themselves or watching it. Most importantly, they took advantage of the face time.

Garence found Chalise's laugh infectious, and everything about her smiled: her lips, her eyes—even her nose crinkled. Somehow, she made him feel alive once again. She looked at him with those brown doe eyes framed by thick curly lashes like an exquisite painting, and her dimples gushed with the simplest facial expression. The light from the overhead torch caught the bronze highlights in her curls and emphasized their softness. Her skin was a rich brown, smooth, and it radiated like gold. As impossible as it was to believe, Chalise's charm outweighed her confidence, and the way she held his eyes made him feel like a man.

On the other side of the table, Chalise allowed herself to continue to fall for Garence. The corner of her mouth turned up as she eyed the fine gray hairs that lined Garence's curls and forehead and speckled his beard. Funny how age flattered men. Nine times out of ten, when a man aged, it suited his long-lost but not missed baby face, and it gelled well with his sensuality. The wrinkles around their eyes and mouth classified their sense of humor, the gray amplified their sex appeal, and with the passing years, their appreciation for women evolved—in the best of men—and spilled into their affections. He leaned against the chair back, and she watched him run his hand through his hair. *Damn, look at him.* Garence was an ordinary guy, but he had the ability to produce extraordinary responses within her. She wondered if the same could be said about him behind closed doors.

Chalise bit her lower lip, and Garence couldn't help but connect this response with someone else he knew. He had seen Sabina do this on countless occasions, and he had always found it erotic. He didn't know if he was feeling self-conscious about being on his first date since Sabina died or if he had imagined Chalise replicating Sabina's inclination. On second thought, what did he do to make Chalise and Sabina bite their lip? He dismissed the thought like it was yesterday's rubbish.

Although Garence demonstrated a genuine interest in getting to know her, a subtle reservation about him slipped in and out of their conversation. Like he wasn't present, which made Chalise realize he wasn't available on an emotional level. She had no substantial reason to support her intuition, but her gut told her that he couldn't give her what she yearned for, a strong and loving relationship.

As disappointing as this realization was, Chalise still didn't want this afternoon to end or to never see him or hear his voice again. How strange that she should feel this strongly for someone she had only just met. She felt ridiculous. If it had been possible for Chalise to kick herself at that moment, she would have done it regardless of how silly she looked. Then again, the mind generally tried to safeguard oneself from making the same mistakes and experiencing heartache, whereas the heart urged its owner to throw caution to the wind and live in the moment. Her head and her emotions always played well together, and they always arrived at the same conclusion, but not now. She was dumbfounded by her inability to reconcile the two.

If she were being honest, she was protecting herself. Her last relationship had been six months long, and it had started out roses. Chalise was at the cinema with Emma when the guy in the row behind her was trying to get to his seat, past the people who were seated, and spilled the topmost layer of buttered popcorn over her shoulder. She took a piss at him by saying she didn't order popcorn, and he apologized. He was cute with a movie-star smile and his ring finger was missing a band, so when he caught up with her after the flick to apologize in person, she didn't refuse him—or his request for her phone number. Chalise and Robson were together for five months before he moved in with her, and it took five weeks for his duplicity to be revealed. He left their flat for a run when his phone kept ringing and ringing. It rang so much that Chalise believed there was an emergency, so she answered it. On the other end of the line was a six-year-old girl, May, crying that her mommy hadn't picked up her and her sister, June, from school and asked if their daddy, Robson Miller, could pick them up. To say that Chalise was thunderstruck was one thing, but hearing this scared little girl sob for her father was a different matter. Robson jogged for an hour, and she knew his route, but by the time she found him, who knew how long those little girls would have been waiting for their parents. So, she picked them up and brought them to her flat. When Robson arrived, he found the girls fed and his belongings shoved into trash bags, and that was the last she ever heard of Robson. As devastating as his betrayal was, she was the most sickened by the ugly realization that she was the other woman. She knew the truth, but she felt as though her own skin had been stripped away, leaving her with a thick coating of bloody muck to sheathe her true self.

Did she need to protect herself from Garence? Should she fear the possibility of being loved by him? She hadn't known him for long, but her gut told her that Garence wasn't going to hurt her malevolently any more than he was going to reciprocate her feelings.

Her eyes were not paying attention to the memories of boyfriends past but gushing over Garence, when Chalise caught the tiniest reveal that would send her on the path of understanding what was tripping her wits. There was pain in his eyes. She wanted to ask him about it, but she didn't think she should. They had only just met. Should she? Good grief, why had she lost all sense of resolution?

She could sense he had deep wounds, as if he had gone through a horrible breakup. No, that piece didn't fit... Had he... lost someone? Her curiosity burst into a hundred fragments. That was it. It felt so right that she couldn't think of any other reason for his demeanor. Chalise couldn't imagine the heartache involved. Breakups were difficult, but to have your soul ripped in two? That was too much. She looked away, wishing she hadn't spotted the tragic truth. He appeared to be forty or so, but he was too young to have experienced bereavement.

Her heart went out to him in an even bigger way. Her mind could understand that Garence wasn't capable of dishonesty. If she was able to listen to her intuition when her thoughts and emotions were aligned, then she should be able to do the same when they weren't. It was settled. She wasn't going to force any romantic notions. She would proceed with the intention of being his friend. There was no harm in hanging out with the guy from time to time. That way both forces won.

She smiled.

She placed the fork and knife down, side by side over her half-eaten meal to indicate to the owner that she was done eating. "Lunch was delicious."

"Yeah. I'm done too." Garence laid his cutlery down, and when the bill was presented, Garence offered his card.

Chalise laughed at Garence's stories and ran her eyes over him, making him feel desirable once again. He couldn't have admitted this before

today, but he wanted to be desired. To feel a desire for another woman.
To feel her against his naked body. But a part of him was still locked inside
a glass room. Was the glass bulletproof? Could he pull the trigger and
see what happened? Garence could not look at Chalise as these thoughts
passed through his mind like flour through a sieve. He liked hanging out
with her, and her positive aura was affecting. Not to mention the fact that
she was sexy… Could they be friends?

Garence fell silent, then he became anxious.

"Have I made you uncomfortable?"

"Me?" he asked, startled. "What, this?" He moved his hands. "No. I'm
not nervous… I'm sorry this has ended so soon. Shall we do it again?"

Surprised, she ran with it. "I'd like that very much."

A small genial smile materialized, and she made herself even more
alluring than Garence had already believed her to be.

Chapter Thirty-Three

ONE YEAR AGO

— MAY —

"You went out"—Henrietta nearly popped her clogs—"with a woman?"

"Have you lost the plot? I know it was unimaginable beforehand, but yeah, I did. She moved to London and she frequents Gloucester where her girlfriends live."

"You mean where she travels to see you."

"No. No. It isn't like that."

Henrietta spotted how quickly Garence covered up the truth—he could lie to himself, but she knew what was going on. But she would let that slide because she was still hung up on the fact that he'd gone out. She was so astonished by his metaphorical moon leap that she was almost afraid he was moving too quickly, but that couldn't be correct. She dismissed the thought. Everyone traveled at their own pace; perhaps Garence needed a little push.

"We had a nice time."

"Nice."

"Mm-hmm."

Garence seemed to be reliving something from their time together because his eyes glazed over. She wondered what he was thinking. "What was nice?"

He would have thought that was pretty obvious. He looked around, slipped on sarcasm, and chuckled. "I dunno, the weather? Being out. The fact that no one stormed in to blow us to pieces. What do you expect me to say? She was nice. We had a nice time."

"That's disappointing."

"How so?"

"Nice isn't an exceptionally strong adjective for someone you of all people spent time with." Now he was defensive and embarrassed, she wouldn't let this slide too. "Does this nice woman have a name?"

"Chalise."

"Oh. That's nice."

"Thank you," he replied, appreciating the cease in her fire. "Wait!" he stammered. "Why do you get to use nice?"

"Because I'm charging you a hundred and forty pounds an hour, so I can bloody well say whatever I please. Not to mention the fact that it's appropriate."

Garence drove his fingers through his hair. "You are unbelievable."

"Thank you. Now tell me about Chalise."

He tried to hide a smile.

That also said a lot. She'd better turn it back a tick. "A sparkling personality to accompany her nice smile then?"

"Chalise is five-foot-three, an American with fine dark skin like the actress Viola Davis. A digital marketing associate, and she has determination to go along with a cheeky personality that complements her mischievous dimples."

Garence raised his chin and relaxed his shoulders the way Michiel did, and Henrietta was reminded of that pivotal night he had abruptly left her house to kill himself. He had not succeeded in that venture; instead he'd worked through his depression, met a woman near Loch Lomond, and married her.

Garence reminded her so much of Michiel it was uncanny, and him meeting a woman who sounded very much like Michiel's own Espen was her validation. Henrietta was not just relying on her gut feeling that Garence's story mirrored her son's and that it would continue to do so now that he'd met Chalise, she was betting his recovery on it.

"Garence, she's more than nice."

"Anything else, Your Highness?"

She didn't need to glare at him. "Yes. You forgot to check your attitude at the door. Be sure to wipe your feet of its awful residue. So, when are you going to see her again?"

"Who said I was seeing her again?"

"Not you, but I presume that you will see each other again because if she was able to get you out of the house on two occasions, then there is bound to be a third recurrence. I can discern from your demure delight in talking about this nice woman that you like her."

A lot, she thought.

Was he really an open book? Henrietta looked pleased with herself for some reason.

"I will see her again."

He refused to look at her any longer; he rested his head back against the sofa and placed his clasped hands upon his lap. He wasn't going to divulge anything further—that's all Henrietta needed to know. He had grabbed a pint and met a woman—*a delightful woman*, his conscience asserted—and then he'd had lunch with her. He didn't know why she was so bloody interested in his outings. It's not like their encounters were romantic or anything.

The word romance aroused certain thoughts. The constant exchange of meaningful words, heartfelt interest, eternal respect, a deep yearning for the other person, endless caresses. He didn't feel anything of these things for Chalise.

His conscience spoke, *Liar.*

Fine, there was mutual respect. Her smile and laughter came to his mind. Yes, he was interested in her, and he looked forward to seeing her again. He couldn't deny this fact. He drew a deep breath. He supposed he understood why Henrietta thought his escapades were somewhat of a revelation. He stole a glimpse of her; she was looking through the window overlooking a water fountain across the way. She appeared to be coming up with another way to poke him in the ribs, but there was nothing left to discuss, so he closed his eyes and said nothing else.

"Does she know?"

This woman was relentless. Of course Chalise knew they were meeting again... Wait. Bugger. Henrietta's severe tone had detonated his bubble and megaphoned the fact that she was asking whether he'd told Chalise about Sabina. Garence squeezed his eyes tight. No, he wasn't going there. He'd rather Henrietta pestered him about dating.

"Of course she does. We spoke of it. It's practically all set."

His senseless avoidance marveled her. "Really?" He knew damn well she was asking if he had told Chalise about any part of his previous life. He didn't have to tell Chalise the whole story, but he could at least tell the woman he was a widower.

The loss of Sabina fell upon his shoulders once again. Perhaps Chalise should know. He wasn't ashamed of his past; it was just too painful to bring up. He could converse with Chalise through his broken heart, and he wondered why she kept hanging out with him, so to tell her even a little bit of his pain would be excruciating. "No."

Henrietta already knew Garence wasn't ready to talk about merging his past with every present day that led to a future, but she had to press him enough. If he was progressing beyond his grief, then she couldn't allow him to remain closed up.

"Garence, you are going to continue to meet women. At some point, you are going to have to tell that special person about your backstory. They deserve to know what happened to you, as you will deserve to hear about their life. What you guys do with that information is your business, but you need to be open and honest in order for any relationship to possess a solid foundation and stand a fighting chance at sustaining a lifetime."

Henrietta heard Garence mutter, "I know."

The room absorbed everything between Henrietta's words, but neither of them spoke. Garence had sailed through this half-numb, but Henrietta was too vigilant and outspoken to not meddle.

"It may not be Chalise or the next woman, but at some point, you are going to have to share that part of yourself with another."

Garence knew Henrietta wasn't trying to be his puppet master or even dictative. He needed to hear these words. Wasn't this what he was paying her for? To help him through this phase of his life. If Henrietta wasn't guiding him, then who was?

"You know," whispered the reverberating voice from his luncheon with Chalise, though this time Garence wasn't receptive.

Why did he feel as though he were on a rowboat gliding across a loch guided by no one he could see? He stopped to investigate the buzz that cruised the airwaves, but it became indistinguishable. Forget it, he was dwelling on this too much as it was. Focus on the present.

"I know," he said.

"When you're ready."

Henrietta was yielding. Garence breathed a sigh of relief.

Nine minutes from their sixty-minute hourglass had got away from them, but Henrietta could tell Garence had been through enough. "Shall we call it a day?"

"Yes," he answered. He was more than ready to head home.

"That was all too quick. Was it something I said?"

Garence snickered. "No and yes. It's been a long day."

"I understand. See you in two?"

"Wouldn't miss it for the world," he said facetiously.

"For the world? I could think of a few things I would bail on you for."

Garence glanced at her sideways; there were indeed a few reasons why he would bail on himself too, but he didn't say this to Henrietta. He'd got her off his back about not wanting to live, he wasn't about to stir the pot.

Chapter Thirty-Four

PRESENT DAY

I'm almost ashamed to admit this, but I didn't tell Chalise about Sabina for a few months. I couldn't bring my wife into that part of my life where she didn't exist, nor could I admit to myself that I seemed to be moving on without her. I met Chalise in the city on several occasions. We had dinner, caught a movie, had drinks, and we even attended an art exhibition. I remember being apprehensive and scared to tell her about Sabina. I had told Chalise I needed to share something difficult with her. She looked me straight in the eye and said there was no rush. It's like she already knew... Nevertheless, I was grateful for her patience with me. She told me that her previous relationship involved a guy living a double life, so she asked if I was married or in a relationship or had children. The way she posed the questions so that I wasn't at all offended by them, was a credit to her charm. Chalise had a way with me. She could make me feel safe when I was vulnerable and happy when I was down. She was my reciprocal, always flipping me into the best disposition I could be under my circumstances.

Chapter Thirty-Five

ONE YEAR AGO

Chalise walked through the glass lobby of Lucky Piece, trying her hardest to battle the grin that yanked her dimples inward to reveal she was eyeing her crush. Garence was leaning against a metal lamp post, hands inside the pockets of his long coat. This time of year was characterized with warm days and cool breezes, which was a welcomed change from her office, so she'd left her sweater behind. She pushed through the doors.

The sound of her heels hitting the pavement like long power strides announced her approach.

She raised an appreciative eyebrow at his fitted, charcoal, long-sleeved tee. "Hey there."

Chalise relished his bold embrace and how his body heat radiated. He smelled like a man too. Woody and honest.

"I appreciate you meeting me," he said.

"Of course. It sounded pretty important. Is everything all right?"

"Yeah." He started calculating. "Everything is as wonderful as it can be. Can we sit on a bench somewhere? Are you okay with going outdoors?" He motioned down the street toward the River Thames, several minutes' walk away from them, then stopped. "You know what? I apologize. I'm a bleedin' idiot. It'll be cold by the water. Let's find a café, someplace warm."

The slight pressure of his broad hand upon her back was a welcomed surprise, and she didn't want him to leave her. "No, it's fine. Fresh air would be great. Queen's Walk?"

They talked about her day before propping down on a planked bench beneath the London plane trees on the South Bank. The jogging path was speckled with very few passersby, with the water waving hello. Chalise crossed her ankles as she faced Garence, who sat rigidly.

"I'm going to come out with it and spill what I came here to tell you."

Eyeing his nervous demeanor, Chalise took a breath and waited for him to speak. She had wondered if her hunch was correct in that he had lost his partner, but she dismissed the curiosity. She wanted to hear whatever he had to say with an open mind.

"I was married... Sabina died after our car was hit fifteen months ago."

Her hands gripped his. "I'm so sorry."

She was put off because he did not tell her this sooner, but she cared for him more than that. It didn't matter that he had already encountered the great love of his life and she hadn't. His marriage was another life, just as her past relationships were. She didn't want to replace Sabina. Life was about living and receiving second chances, and she wanted a chance to be with Garence.

She had yet to feel the full scale of the great love that Garence had; she envied him. She envied Sabina for having been the object of his affection no matter how short their relationship was. At least they had experienced love.

"Everything about my life with Sabina was beautiful, even the downs. It's been difficult."

"Of course it has." She reached over and held him, and he said nothing more.

"We wanted children. We tried... but they never lived. I'm sorry I couldn't share this earlier. I hope you understand."

"You can talk to me." She wasn't accepting his glossing over his loss with her. The man she had fallen in love with had lost everything, and she wished Sabina were alive, and their children, in order to see him blissful.

"Why?"

"Because you could use a friend, and I'm here. I think it would be good for you."

"I appreciate that." He looked off into the distance, then returned to their conversation. "You know what? I'm going to head home. I'm pretty tired."

"I don't think you are. Maybe you don't want to discuss what's going on with you."

"And you would be right because I bloody don't," he said matter-of-factly. He retrieved an envelope from his back pocket that looked as though it was ready to post and handed it to her. "This is for you. I'll see you around."

"Garence." She watched his long strides pull him farther and farther away. "Well, that was awesome."

Chapter Thirty-Six

ONE YEAR AGO

Chalise waited to open the letter until she arrived home.

Dear Chalise,

I write letters as a means of therapy, and I would do it more if you would indulge me a little and we wrote to each other. It's been hell living alone, and I find I am too eager to fix my neighbor's home for the distraction it provides. All in all, thank you for crossing my path. I can't say how long it has been since I have had a friend. I'm sure some of my awkward silences have made your imagination wander, so thank you for never pressuring me to speak more than I wanted to. I'm sorry I haven't been more myself. The self I'm trying to recover, but I'm sure the two of you will meet in divine timing.

Sincerely,
Garence

Dear Garence,

Friendship is as special as the sun, moon, and stars.

Like guiding lights, you will always have mine.

Yours Truly,

Chalise

Chapter Thirty-Seven

ONE YEAR AGO

— SEPTEMBER —

Chalise didn't care if Garence wanted a pen pal. She wanted to be there for him in the now, get him out of the house, and spend time together. There was so much to see and do and to live for. If he didn't see that, then she could open his eyes to what was possible.

She had his cell number, so she texted him.

Hey, globe-trekker.
Is there anything you've wanted to learn?

That's random.

Begs for an answer.

Learn to surf.

Whaaaat? You don't know how to surf?

And you do?

Duh? LOL. No.
Figured you would have during a trip.

Wake and paddleboarding,
but not surfing.

Anything you haven't done in a while.
Do you have allergies?

What are you on about?
Are you going to kidnap me? Ha!

You wish. Final Q.
Do you have plans next weekend?

I'll be on assignment.
Leave tomorrow, but I'll be back the following week.
What are we doing? Can I help?

Nope. I got you.
Just clear that weekend. Got it?

Loud and clear.

The sun caught Garence's eyes, and he was double-blind in the moment. Chalise was driving, so he didn't have to be vigilant. He put on his sunglasses, thinking how much better it felt to be looking through dark lenses, then he used the visual mask to examine her attire for hints as to what they were doing. She had suggested he wear comfortable trousers and closed-toe shoes, but this didn't leave him with a single clue. She, on the other hand, had her hair wrapped in a white scarf, and she wore riding tights, which led him to believe they were horseback riding, but she also wore trainers, which confused him. He was out of his element. No one had ever arranged a surprise excursion for him. Silence had befallen him, and he allowed events to unfold.

His face warmed when they pulled into Wimbledon Village Stables, where over three thousand acres were available to them. He exited the car and walked over to her. She was leaning against the car as she swapped her trainers for tall, worn riding boots that looked as though they had been cleaned.

He shook his head. "This isn't your first rodeo, is it?"

"Ha. Ha. I've never participated in those." She tossed her trainers in the back seat.

"And you belong to a riding club? How long have you been riding?"

"About a year and a half. I wanted to learn something new and unexpected. I walked by a display window with paddock boots, half chaps, and tall boots. I knew I'd be a poser for wearing the boots without knowing how to ride. And ta-da! Here I am."

"Sounds like a manifestation," he said.

"I don't know about all that, but I've been enjoying it. Life's too short to get stuck in a rut. What about you? Know how to ride?"

"I rode a lot on my grandparents' property. It's been six years or so."

"Cool. So, we can skip the lessons, but you'll need a riding hat and chaps. Are you going to be comfortable riding in what you have on?"

Garence looked at his attire. Gray tee, blue jeans, and leather boots. Not much to complain about, and he said as much.

He followed her around the facility, impressed by the friendliness of the staff. Then again, he imagined anyone interacting with Chalise would respond in this manner. They picked out their horses, and he trotted beside her. Even with his sunglasses on, his eyes were getting used to the sunlight. Being confined to his home was proving to be a growing habit to kick. It was a wonder he didn't have this trouble during his travels. He'd hiked Table Mountain in Cape Town, South Africa last week, and he didn't recall being bothered by the sunlight. Strange. It was like an allergen, but who could be allergic to the London sun on an outing like this?

They were riding past an ancient tree in Richmond Park, and a soft breeze gave Garence a breath of fresh air. "I don't know if it's the day or if this is the horse's natural demeanor," he said, picking up on something less peculiar instead, "but my chap is pretty chirpy. He's having quite an effect on me."

"Dirby? Definitely. Riding is a great stress release. But all the horses are well cared for," she said, adjusting her sunglasses. "Mimi, here, is a breeze to ride."

"There's stables by my place. If I had known we were riding, I could have also set this up."

"Ah, but a change in location couldn't hurt ya."

"True. This is a nice change of pace."

"How's this for a change of pace?" She clutched the reins, leaned forward, and pressed against her horse.

The corner of his mouth turned up, and he stormed after her.

They galloped around the bend and ducked beneath the tree leaves, passing each other at different openings. The fresh air, the wide terrain. It was new and exhilarating and something else that Garence couldn't quite put his finger on, but it was an odd sensation. A release after all he had been through. And then it hit him. Today was freeing. An escape from the charming walls that were a chamber of eternal shadows closing in on him. Yet here he was. Outdoors with a friend, experiencing a new take on something familiar. Perhaps that's why he was having such a good time. It was familiar with a familiar person. He could go on and on about his amazement, but it was faltering. This was a temporary situation, and no matter how much he wished circumstances were different, they never could be different.

They left the stables to eat dinner at a rooftop restaurant near her flat. Her eyes were fixated on the colorful horizon when he found himself looking at her. He struggled with how her gift of today made him feel versus where he was in his life. Chalise was a breath of fresh air. A vivacious younger woman, an American, who knew nothing about the commitment of marriage or the dark trappings that losing someone had brought to his doorstep. She had shown him that possibility was possible and that was a gift only a friend could bestow. And she was just that. A friend. A wonderful human being who wanted nothing but the best for him, and here he was slipping away into the evening midnight like the sun.

He followed her gaze. There was beauty in the night, the stars and the moon, but there was beauty in the light, and that's where his greatest love resided. Today was an example of what life could be like when he left his own doorstep to breathe. To exist and live. It was an attainable manifestation he could conjure like a magician.

He hadn't thought of Sabina in several hours, but she weighed heavy on him now. *She would have loved today*, he thought. He ran a hand through his hair and pulled at the roots. What was he thinking? Today was going so well. How could he ruin this moment? He was with Chalise, not Sabina.

He sat frozen at the thought of him being "with Chalise." Were they a thing? *No*, he said to himself. With tight lips, he took a deep breath, then released it. *We're just friends. This is what life would be like if I... lived. Moved on.*

His chin trembled.

"This sunset is one of the most beautiful ones I've seen as of late." She placed her hand upon his. "I'm glad you're taking it in too. Ooh! Look at that hue."

"From fuchsia to plum to midnight blue. Is this what friends do for each other?"

He watched her survey the day as if it were splotched on the skyline. "Yes," she admitted. "I can't say they all take their friends horseback riding, but they're there for each other. I'm always here for you."

"And I am grateful for you. No question."

"You don't have to go through anything alone. You can talk to me about anything at any time. That's what friends are for."

"I know."

"Do you? 'Cause you don't act like it."

"I'll phone a friend. Shoot you a letter. How about that?"

She laughed. "Hey, do you. Are we good?"

"Yeah, we're good."

She was a mirror image of the sight before her, and the sky seemed to kiss her face. All he could do was grip her hand.

Chapter Thirty-Eight

PRESENT DAY

We were open and honest with each other about everything, and although we weren't exclusive, Chalise reduced the number of dates she went on because of her love for me. Yes, I'll admit it. I knew she had a thing for me. I pretended not to notice, but I had a feeling about her.

No one could fill the void Sabina left... Well, perhaps one person, but I don't want to get ahead of myself.

Garence removed a handful of envelopes from an elastic pocket on the inside of the luggage lid. Most of them were in Chalise's neat and uniform handwriting, a quality indicative of her personality. Always on point, collected and enchanting—like the content of her letters—and he had enjoyed them from the first word.

Chapter Thirty-Nine

ONE YEAR AGO

— SEPTEMBER —

Dear Chalise,

There were days when I never thought I'd move past my sorrows. Weeks and months when I never thought I would feel connected to another human being, but that has changed. Without you knowing me or my past, you have extended your hand toward me and coaxed me out of a very miserable burrow. I can't thank you enough, Chalise.

I look forward to our friendship.

Your friend
Garence

Garence,

Light has triumphed over the night, shedding light on a new day as it stretches its brilliant fire and gold across the sky.

The temperature increases.

The goldcrest birds that chirp in the royal oak greet it all with a song that is a yawn.

Nothing is not possible.

The yew and berry air are filled with hope and a fresh promise of possibility; a new day.

Yours Truly,

Chalise

Dear Chalise, Miss Sentiment Weaver,

Allow me to bow before you.

I enjoyed your letter. It encapsulates so many images, images that I'm not sure are possible, the very best of what the morning brings, what new beginnings mean.

The more time I spend with you, the more I realize how closed off I am, how lonesome I have been. Your friendship and your words are a beacon on a coast I am having trouble seeing from angry waters. Beyond this point in my life is another world I have yet to explore, but I am not sure if I am ready for another journey. I catch glimpses of you and feel a spark of inspiration within my chest.

Thankful,

Garence

Chalise took the initiative once again and invited Garence out for a drink, which he accepted, but stated he would meet her. Two hours later, they were on their third drink at the local when Chalise sat up from her seat.

"We should do karaoke!"

"Okay," he said, almost mocking her. "First thing in the morning."

She gave him an odd look, then threw back her head. "I mean it. It's Friday night and we're *totally* buzzed and you're in town and we're alive, so let's live it, baby!"

"And. And. And you can't stand." He got on his feet and felt as sturdy as ever, but he played the part. "Wait, that's me."

"Lightweight." She gave him a discerning look, judged his body language, and replayed his clear speech in her head. "You're fine. Have you ever done it?"

"I've done *it* plenty of times, lightweight."

"What are you?" She shook her head, almost disgusted at his innuendo. "It isn't a contest, creeper. Karaoke. Have you done kar-a-oke?"

"Of course. All over the world."

His touch was unexpected, but she enjoyed having his arm around her.

"And I'm killer on air guitar," he said, "but you didn't hear that from me."

"All right. Maybe you can be my accompaniment on stage, but I'll think about it for a bit. Let's bounce."

They split the tab, then walked over to the bar at the corner of the street. The bass could be heard from outside, but moreover, so could a pitchy voice. Chalise left her song request with the MC as Garence bought them each a shot of whisky, and she jumped on stage.

"There's no guitar on this one. So, you're gonna have to cool it."

"Damn. I guess I'm out."

"What? You're surprised? I can't have you upstage me."

"I see how you are."

From the second "SexyBack" hit, everyone in the hazy bar watched Chalise coil her curves to the lyrics as she and Garence switched on vocals. There were more opportunities to touch each other. A light finger over his shoulders. His hand and thumb running down her spine. The audience's applause doubled when he sang along with JT about letting her whip him while giving the crowd a wink. Chalise shouted her approval, then leaned in close.

"We need to do this more often."

— FOUR DAYS LATER —

Garence,

Dark corner,

Shallow breaths,

A dragon slumbers.

His internal furnace kicks on,

Sparks ignite,

First breath of fire.

His wings give him flight,

The horizon,

A new day.

Yours Truly,

Chalise

THE NFXT WEEK —

The morning was fine, and a coworker had texted Chalise a meme about a cowgirl falling off a horse. She belted a laugh and forwarded it to Garence with a simple "LOL as if" caption. Her message went unanswered.

— ANOTHER WEEK LATER —

Garence,

Fun times visiting friends.

You're trekking majestic summits, but Gloucester isn't the same without seeing you, my friend.

Yours Truly,

Chalise

Chapter Forty

ONE YEAR AGO

— OCTOBER —

The following week, Garence showed up at her door. He hadn't notified her of his arrival, and she was glad she was home. The London clouds had welcomed him with showers, and his clothes were spotted. His shoes were wet, and she was glad he left them at the door, where he shook the wet from his hair with his hand. She offered him a glass of water, but he refused it. She had two bottles in the refrigerator, Cabernet Sauvignon and Pinot Blanc, and he opted for the red.

Chalise recognized the bags under Garence's weary eyes from when they'd first met. They had disappeared around the time they went horse-back riding, but now they were back with a vengeance. He didn't have any luggage with him, so he wasn't coming from travel. Not that it mattered that he'd stopped by. She was glad he'd thought of her.

"How are things?"

"Things? Things are good. I was in town meeting someone when I took a walk and it started to rain. I stopped in a museum…"

"Did you?" she said from the kitchen, pouring the second glass with Cabernet.

"I didn't stay long. I found it difficult to relax long enough to give the creations the attention they deserved. And I thought of you."

She wasn't sure if that should have been received as a compliment, but she wasn't going to overthink it. It was clear he needed a friend and that was the matter at hand. She handed him a glass. They clinked them before taking a sip. Rather, Chalise sipped while Garence drank the entirety.

"Would you like another?"

"No. I was thirsty. Thank you, though."

He rubbed his face, and she was taken aback at how much pressure he was applying.

"Would you like to lie down and sleep? You're more than welcome to my bed."

"No. I needed to escape my four walls. Thank you, though."

"Is there anything I can do?"

"A massage would be nice." He shook his head as if to wield the thought. "I'm fine. Thank you, though."

She wondered if he knew that he was repeating the same gratitude expression. She got up, laid down a yoga mat by the fireplace, wishing she had it going, and set a pillow down before beckoning him.

He obliged and rested on his stomach.

She kneeled beside him and rubbed his shoulders, the length of his spine, neck, legs, arms, and feet. She asked him to turn around, where she repeated the process, finishing by caressing his skin with her fingertips, drawing everything out of him from his center outward.

She expected him to say something, but elongated breaths entered and left him. She draped a throw blanket over him and started that fire for him.

Chapter Forty-One

ONE YEAR AGO

— OCTOBER 11TH —

"Yes!"

Chalise raised her arms in celebration as she completed her analysis on a jewelry advert she'd received from a folk artist in Stockholm and another artist in Santiago de Querétaro, who specialized in sterling silver designs. She loved how the artists fused their unique cultures with contemporary flares, and she decided she would accept their lines of rings and earrings and necklaces and bracelets. It was half past seven when she released a sigh of satisfaction. Now she could take the evening off. She powered off her laptop and turned her back on what was a minor extension of the workday in her apartment.

Her steps were light and audible against the concrete floors and even more muted when she traversed the black-and-white striped area rug; her toes caressed the soft fibers in warm welcome. She retrieved her cell phone from its pedestal of novels with scratched protective covers and curled cornered paperbacks on the glass coffee table. She replied to several texts, then began to delete older conversations when she came upon Garence's.

She hadn't heard from him, but something within her suggested that she should call him today. She pressed upon his name when her phone rang and his name appeared on the screen.

"Garence."

"Hey, Chalise. I've been meaning to contact you."

She didn't have a reason to believe or disbelieve him. "No worries. How have you been?"

"I've been… Um. I can't say that I've been busy or anything because I haven't. Not traveling or renting or doing anything."

Chalise closed her eyes as if to shield herself from the truth. She shook her head. Was he implying what she thought he was implying? That he was avoiding her. She wished she could say this was out of character, but it wasn't.

"I'm sorry. I don't quite follow you."

"There's no excuse for my absence. I've been in what I've come to think of as my burrow."

She sat upon her leather sofa, dropped her head, and released a small "Oh." She wasn't sure if he meant to liken himself to an animal lodging in some buried haven, but her mind scurried to wonder why he had retreated when he had been fine for a long while. Furthermore, she didn't understand the subtext. Why was he leaving her out this time? He was dealing with the loss of his wife, and he was seeing a psychiatrist. Chalise wanted to be there for him, but he kept shutting her out, and she couldn't help but feel hurt he didn't reach out to her. She swallowed her pride—not everything was about her.

"Tell me what triggered you?"

"I should start by saying that my wife had suggested I write short stories about dragons for our unborn children based upon some renderings I had completed. I never wrote anything, but I didn't stop drawing, at least not until we decided to stop trying to conceive."

Chalise gathered the scattered puzzle pieces that belonged to her and those that belonged to Garence. "So, when I mentioned dragons in my letter, my declaration that you have new days ahead of you implied…"

"That I'm turning my back on them," he finished for her.

Her shoulders slumped, and she brought a hand to her forehead.

"Why is it that everything I say reminds you of your past? I feel as though I'm tormenting you. I don't want to remind you of what you lost."

"I know you don't. It's difficult for me to be in the present sometimes. I don't feel like I'm allowed to live. And feel. A large part of me feels like I'm betraying Sabina."

Chalise couldn't help but notice that Garence didn't argue against her assessment of her reminding him of his past; the affirmation bothered her.

"You are allowed to live in the present without feeling as though you loved Sabina and your children any less than you do." She wanted to say that Sabina wouldn't have wanted him to live in solitude, but she was afraid of treading on her sacred ground. "You shouldn't feel guilty for living, Garence."

"I know." He released an exasperated sigh. "Today is her birthday," he said, rubbing his face with his hand. "She would have been thirty-seven."

"I don't know what to say."

"I'm not expecting anything from you. Just don't tiptoe around me; I wouldn't want you to act differently toward me."

He was tugging on her heartstrings. Not walking on eggshells would be easier said than done because she cared too much for him.

"All right."

Garence called out the buzz in the air. "You're tiptoeing, Chalise."

"I'm sorry. I... I don't know. These past few weeks have been silent. It sucked, royally!"

"I'm sorry I've been dodging you."

"Can't imagine why. I keep striking your chords."

"You're fine. I'm not feeling my best. I'm going to let you go?"

She didn't want to release him, but she was more disappointed to hear he was unwell.

"Yeah. Can I do anything for you?"

"No. I'll be all right. You take care."

"You too," she said hesitantly.

Garence parked his car down the row from Henrietta's office; he turned the engine off. His head fell against the headrest as if it were heavy with rush-hour contemplations. He was tired of Chalise's words revolving inside his mind and dizzy with nausea.

"Light has triumphed over the night," he recalled from one of her letters. Hmph, the night had trumped over the day. His blood had cooled, and yesterday's shadows had stretched into his consciousness. At some point, their thin claws would strangle him.

He then thought of Chalise verbalizing how he was allowed to live in the present and that he shouldn't feel guilty for living. How could anyone know what he was feeling or what was best for him? Living a life where no one he cared for mattered was not what he desired.

"I am betraying Sabina," he said out loud, too preoccupied to feel the pinpricks of agitation on his skin.

Garence had good days with speckles of bad ones; the noises in his mind seduced him into the latter. He released a small request for a quiet, good-humored session.

He entered Henrietta's office and greeted her with silence apart from rallying enough decency to raise his dark eyebrows in hello.

Garence didn't say much for the next forty minutes, and he knew it was irritating Henrietta. There was no point in enduring a meaningless session when he needed a release.

"What would Sabina want?" she asked.

A disturbing hush fell over the room.

Garence glared at Henrietta. How dare she bring Sabina into this! Of course he knew what Sabina wanted, happiness, but it wasn't what he wanted, so why was Henrietta bothering to step on Sabina's ground?

Happiness was not possible!

Frustration built, and he was almost afraid of his words exploding from his mouth. His cool nature had recently been fine-tuned from grief. He didn't offer Henrietta a reply.

"Has that crossed your mind?"

He said nothing.

"Are you all right, Garence?"

"I was."

Her brow creased. "You were? What happened?"

"You decided to bring Sabina into all of this."

He could feel her eyes narrow on him.

"Isn't she the reason why you're here?"

"No."

"No? That's strange. I thought you were here because you lost your wife, Sabina?" Henrietta seemed to jog her memory. "I'm sorry. If you're not here because of Sabina's death..."

"Stop saying her name."

The reason he was seeing a psychiatrist was to try to gain some semblance of his former self again, but that wasn't in his favor. He damn well didn't appreciate Henrietta speaking about Sabina as if she knew her. He scoffed. He wasn't playing into her hand.

"If you're not here because of Sabina's death, then why are you here, Garence?"

"I asked you not to say her name."

"You didn't *ask* me not to say Sabina's name, you flat out demanded..."

"What am I, fair game now? Some bloody target?"

"Of course not. Don't be ridiculous. That's not what I'm getting at, and you know it."

"Now, I'm supposed to know what your angle is?"

Henrietta wanted to slap him, but instead, she threw her notepad down on the floor beside the armchair; it smacked against the floor like a whip.

"Garence, what the bloody hell has got into you today?"

Garence covered his face with his hands, wiped his eyes, and leaned back while running his hand through his long hair.

"Here's a bottle of water." She pushed the bottle across the coffee table with her fingertips.

"Thank you." He accepted the peace offering and took one sip. "Before I go, I will say that Sabina would want me to be happy. But I can only do so much without her..."

And only so much when she appears, Garence thought to himself. He didn't disclose this. He had never shared with Henrietta the fact that Sabina visited him.

"I understand," Henrietta said, almost regretting pushing him as hard as she had. But she wanted to hear him say he wanted to get well.

Garence drummed his fingers against the side of the bottle and nodded his readiness.

Henrietta looked up at him, anxious. "I'll see you in two?"

"Yeah..."

He seemed to search for a reason to come back for another session or to quit altogether.

"Yeah. I suppose you will."

Chapter Forty-Two

PRESENT DAY

I had never imagined in a million years I would be as vulnerable with myself in the way I was with Chalise. Even the settings in which I rolled everything out were momentous and quite symbolic. At first, I was guarded and rattling within myself when we were in an enclosed space, the Raucous Pint and at Shannon's Pub. In the most recent conversation, I was exposed and allowed Chalise to hear the currents of truth, and it all took place outside, along the Thames.

To say that our next excursion was a bash is not only an understatement, but it proved to be the lift to an unfathomable dimension.

Chapter Forty-Three

TEN MONTHS AGO

Garence and Chalise hadn't seen each other for months, but he couldn't miss celebrating her birthday. When he arrived at her flat, not a single moment was lost between them. They kissed the other's right cheek, lingered, then moved to the other side. Chalise placed a hand on his dark, textured coat. She rubbed the collar of his white dress shirt where the top button was undone and smiled. The thought of his sex appeal crossed her mind, but she remarked on how smart he looked instead.

With her hand in his, Garence raised it to get a better look at her in black leather trousers and a velvet, fitted, military-style coat. "You look every bit the loveliest birthday girl there was."

She dropped her eyes and dipped into a graceful curtsy. Chalise took his arm and guided him down a brick row in Pembridge Square and straight to the doorstep of a three-story mews house. Laughter coming from above caught their attention. They looked up and saw the roof terrace lit by a glow coming from several strings of clear lights.

Although the pair had arrived on time, the majority of the guests were already in attendance to greet the birthday girl with hugs and cheek kisses. Chalise introduced Garence to everyone as intrigue marked their faces. Their age gap was as clear as day, but that couldn't have been the reason for their interest; Chalise grinned, knowing that Garence was the real star of the night. The hosts, Hugh and his wife Elin, offered to take their coats. Chalise took hers off, revealing a silver sequin sleeveless blouse with a low back. An array of hors d'oeuvres made the rounds by a few party staff, and a couple of the bartenders set up in the dining room prepared drinks whilst the smart home played a mix of Chalise's favorite music from her shared playlists. Hugh and Elin came out of the kitchen, pushing a cart and a round cake with whipped coconut cream frosting. A crown of twenty-eight sparkler candles illuminated every quality of Chalise's gobsmacked face from the time her jaw dropped to the instant it altered into a brilliant smile.

Dancing and indistinct conversations went on, but all inquisitive eyes were on Chalise and Garence. The pair danced the entire evening, with a bottle of beer or a glass of wine rotating between their hands, and they looked every inch a romantic couple.

Emma and her partner, Launa, swayed nearby. "Hey, lovebirds."

Chalise contested the remark with a roll of her eyes, leaving her arms around Garence's neck.

"Did you know that most of your guests have gone?"

She surveyed the home and discovered it was almost empty. Wonder befell her. She laughed into Garence's chest.

"It's funny, isn't it?" Emma was wide-eyed and impressed by Chalise's inebriated state. "I'm heading out. We're going in different directions, but I can call you guys a car?"

Hugh approached. "I don't mind driving them."

Chalise pursed her lips and shook her head as Garence hugged her waist with unexpected ease.

"I'll see her home safe," he said.

His no-nonsense words convinced Emma he wasn't as sloshed as Chalise.

"Emma, my dear. I'm not as stewbummed as you think." Chalise meant to place a hand upon her friend's shoulder when it missed and swept her chest instead. A look that said "nobody saw that" crashed her face. "On second thought. Hugh, darling?"

"Yes, dear?" he said, entertaining her.

"I'd like a cup of water, please. Just in case. I don't wanna feel like shit tomorrow."

"Comin' right up."

"Maybe a whole kettle and some migas," Emma hollered. She stayed with Chalise and Garence, eating from their platter of torn pieces of corn tortillas fried with eggs until she sobered up.

Garence and Chalise walked to her flat, howling their embraced laughter into the midnight hour, peeled their coats off, and dropped them on the hooks by the door.

Chalise headed straight for her bedroom, hollering, "Make yourself comfortable."

Garence entered the kitchen with a pang to quench his thirst. "Thanks. I'm gonna get a drink. Is that all right?"

"Make yourself at home," she said, changing into leggings and a tank top.

Garence opened the fridge. As for beverages, his options encompassed a beer, a pint of orange juice, bottled water, and milk. It'd be best if they hydrated, so he pulled out two bottles of water, then plopped on the couch. Chalise entered and sat beside him, pulling her legs up on the cushion. Her face had been washed, and now her skin was fresh and without a lick of makeup.

"What a fun night," she oozed, beaming.

"Did you have a nice birthday?"

"Mm-hmm."

Garence reached into his trouser pocket, pulled out a small, flat turquoise box, and handed it to Chalise.

"You didn't have to do this." She pulled the white ribbon from around the box and opened it. A pair of olive leaf hoop earrings in sterling silver gleamed back at her. "These are gorgeous. You shouldn't have." Her enthusiasm mirrored the earrings' brilliance. "I have to try them on."

"Here, allow me to hand them to you. There's the first, and the other's backing. Now they're gorgeous."

Her doe eyes dropped as she leaned forward to embrace him. "Thank you." She met his eyes. "I love them."

To Garence, Chalise was as fresh as morning radiance with all the comforts of having experienced a good night's rest after mind-blowing sex. He imagined her soft skin against his body, cupping her breasts as he dropped his mouth to them. She was sweet and sexy, and she was inches from his face. Vigor pushed him toward her.

Chalise was taken aback; Garence was kissing her, and there were no butterflies in her stomach urging her to flee from the situation, nor was there any fear of what might happen if she kissed him back.

So, she did.

Their breathing crescendoed. Chalise wrapped her arms around Garence's neck as he caressed her curves. Tops and bottoms were tossed to the side like beads at a Mardi Gras parade. He stroked her cheek, relishing the velvet effect it retained. He placed his hand upon the back of her head, then drew her in again.

Chapter Forty-Four

PRESENT DAY

*At Chalise's birthday party, I could sense the cogs of time
rotating and punching into the next, but I had disregarded them.
And I had been drinking. A lot. I was disoriented by the end of
it, but the coffee helped. What I cannot distinguish is whether
the gears were cranking with some resistance or if they were
clicking like a well-oiled machine. I would have thought the
differentiation would have been as clear as a bell, but it wasn't.
It doesn't really matter; it's an insignificant afterthought. But
time was most definitely speeding up and slowing down all
at once—please, do not ask me to explain this further. I have
had little sleep, and I've downed over nearly a dozen bottles of
wine in the past two days because I cannot bear to leave behind
excellent wine that my dearest Sabina was saving.*

*Anyway, some point that night, after we arrived at Chalise's
flat, I became more aware of the shifting planes of time that
converted into energy. It was a flicker, but it activated that
evening. My life was being guided by something bigger than me,
because that night was as liberating as it was life changing. How*

strange that I can remember this faint awareness, so that I can almost sense it now. It was a deep sinking feeling I had shoved even deeper because I wanted to feel again.

With Chalise, I experienced that. In more ways than one, and without getting ahead of myself too much, I got <u>exactly</u> what I had been secretly projecting to the universe.

As hard as I was on the night of her birthday, I had mastered the art of the lull long enough to consider the woman before me. Chalise was sitting on her heels on the leather sofa, her palms resting upon her thighs. Her eyes were on me as if she didn't care if I ogled her, but then her dimples flickered; her grin could propel sea-devoted crew members overboard. She was a vision of seduction in a black lace and mesh bra and knicker set. Her nipples were visible, as were the bare point at which her thighs met; I couldn't help but give in to her. I reveled in her fingertips fondling my chest, telling me how desirable I was. Her hands slivered down to my groin, where she gave me a mind-blowing kiss, and then I returned the favor.

I committed a crime by not loving Chalise. We were always keen on each other, and I'm sure there's nothing either of us could say to sway each other.

No, that's not true.

Knowing what was to come, Garence tried not to get ahead of himself again.

Little will be said to dissolve her love for me.

Chapter Forty-Five

NINE MONTHS AGO

— FEBRUARY —

Chalise was lying on her bed, thinking about a meeting that had transpired earlier in the day, when she realized she needed to make a grocery list. She grabbed her cell phone from the end of the bed, pulled up her memo, and typed in the items she needed off the top of her head before going through the cupboards. Clingfilm, Fairy Liquid, hairspray, tampons.

Wait.

It seemed as though she should have needed tampons a while back. She pulled up the calendar on her phone.

She sat straight up, clouded in a state of disbelief.

Was it really the 25th?

She was one, two, three, four, five… six days late.

No, it hadn't been that long. Her last period was… She scrolled, frantic, through the weeks, looking for her last period, and compared it to the events on her calendar to verify that she had entered the correct date. The night she had dinner with Emma and Launa she'd been on her period, so her dates were right.

Shit.

She should have started February 19th. She was six days late. No, she had dinner with Emma the week of her birthday so that meant she was supposed to start today.

What?

No, that would have meant she was on her period when she slept with Garence, which she was not.

The dates were correct.

Her stomach somersaulted, and she lay back down on the bed. Her period was late for the first time in her whole life, and it had been twenty-five days since she slept with Garence.

She was pregnant.

What was she going to tell Garence? How would he react?

He didn't want a relationship with her. They were attracted to each other, but that moment wasn't a gateway toward some future together. A child would mean a new beginning for Garence.

The corner of her mouth turned up at this thought. He had always wanted children... with another woman.

Chalise shook her head. *Don't bring yourself down with these thoughts*, she told herself.

A child would also mean she and Garence were linked for the rest of their lives; she was afraid of what this all meant to Garence. Chalise placed her hands to her forehead.

A few days later while out shopping, she received a telephone call from her doctor's office with the confirmation. She stopped in the middle of the pavement in busy, cold London. She was four weeks pregnant. She turned her head toward the store's display window. She should have seen the mannequins, a woman and a girl, before her, but she only saw her cloaked silhouette reflecting back at her from the glass of what might be possible.

She had befriended Garence after the mere mention of his having new days ahead sent him running for cover. Would he retreat again? Would he resent her or the baby for what he never had with Sabina? These thoughts were nauseating. Would he want to be in the babe's life? She would lose him again, that was a possibility. She wondered why this crossed her mind. They weren't a couple, they were friends. Friends without any spoken words of romantic love, just exchanges of mutual admiration for their companionship. Her fingers intertwined into a single mighty fist, and she hoped Garence would remain in her child's life. That was all she wanted.

She continued to walk toward the tube, acknowledging that with every step, she was walking toward the man she loved, one who cared for her, but who was certainly not in love with her.

She couldn't dump this on him as if she were bestowing a gift, although she already thought of the child as such. She slowed her step, then continued to stride onward. Should she wait a while? No, of course not. She would tell him straight away. She stopped at the bustling corner of Kensington Park Road and Elgin Crescent and waited for traffic to clear. He was flying in from Thailand in two days. She could catch him in the city, arrange to meet at a restaurant, or, better yet, cook him dinner at her place, enjoy a fire, share a nice bottle of wine—scratch that—a nice bottle of, um, water? That was daft. A kettle of hot cocoa. Better! She could envision it all now. Dinner, fire, cocoa. Garence would arrive with his duffle bag in tow, jet-lagged—why was she conjuring these aspects into what was a picturesque illusion? She'd have the brick fire burning, a candle in one of Garence's favorite scents burning in the distance. The scene was becoming way too romantic, so she'd scramble it with some rock music or something. Yes, that was better. It'd be perfect. They'd eat. Catch up. Then she'd tell him she was pregnant. Bob's your uncle! Nothing to worry about.

Garence indeed arrived with a large duffle bag over his shoulder and rings under his eyes and an expression that screamed, "I barely made it here!"

"Hi. Gosh, you look knackered." It was not how she wanted to greet him, but the words flew out of her mouth before she could stop them.

"I am." He welcomed her invitation to drop his belongings. He said hello and kissed her cheeks, then peeled off his jacket.

The living room should have given him a flashback from his last visit, but he was too tired to process any visual cues.

"Can I make you a cup of tea, coffee, cocoa? Perhaps a good stiff drink to take the edge off."

"If I had any edges, I would take you up on that offer. I'll have whatever you're having. Even if it's hard. I'm up for anything. I want to relax."

From the kitchen, Chalise could feel his weariness, and her body stiffened. "Rough flight?"

"The flight, the hotel, the people, and the attendants. Everything was bloody horrendous." He rubbed his face with his hand. "I'm glad it's over though." He rose and walked over to her. "You are so sweet for inviting me over. There's no way I would have made the journey home after all of this."

"Of course," she said, forcing a smile.

Garence entered the kitchen. "Hot cocoa?"

"Yeah. I feel like something sweet. Still wanna share?" she asked, anxious.

"Of course." He was leaning over the counter as if his life depended upon it. "Be sure to shake in some chili powder."

Intrigued by this suggestion, she smiled. "Really?"

"Oh yeah."

Her smile faded when she realized he'd drunk his cocoa with chili with Sabina. Her stomach somersaulted with dread, but she obliged. She poured the hot drink into two celadon mugs that were stout in size and capacity and could have rivaled the size of the small pot from which they were derived.

Garence took a sip, then rolled his eyes back and an expression of pure delight covered his face. "You are a woman of many talents."

"I see you forgot my element of surprise," she said with a wink, then regretted these words, knowing full well what she was going to reveal that evening. She sat beside him on the sofa and pulled her thermal-clad legs up against her body.

"I suppose I did, but that's what I like about you. You do always surprise me."

He hadn't seen Chalise since her birthday, a memorable way to part ways. Since then, he had taken full advantage of their day-to-day conversations, and he was honestly pleased to set eyes upon her again.

She took a sip of cocoa.

"I've been missing your letters."

"Have you?" she asked, astonished. She had stopped writing ever since she sent him running for the hills with her optimism.

"Yeah. You have a way of seeing things and sharing that vision with me in your letters. I've never met anyone who took to writing the way you have."

"Is that right?" she said in more of a statement drizzled with disinterest. Not even Sabina? She bit her tongue, forking her jealousy.

"It is. I've missed you, Chalise."

Even as dog tired as he was, Garence smoldered in that unintentional way that made her heart skip a beat. Goose pimples erupted all over her skin. With the atmosphere as idyllic as it could be and the life within her yearning to be a part of it all, Chalise couldn't wait another moment to tell Garence about her news.

"I…" Her voice caught in her throat, and her breathing shallowed. *You are about to ruin everything you two have built*, her conscience jabbed, but her emotions retaliated, *It's not within Garence to refuse you or the child— no matter his history.* Everything had changed, and he needed to know.

Over the rim of his mug, Garence observed her tension. He licked the cocoa residue from his lips. "Is there something wrong?"

Alarm struck her face. "No!" Dammit! She couldn't have his thoughts strolling on a path that stunk of problematic difficulties. "Oh, no," she said nonchalantly. "In fact, it's rather the opposite." She swallowed. A smile warmed her face, and the announcement fell from her lips as smoothly as it could possibly be delivered. "I'm pregnant."

"What?"

He couldn't have heard her correctly. He swore Chalise had said she was pregnant, but that was absurd. Then their last interlude flashed in his mind. Fine, so it wasn't quite as absurd as he first thought. His focus cleared, and he blinked several times.

"You're... pregnant?" He placed the mug on the coffee table. He was half-excited about the prospect of being a father but shocked.

"Yes."

He forced a smile.

Chalise knew this was too bizarre for his words. A dream. His hands were rough against his face. He drew a deep breath and peeked through his fingers... Chalise was still before him. Still smiling.

"Why are you hiding?"

"I'm not hiding."

She chuckled. "Yes, you are." She was grateful he wasn't leaving so that she could appreciate how adorable he looked as he grappled with her announcement.

He was perplexed. "I don't understand how this happened?"

She looked sideways, then met his eyes. "Well," she cleared her throat, still able to recall the evening's details, "it was my birthday, and we rang it in, all right." Nerves made her mouth twitch after realizing Garence wasn't saying anything, and her imagination ran rabid. "We had been drinking, but, um, I'd say things turned out pretty well."

She blushed.

Shut up, she told herself. Stop talking, now! Why was she explaining? He was there. They had sobered up by the time they walked through her front door!

Garence clasped his hands and pressed them against his forehead. This was the one thing he and Sabina had hoped for. It didn't make any sense to him. It wasn't fair. All he could do was remain silent.

Chalise placed a hand upon his knee, breaking his trance. How could he resent her? His friend. The one person who had brought joy to his miserable existence. He met her doting eyes, and his heart melted. Although her dimples were fading, they still brought a smile to his face. If the baby made her this happy, then maybe he could be happy too.

"I'm going to be a father," he said with a spark in his tone that kept burning.

"You are."

"I can't believe this. I'm going to be a father!"

Chalise clapped her hands together and tilted her head back, amused. Her curls danced with her laughter. This was the side of Garence she had always suspected existed, and she was dying to see it emerge from the depths of his grief. Her spirits rose with the hope their child would breathe new life into Garence. She gazed into his eyes to validate what she was seeing and rubbed his cheek with her hand. She loved him with every fiber of her being, and she was desperate for him to love her in return.

He jolted off the sofa and nestled his face in her scent and embraced her.

She was taken aback. It took a second for her to return his hold, and she released the breath she hadn't known she was holding. When he laid his lips upon her forehead, she had to wipe away a tear.

It was a brisk March morning and rain was expected this week, so Garence fertilized the lawns around the most common areas of his property. Moss spotted the soil nearest the trees and enveloped the trunk like a coat. He should have done some maintenance there last autumn, but he'd been too busy trying to preoccupy his saddened mind to think about stuff like that. Satisfied with the idea that the feed would help, he wondered what Sabina would think of him becoming a father. Would she be happy for him? Ecstatic, perhaps? Or would she be mournful or resent not being the mother? He winced at the possibility of causing her pain. He couldn't tell her about Chalise being pregnant. Then the second wave hit him, and he dropped to a squat, hands covering his face. He'd never even told her about Chalise! What had he got himself into? His nails dug into his scalp as stressed fingers grabbed at the roots of his long curls. He'd never had a reason to mention Chalise because she was never on his mind. Now she was pregnant! What *had* he got himself into?

Surprisingly, Garence never noticed, or put two and two together, that Sabina hadn't appeared in some time. Not even after he found himself lost in that cursed dark dream that night.

The tunnel was as cold as it had been the weeks before, but there was something different this time. His boot soles seemed to melt into the gravel as he tried to pinpoint what he was sensing. One thing he knew for sure, he wasn't shaken this time. Curious was more to the truth. With an unstable left leg to stand upon, Garence lifted the other enough to drag it over the gravel without putting all of his weight on the left, feeling for the train track he'd tripped over. It was about a foot and half away from him, and it felt as though it was straight. He might be able to make a better attempt at finding a way out of this dream. *I have to try.* He prepared by taking a deep breath.

Was that a spark?

He stopped in his tracks as the cracking sound echoed off the walls. That was a flare! He cocked his ear and tried to isolate the source when a light appeared behind him. He covered his blinded eyes as the flame burned more brilliantly, the desert sun causing his head to ache as if he were hit with a hammer, then it and the searing pain were summoned to a subtle glow. Before Garence could gather his bearings, he was ripped from the dream. He turned his head away and covered his eyes as he had done in the beginning of the dream; the sun had risen, finding a gap in the blinds to laser his closed eyes open.

That was bizarre, he mused. He hated that tunnel and everything it represented; why wasn't he afraid of it this time? And who was responsible for that flare and what did it symbolize? His arm was getting tired of being held up, so he returned the sunlight's good spirits with a grimace and climbed out of bed.

Chapter Forty-Six

EIGHT MONTHS AGO

— MARCH —

Henrietta was intrigued by Garence's dark dreams. "How long have you been having these dreams?"

Garence closed his eyes and tried to remember what had been happening when the dream first happened so he could associate a timeframe to them; Sabina had died, and he'd forced her to disappear because it ached to see her. "Eight months," he said offhandedly.

Henrietta stared daggers at him. "Curious. You didn't mention them before." She removed her glasses, then placed her fingertips upon her forehead and waited for his reply.

"No, I didn't."

"What else haven't you been telling me?"

Everything he never shared with Henrietta burned his skin, Sabina's visits and his suicidal ideations, and the resonating voice, but he pushed through the flames. "I'm sorry." He was sorry he couldn't tell her about his mental state, but he in no way meant that he would.

He cleared his throat.

"All right."

Garence didn't realize his chin had dipped when he met her eyes. "Chalise is pregnant. I'm the father."

Henrietta jumped out of her skin; she'd had no idea they were sexually involved. But something was off, and it gave her pause. The unspoken truth permeated her consciousness, and she sensed they were not lovers but friends who had allowed a heated moment to seethe them. She was intrigued to learn that Garence had progressed toward a sexual relationship, but a baby. That was a different matter. Mind-boggling. She was curious as to how events would unfold for a beaten man who had lost so much.

"Congratulations. I wish you both a great deal of blessings."

"Thank you," he said with a small grin.

She reflected upon the whirlwind that Garence had found himself in when a thought occurred to her. "Did you know Chalise was expecting when you had the flare dream?"

"Yes. It was the same night."

The corner of her mouth curled up.

What the hell did that look mean? he wondered.

"You've been granted a gift, Garence. Even your subconscious recognizes it."

Garence was too tired to participate in repartee, and he wished Henrietta would spit out whatever she was going to say; he rubbed his face with his hand. "Is that right?"

She recognized that she'd have to lead him through the maze. "Sabina was the light of your life. The light at the end of the tunnel, correct? All right. You hated being without her even when she was alive, so you dreamt about being in a tunnel, searching for her light at the end of the tunnel. Then you learn you are to become a father, and you see a spark in that tunnel—a flare. Flares are utilized as a signal or guidance, in times when one needs rescuing from distress. It's clear your child is your saving grace."

"My light," he whispered from his core.

Henrietta couldn't make out what he said, but she suspected he understood her.

It all made sense to Garence now, but he wasn't sure it would make the next bit any easier. He rubbed his eyes. "On that note, Henrietta, I have the sign I've been waiting for."

"Oh?"

"I was undecided before, but now I'm quite certain I am taking the right course of action. I won't be coming to see you anymore. I have a great support system in Chalise; she's been a brilliant friend. Now that we're expecting, I won't have time to come to Gloucester. I have my work, the holiday let, and Chalise and the baby in London." He saw a hint of sadness in her eyes, but he had to do this. He couldn't decipher whether this move felt right or wrong, but it was logical. "I will miss you, Henrietta."

She scratched her head, muttering an obscenity. "I did not see that coming at all."

"I'm sorry."

She waved her hand. She wanted to ask him if he had thought this through, but deep down inside, she detected it would have been a waste of her breath; she gritted her teeth. "I support you no matter what." She looked straight into his still, hazel eyes, uncertain about his future. "If you ever need someone to talk to, I want you to blast my telephone line or burst through those doors—I don't care who you interrupt."

Sentiment warmed his lips.

Henrietta rose from her seat and went to embrace him.

Garence stood and hugged the woman, another special being, who had helped him during a dark period in his life. "Thank you for your guidance," he said, placing a delicate kiss on top of her head.

"You are most welcome." She sniffled, then pushed him away. "Now bugger off before I make you share whatever else you've been keeping from me."

He grew solemn. As the hope of his being all right without Henrietta's counsel plummeted, Garence was forced to say goodbye with a heavy heart.

Chapter Forty-Seven

EIGHT MONTHS AGO

— MARCH —

Chalise,

I am dumbfounded.

For once in my life, I do not know how to execute a letter... Yet, I feel a very deep need, a compulsion, to write to you. So, I'm going to write whatever moves through me. I could rewrite this letter until I get it right, but it would sound forced or scripted— and that is the last thing I want.

I hope you'll bear with me... and excuse any strikethroughs that may arise.

I am sitting on hardwood floors with my bare back against a wall in a room that Sabina and I defined as the nursery. This room was fit for a country princess with inviting whites and beiges and cozy blues, and lots of light and books and games. Now it's been stripped of all those things and the two living, whole hearts unmarred by grief. I'm near French doors that face north. It is an unclear day, and I am feeling most unclear. And quite uncertain. I cannot guess what the temperature is, inside or out, but my nails are a bit purple, so I suppose it is cold enough. I am barefoot with only my jeans to warm me, but I don't feel the need to dress when I'm going to go to bed when I finish writing to you.

I've ambled through each room in this cottage like a lost soul searching for something or someone. I don't know what I am looking for or what the point is in my sitting here. Perhaps if I am stationary, someone or something will find me, and if it succeeded, I wonder what would transpire? Would that experience transform me in some way? I wish things were different. If someone asked me what my one wish would be, I would say that I want everything that I lost. But no one is asking, so who cares what I desire.

I've been thinking about that, everything I have lost, that is. I know I shouldn't, but I can't help it. I am dead inside and will continue to feel nothing for the rest of my days. Then I become angry because I want the family promised to me on four occasions. The first being Sabina and then each of our three children. I want the woman who gave me purpose, whose light gave me guidance.

Fuck me!

I want to say something, but it's such a horrible thing to admit. I can't believe I am even thinking this, but ~~fuck, what's wrong with me~~ I might as well ring it out. As much as I loved my children, I would have had a life without them because I had Sabina. Please don't think that I never wanted them, because I did. I grieved for Sol, Luna, and Estrella (Spanish for sun, moon, and star, respectively), but it's not the same thing as losing a spouse, my twin flame with whom I was building a beautiful life. I would have kept trying for children if Sabina wanted to, but it wasn't in our stars; I accepted that. I could have lived without the kids, but not without my wife. I suppose that makes me selfish, but I don't give a flying fuck!

I know she is now a pure, nonphysical energy. I shouldn't be grieving for her with this knowledge, but I cannot get out of this single-mindedness. I am bound by my own deprivation.

I guess that means, if I'm being honest, I'm choosing bondage over living.

~~Ever since~~

~~I'm~~

Ever since my wife died, I've been lost. I don't even feel like myself most of the time; it's quite a bizarre sensation. Sometimes I don't know what I'm doing. I've not been able to open up to anyone. Not completely. Not even to Henrietta, my psychiatrist. I can't have her knowing every private disturbing thought and emotion. I've never told anyone this, Chalise, but I don't know what the point of my life is.

I'm dying to know.

I miss my wife, Chalise. I miss my lover and my best friend. I miss her so much my head and my chest ache with emptiness. I've told Henrietta this bit, that it felt as though my heart were absent, excavated from my very chest. To add to my misery, I haven't been able to take a full breath since she died. It hurts so much. I dream about her every night. I dream about when we were blissfully happy. When we lay beside each other in silence and our breaths were in synchronization. I dream about how distraught we were each time we lost a child, when we were sure of nothing but each other, and I dream about how alone I felt all those times she shut me out after we miscarried.

Chalise, my wife died two years ago, and it feels as though it happened yesterday.

I have written countless letters. ~~And~~ I want you to know that I've never written one of this length before.

Ever.

I don't know why...

I suppose it must mean something. Or nothing.

We were together four and a half years, way too short, and she was the one person I wrote the most to in all my life, but they were never more than a page. To see myself writing past the first sheet is amazing even to me.

In this cottage, I spent the happiest and saddest times of my life. I was invited to a couple of friends' houses and Sabina's parents' in Bilbao, but I declined. If anything, I saved them all from watching me struggle to express a genuine grin or something. Now, March 11th approaches, and it knocks the wind out of me to realize it's Estrella's birthday.

It wasn't possible for Sabina and me to hold our first two children in our arms because of how early in the trimester the miscarriage occurred, but I had the opportunity with Estrella. She was much further along, stillborn at nineteen weeks. She was so red, and her skin had deteriorated. I was scared to look at her in this condition, but I could never look away from my darling little girl. She was so beautiful. She sort of had Sabina's face. I'm glad we each experienced that moment with Estrella; it provided us with some closure, and I got to kiss her goodbye.

I'm sorry that I cannot write you a better letter or that we can't meet in Gloucester. As much as it pains me to be here, I am glad to be home and not anywhere else in the world.

I'll see you,

Garence

Chalise was curled up in bed, gripping the last page of Garence's letter with enough force to crumple it. Her bedroom was filled with morning sunlight equivalent to what appeared in orange juice commercials, but the diaphanous curtains shed a cloudy vibe upon her. If she could eradicate his grief, she would. It was irritating to want to help someone more than they wanted you. Why the hell didn't he reach out to her? He shouldn't be alone right now. She had so much love to give, there was no reason for him not to confide in her. It hurt to think he didn't want to. She wiped tears from her eyes, imagining him all alone in a house filled with memories. She had no idea what he was going through, but she wanted to comfort him.

If the tables were turned, she would talk to someone or seek help. Garence was seeing a psychiatrist, Henrietta, and she was certain he still was.

Or was he?

When did he mention an appointment?

A month ago? She tried to remember, but her anxiety prevented her from focusing. Goodness, could it have been longer?

He could still be going to his appointments and he was super busy, or he could have stopped seeing Henrietta and now he was alone.

Her stomach dropped.

If she were in his shoes, she wouldn't want to be by herself. If she knew where he lived, she would drop in, but she had no idea where that was. The one thing she knew for certain was that he lived in Bourton-on-the-Water and he owned a rental... down the road from... the Whitmore Estate! The thought of Garence suffering in silence was too much to bear.

Her mind was made up. She was going to see him right now.

Chalise grabbed her laptop from the bench at the foot of her bed and awakened it to Google "Whitmore Estate, Bourton-on-the-Water, Gloucestershire county." Her eyes scrolled down the search results, where she could navigate to Wikipedia, the Cotswold District Council, the best-rated hotels, the Tea Festival going on today, March 11th.

Chalise's jaw dropped. Today was Estrella's birthday.

Rather than pause on whether she should visit Garence on Estrella's birthday, and change her mind, Chalise forged on. She located the property, the address, and saw Garence's house and the holiday let next door. It would be easy enough to find.

Her mouth twitched.

Should she invade his privacy, his home? Sabina's home? She winced.

She stared at the slate roof; Garence was in there. Alone and suffering.

She shut down her laptop to jump in the shower.

Chapter Forty-Eight

EIGHT MONTHS AGO

— MARCH 11TH —

Chalise had never been to the town of Bourton-on-the-Water, but she followed the instructions spoken to her by the navigation system without difficulty. She turned onto Moonlight Road, Garence's road, with the caution of an underage driver. Everything inside her said she was doing the right thing by visiting him; granted, it was unannounced, but nevertheless, she was doing the right thing.

From inside the car, she could hear the gravel crunch beneath the weight of her visit, or was it the weight of her car? Around the left of the cottage were shrubs fringed with bluebells. She parked next to a car she didn't recognize at the side of the house, unbuckled her seatbelt, and sat there. Now that she was here, she didn't know what to do.

What was she doing here?

Should she call him first? No. If she was going to do that, then she should have done it when she was in London.

She looked back at the cottage and felt nauseated. What if he was out for a walk and she ended up sitting here for ages? Or worse, what if he saw her surprise appearance as an intrusion and was annoyed?

She looked over her shoulder and at the front door. Goodness, she hadn't thought this through. What the hell was she going to say to him?

The sun was masked behind sea-gray clouds, but nothing could extinguish the uplift she felt when she saw Garence exit the cottage. Then two other people followed him. A man and a woman. The three of them were too preoccupied by the horizon to notice her or her widened eyes. She crept down in her seat, hating her tenacity.

In the rearview mirror, she watched Garence turn his head toward her car, surprised at seeing it. He tilted his head, and she was mortified by his pause, and then he raised his hand.

She mirrored his gesture, only hers was a nervous twitch muffled by her gloves. She heard the woman ask, "Whose vehicle is that?"

He inched closer and closer without the faintest trace of an expression. She exited the car, shut out the cold by fastening the two buttons of her wool coat, and pressed the door closed with her hand.

"I'm so sorry for the intrusion."

"That's not necessary. They're leaving. Come over. Gael. Clara. This is a friend of mine, Chalise. Chalise, these are Sabina's parents."

Chalise's smile froze the shockwaves that emitted from her as she shook their hands.

"Congratulations. Garence tells us you're expecting?"

Chalise attempted to conceal her surprise, but it wasn't a shock to learn that Garence had recognized her and the baby to another.

"It's such a comfort to know Garence has someone by his side," said Clara, giving her a hug.

Chalise was silent as she allowed the trio to say their goodbyes. She and Garence watched them drive away, and before he could ask her why she was there, she jolted the cold chill forming on her coat's lapels and turned to him.

With no idea of what to say, one of the most prominent aspects of Garence's letter popped into her head, and she echoed the very question he'd written in his letter, the one he wished was posed to him.

"If you had one wish, what would it be?"

Something in his demeanor shifted, and it calmed her.

"I want everything I lost."

Although she would have never guessed, his composure bobbed above and below the line of solidity. Garence stared at her as he tried to grapple with the fact that she always managed to say and do the right thing. Her heart was one of the many things he liked about Chalise.

He broke the silence with amused curiosity. "How did you know where I lived?"

She tugged on the collar of her coat; her dimples dared not to blush. "I cannot disclose my source," she said, mocking factuality.

Garence sensed the vibration of her easy nature. "Classified information from your secret task force, is it?"

"I can neither confirm nor deny such an alliance."

He grinned, motioning toward the cottage before placing his hands in his pockets.

"I remembered you mentioning that you live next to the Whitmore Estate."

"Yes. The Whitmore Estate. I think they're having a festival of sorts today. Must be inside with it being so bloody cold out."

She entered the house, and he took her coat. The cottage welcomed Chalise with the delicate scent of sweet, crisp apples and a low-burning fire. She absorbed the interior of the space, where Garence spent the majority of his time. She liked the texture that the ebony-and-sangria-red Jaipur area rug added to the room, and she already wanted to curl up on the couch with one of those throw pillows misshaped from frequent use. The oversized back windows framed the English countryside like a gallery piece. The massive mantel over the stone fireplace held a dozen framed photographs. Amongst them were some intimate shots with two half-burnt candlesticks in unique brass chambersticks and a Victorian pocket.

One photo caught her attention. Chalise walked over to the mantel for a better look, and there she was. Sabina. A woman, smiling, clad in hiking gear, near the edge of a cliff, with Garence's arm around her; the breeze blew her hair behind as if it were embracing him. Both of them swimming in the ocean near sunset, with the sun glistening off the ripples and mirroring the liveliness of their smiles. Garence and Sabina kissing each other with cake frosting smeared on their cheeks and noses in a bright forest. Last, the photo of Sabina in a carnation-white, halter shift dress in Australia.

Chalise couldn't hide her admiration even if she tried. "She's beautiful," she admitted.

"She was a brilliant person." Garence stood beside her now. He took a long look at his wife, then turned his attention to Chalise, the corner of his mouth turned up.

His gaze seemed to search for something, but it wasn't for her. Chalise grew anxious. "I, uh, brought us a few things." She lifted the paper bag from behind her.

"Thank you. Shall I open it here? Looks like there's some consumables. Let's go to the kitchen instead."

Garence took the bag while Chalise surveyed the house as she followed him.

The kitchen was small, but the simplicity of the cabinetry and the lack of small appliances displayed on the butcher block countertops granted the area a broader feel. Pod lights caught the copper pots and pans that hung over the stove.

Garence placed the bag on the counter beside the apron sink.

"Let's see what gifts you brought? We have a bottle of Rioja Alta. Mmm, this is from the north-central part of Spain, which is a couple of hours from Bilbao." He looked at the label to confirm his suspicion, if only to see Sabina in the verbiage. "I've had a few of these before. Have you?"

"No," she answered flatly. "I thought I'd try something new but keep with the theme."

Garence maintained his unruffled tone and accepted the bait that there was more to be revealed.

He scrutinized her. "I am now more curious than I was." He set the bottle down and pulled out a white baker's box. "Then we have," he lifted the lid, and his brow raised when he caught sight of the golden pastries, "empanadas! How? Where did you get these? No one in town makes these."

"A bakery by my place."

"I'm impressed. What's the filling?"

"An assortment, but there's two of each, chicken, beef, cheese and onion, pumpkin, mincemeat, and pineapple."

"I am salivating. I've never had a mincemeat empie, but I'm sure it's good."

"I thought so too. Nothing like blending two cultures into one savory treat."

Garence peered into the bag. "It looks like there's something else in here. A card. Whatever for?"

The gleam in his smile made the corner of her mouth turn up.

Garence untucked the flap from inside the envelope and withdrew the thick cardstock. The front contained a sphere with a bright nursery-like moon in the sky overlapping another sphere with a cheery sun in it while a shooting star burst through the two orbs.

Garence smiled at the sweet scene, then read Chalise's message written on the inside. "There are billions of stars in the sky, but none shine brighter than your darling Estrella." Garence froze; the emotions stirred from the aftershock of reading his daughter's name made it difficult to continue reading. "May she be a ray of eternal light. Happy birthday."

Beneath the hood of his brow, Garence stood before the gifts. "I can't believe you did this."

The silence that vibrated between them was enough to make their ears bleed.

"You truly get me."

He turned to Chalise, and he embraced her for a long while, then said, "Thank you."

A tear fell from her eye without a trace of its existence. "You're welcome."

He released her, and he couldn't help but gaze upon her; she was meaning more to him with each passing moment.

How did he get so lucky as to come across two wonderful women in one lifetime?

"Are you hungry?"

As if on cue, her stomach rumbled. "I am."

"So am I. I'd suggest sitting out on the back patio, but it's pretty cold."

"Too cold. We can eat in here." She motioned to the eating area behind them.

"No, let's go into the living room. It'll be more comfortable. I'll put another log on the fire."

"Okay. Where are your plates?"

"Cabinet to the right of the stove."

Chalise grabbed two ceramic plates and some napkins from the table while Garence transferred everything to the next room.

"Have a seat anywhere," he said, placing the card on the mantel next to Sabina's Australian photograph.

Chalise sat on the couch's middle cushion in front of the fire. "Which empanada would you like?"

"The beef, please."

Chalise chose the chicken, and the pair took a bite.

"Mm. Mine is so good," Chalise oozed, covering her mouth with her graceful hand.

"So is mine. You've gotta have a bite."

She leaned over and took a generous taste.

"Was I right?"

"Oh yeah. Try this one. You like it better, don't you? Good thing I bought a second. Do you mind if I have one of the dessert ones?"

"Not at all. They're yours."

"They're not mine. I bought them for us," she said, giving him a side glance.

He, too, had once made a point of using the pronoun "us." Garence dismissed the reflection. "Thank you."

"You are welcome. This mincemeat one is pretty good." She looked through the back window. "You've got a gorgeous property."

"Thank you. It's a sanctuary of sorts."

Chalise couldn't argue with this statement.

"This place is haunted."

Her eyes drifted to Garence as she juggled with the options of the ghosts that could have plagued the area. The property was old enough to have had spirits residing on it. She took that back. Age had nothing to do with the possibility, it only increased the odds. No, she had a strong feeling Garence meant Sabina was occupying the property.

"Is it?"

"I think so. If I'm being honest, I'm not sure I mind it."

"Who's haunting?"

He pondered his reply. "Someone who cannot move on."

She wondered if he meant himself. "Well, that's obvious. As long as you're okay, then I don't see anything wrong with it. At least you have company."

His laughter charged her spirit.

"I've missed you," he admitted.

"I've missed you too."

"I am sorry I've not maintained contact with you."

She accepted his apology, then set her plate on the aged coffee table. "I want you to know that I understand why you isolated yourself here. I mean, if I lived in a burrow like this, I wouldn't want to leave either, but in all seriousness… I empathize with you. I don't need to have experienced the amount of loss that you have in order to identify how difficult the past few years have been for you. I want you to be able to talk to me. Tell me what's going on in your head, because I can't read minds."

Garence smiled. "Well that's a relief."

The uplift in his voice melted her agitation. "I must admit it would be helpful."

"Trust me, it wouldn't."

She was so tired of this heavy roller coaster that she laughed off the dismissal. "Fine. Changing the subject."

"Brilliant."

She looked outside and acknowledged how dark her drive home would be if she didn't leave soon. "I should head out."

"All right."

Chapter Forty-Nine

SEVEN MONTHS AGO

— APRIL —

The pregnancy was a surprise. But was it a welcomed one? It was overwhelming, for sure. Suffocating. Terrifying. He could not believe they were pregnant. They'd had sex once, and all of a sudden, he'd created a human being with a woman who wasn't Sabina. He'd created an opportunity to launch a new future for himself with them. He didn't want a new life. He wanted the one he had. The one he embraced. The one that was intentional and awakening. How was he supposed to live with himself now?

Garence spent the next month preoccupying himself by working on his neighbor's land and remodeling Cosmos Place. In fact, when he dug into the numbers, another preoccupation of his, Garence discovered the property could rent for fourteen percent more with a few updates. Desperate to immerse himself into a project between travel assignments, Garence rolled up his sleeves and replaced the kitchen cabinets, bathroom vanities, and installed new light fixtures throughout.

Although he made every possible attempt to distract himself from seeing Chalise, he made a habit of calling her every night. They'd ping-pong baby names for boys and girls, but neither of them ever hinted at which gender they'd prefer the babe to be.

Before Chalise could verbalize his persistence in delaying a visit, he showed up on her doorstep on a Friday night with dinner and a bouquet of blushing flowers.

She inhaled the sweet pea and peony and made a fainting expression. The arrangement was full, fuller than any flower stand would have had on hand. "You picked these yourself, didn't you? You're a dream. Muah! What's with the bags?"

"Dinner."

She eyed him. "Dinner?"

"You still eat, right?" he quipped.

His mere presence was appreciated, but the excessive gifts were unwarranted, and they deepened the undertones that he had been eluding her. He didn't want to come out and say it, but one way or another, she would get him to recognize it. "You're cute, but you're not that cute."

"Chicken and lamb kebabs, rice, and vegetables." He set the bags on the dining table and took out the food containers while Chalise placed the flowers in a column vase.

"Yum. Is this supposed to make up for not coming by in over a month?"

His jaw dropped when she called him out. "In a way."

"I appreciate you calling me every day. It means a lot to me." She placed the bouquet on the table, bare feet tapping the floor. She made a few minor adjustments to the arrangement, then advanced to his side. "But I don't want to go through this pregnancy alone."

"You're not alone."

"Yes. I am. I haven't seen you in a month. I know you've been planning these renovations for some time, but that's no excuse."

She allowed him to stew in his own muck long enough to grasp the enormity of his negligence.

"I am sorry I haven't come by to see you two sooner." He drew her close with one arm, close enough for his fresh breath to be felt upon her skin. "It won't happen again." He placed her hand in his and kissed it.

Ever since her birthday, Chalise couldn't help but replay the instant his intoxicating lips had touched hers and the incessant waves of ecstasy that supervened. The way his eyes narrowed on her made her toes curl. She could never handle his expression or the way her body responded to his mere presence, so she broke away, declaring her hunger for food.

Garence recognized that flare in her eye, the twinge of pining that seemed to mist behind her glowing doe eyes, and he was glad she left when she did. Otherwise, he would have had to kiss her or be the brute who pulled away once he caught himself enjoying the interlude.

"Seeing as we have our own separate lives, we should discuss what our intentions are once the babe is born."

She strolled over to the dining table. "Well, I have the option of working from home most of the week, though I would hate to miss out on the impromptu meetings and the interaction with my team. I have no desire to reduce my hours or to leave London once the baby is born."

"I'm glad to hear it. You love what you do, and you've worked hard to get to where you're at; I would hate to see you step away from it."

"Though it would be a worthy cause. I admire parents who are able to tend to their children round the clock," she added, knowing that if she and Garence were a genuine couple, she would give up her life to raise a family with him.

He met her gaze. "I meant to be supportive."

She supposed she understood where he was coming from. "I also don't want to impose upon what you have going on in Bourton." Because it was Sabina's home, and she knew nothing could ever change that fact. As difficult as it was to swallow, Chalise knew that if Garence really wanted her in his life, she would have been more involved in it by now.

He eyed her. "I'm going to keep the holiday let running."

"As you should," she said, wondering if he thought she expected him to change his life.

"I'd like you to come out again, and I want our child to love it."

Her gut told her that Garence couldn't be extending this invitation from a place of sincerity but rather out of obligation. They had been friends this whole time, and he had never invited her over, but their baby should be involved in his life, and that meant living with him at times… in the home he'd built with another woman hoping to bring home their own children.

"Yeah. That sounds nice," she said flatly. She knew full well that Garence wouldn't follow through with his intention—not that she would have enjoyed it. She made a mental note to never bring it up. "I sometimes wonder how this is going to work or where we stand."

"Allow me to try to alleviate your apprehension." He dropped his chin and teased her with a grin. Chalise smirked. He placed his hand upon hers, squeezing it slightly. "I don't know where I'd be without you in my life. I've been to the depths of hell, figuratively."

"Right, because you can't literally go to hell, can you?"

He dismissed her sarcastic tone. "I have every reason to believe that I have been there, but I know better because I don't believe in hell."

The corner of her mouth flickered.

"You're lifting me out of a very dark place. I mean it. I do not always act like it, but you mean a lot to me. We're going to make this work."

The last bit made her heart flutter, but rather than respond to him by squeezing his hand, she removed it, grinned, and shifted a stray curl away from her eye. The fact that they were bringing a child into the world while living separately was not ideal, but she was glad Garence showed interest in their child—that was her number one priority. She knew Garence had no intention of solidifying their relationship; she couldn't help but feel foolish, more like a damned fool, for wanting more from him. This was her sole liaison, unrequited as it was, and now she was pregnant.

They ate dinner at the dining table, then plopped on the leather sofa, where Garence massaged her feet. This scene would be repeated every Friday and through the weekend and always at her flat because Garence never welcomed her into his home.

"Have you thought about any more baby names?"

"Nope."

They met each other's eyes, and Chalise was reminded of the fact that Garence didn't love her. At least not in the romantic sense, and that their one night of heated passion was just that. One night. One night with a living reminder that would bond them forever in this lifetime. His heartfelt attempts to partake in their parenting-to-be relationship were sweet, but she still loved him, and she desired more.

"Have you ever imagined the person growing inside you?"

"What? Oh, yeah." Her eyes fluttered as she came out of her trance. "Of course. You?"

"I have. Tell me your thoughts, and I'll share mine."

By this time, Chalise was a few weeks from their All Hallows' Eve delivery date, and her belly button was poking out. Having never experienced this stretch of the pregnancy, Garence was overwhelmed with the babe's development, and his hand was always upon Chalise's stomach.

"She'll have her mother's skin tone and lips." She emphasized her own pout. "Her daddy's silky hair, and his eyes, and somewhere between our height."

Her eyes sparkled, and it was obvious that Chalise wanted their child to have a bit of both of them, but Garence wanted his daughter to be her own person. "She'll be kind and humble, responsible, generous, and intelligent."

"Is that all?" Chalise asked after realizing Garence had left out the superficial qualities, though she should have known better than to ask.

"Humanity over appearances. Always."

PART FOUR

ALL TOO FLEETING

Chapter Fifty

TWENTY-EIGHT
DAYS AGO

Garence landed at Heathrow Airport more than longing to lay his head down at Chalise's flat. He figured by the time he arrived it would be ten in the evening, and she would still be awake. He waved his Oyster card at Terminals 2 and 3; he was certain he'd added additional funds a week ago. Or had he? His memory was foggy after a twelve-hour flight from Tokyo—it was staying up all night with an old friend, Ryo Takeda, that did him in.

But it couldn't have been helped!

Garence tousled his locks as he reflected upon the evening he'd had. He exited the lift and walked toward the underground. They had been celebrating Garence becoming a father right after Ryo did a fine job of tempting Garence to open a set of luxury bed-and-breakfasts with him in the region. He then remembered the beautiful woman at the bar who'd been eyeing him. Long dark hair. Gray-brown eyes. She reminded him of Sabina. Garence had almost thought it was her at first glance, but she was too thin to be her. Sabina hadn't visited him in eight months, since he learned Chalise was pregnant, and he should have been floored by the sight of her, but he wasn't. He knew it wasn't his love—that and he was too preoccupied by the pregnancy and his buddy. He had turned his body away from the woman and toward Ryo.

Garence entered the train, set his case in the designated area, and drifted off to sleep for what seemed like a split second when the vibration of his phone shook him.

"This is Garence... Yes, I'm Chalise's partner."

Was he?

"She's where?"

Garence stood up.

"In labor? Now? Six centimeters!"

He jabbed his fingertips into his sockets and rubbed his eyes.

"Why didn't anyone ring me sooner?"

Why wasn't I at Chalise's constant side? he asked himself. Garence closed his eyes and visualized the train and underground tube routes that would connect him to the Great Portland Street underground station, and that would get him seconds from the Portland Hospital if he sprinted. He strained to widen his eyes; it was a marvel he could think.

"Yeah. I'm in transit. I'll get there as soon as my angels will get me there. Fifteen minutes... Thanks again."

Thanks again? he pondered. He'd never said thanks in the first place to justify a repeat utterance.

The minutes couldn't fly by fast enough as Garence swore he'd never forgive himself if he wasn't at the hospital in time for the delivery. He continued to look out the train windows and then at the upcoming tube stops as if he would arrive at his stop at a glance. At Great Portland Street station, Garence gripped the lapel of his coat as an unexpected gust of wind forced his head down; he greeted the night with a sniffle. He whipped his long hair out of his face, braving the chilled air, then hastened to the hospital, fastening the width of his case under his arm.

The registrar at Portland Hospital's maternity ward took his coat and luggage, then directed him to Chalise's delivery room around the corner. He entered the room with a reminder of how to coach through Chalise's final hour of labor.

He held Chalise's hand while his heart raced. She screamed and cried, but Garence never wavered. He had emotionally prepped for this moment for years, and he'd never thought it would happen. With every breath, he was one moment closer to being a father.

Garence saw his healthy daughter being born through welled eyes. He gave Chalise a firm kiss on the cheek. His hands went to his temple in amazement at the sight of her wiggling body.

The baby wailed, and beyond his broad smile, Garence's chuckle bellowed.

Chalise held her daughter in her arms. She was swathed in a white-and-yellow striped blanket and wore a hospital bracelet with a barcode and the name Leitner, NBF. Luz was born in London's Portland Hospital at 11:11 p.m., and she weighed 3.3 kilograms. Chalise appeared awestruck when in fact, she was struggling to hold on to her initial excitement that had slipped through her fingers like water. If she hadn't been handed the baby right after the delivery, she wouldn't have believed that she had birthed it, and if she were Garence, she would have assumed the child was not his. But she did deliver her, and she had only slept with Garence, so there was no doubt that they were the parents. Then how was it that the child looked nothing like Chalise? She didn't recognize the tiny face in front of her; she didn't have her pouty lips or her skin color. She supposed the baby had Garence's dark curls. Chalise gazed into the strange eyes that did not belong to her or Garence.

She was frightened.

The grayish brown belonged to someone else. And the olive skin and rosy cheeks. No one in her family shared this little girl's traits, and she wondered where she had come from.

Having never met any of Garence's relations, she made an assumption. She turned to Garence with hopeful eyes, hoping against all hope that the child she'd carried for nine months resembled someone he knew.

She forced a smile. "She must take after your family."

Garence didn't register this comment. The instant he clapped eyes on his baby girl, he was overwhelmed with the love he felt for her, and he was certain he would burst at any second. A silent piece of Garence recognized this little person for who she was. The second love of his life.

He smiled.

A nurse, Wendy, entered the room and informed the new parents that visiting hours would be over in thirty minutes. Chalise sat on the hospital bed with Garence beside her. The baby became fussy in Chalise's arms, and nothing seemed to settle her down. Chalise was distressed by her inability to provide solace for her daughter when Garence offered to hold the baby and walk her around.

The baby was content.

Wendy then suggested Chalise get some sleep so she could have her strength to feed the baby in a couple of hours, while Garence was eager to leave and have the baby to himself. He kissed Chalise on the forehead, said he would see her first thing in the morning, and exited the room. Wendy looked at Chalise with tears in her eyes as she watched Garence leave the room; she placed her hands on Chalise's shoulders and urged her to lie back and rest. Weariness caught up with the new mother, and she surrendered to the welcoming pillows and then turned her body toward the window and the evening sky beyond, hoping her little girl would take to her feedings better than she took to her arms.

Garence gushed and cooed down the corridor. This was the person he had been waiting for so long to meet. How could he have endured so much pain after losing Sabina, then feel whole at the sight of this new person? Garence wept as if touched by an angel. He could feel the energy strengthen more than when he had first sensed it on Chalise's birthday. It flared inside him and within this child. Somehow, all was clicking into place. Everything happened for a reason, and here was the living proof within his hands. His guiding light in a very dark tunnel of impossibility.

He rubbed the back of his hand against her velvety olive skin. "Hello, darling. I'm your father."

Garence chuckled at the sight of her grin. He surveyed her face, her tiny fingers, and he placed his thumb within the palm of her hand. She gave it a squeeze, shrieked with delight, and he swore she shook her hand.

"Oh. It's nice to meet you too. That's a firm handshake you have there. Yes, you do," he gushed, showering radiant smiles upon her.

Wendy later found Garence. "She is an angel."

"Yes, she is."

"Does this young lady have a name?"

"Luz."

"Light, correct? Why, hello, Spanish princess. It's time for your evening rest."

Garence didn't want to let go of his daughter. If he had it his way, he would take Luz from the hospital this instant. He would dance with her in his arms beneath the groin vault ceilings of his study, walk her outside to absorb every sight, temperature, and fragrance the English countryside offered. He would teach her Spanish and French, and about her rich history, and how to engage with the world. He had endured too many trying years to let Luz go the moment he was acquainted with her, but she'd had such an arduous journey into this world that he had to allow her some proper sleep.

Garence closed his eyes and nestled his nose against Luz's as he had done before, and he seemed to press the pause button on time. He memorized the weight of 3.3 kilograms in his hand as he snuffled her pure, sweet scent. A scent that reminded Garence of a soap Sabina once tried, and for a fleeting moment, he recalled that he and Sabina had considered surrogacy. He then kissed Luz's crown and absorbed her skin's gentleness and its moss-like texture. *This is what cloud nine is like.* He tucked these memories into a special place, deep within his overcome heart where nothing and no one could extract this magical moment from him.

"I'll see you soon, sweetheart." He sealed the promise with a kiss on the cheek.

"Chalise is asleep. You look as though you could use a few hours yourself. You're welcome to..."

"No, I'm going to head over to her place. Drop off my luggage. Though some Zs sound pretty nice."

"Then I'll see you soon. Bright-eyed and bushy-tailed."

"I'll see what I can accomplish. Good night."

He watched Wendy turn the corner with his bundle of joy, and then he saw her. Sabina. It was only for a moment, but it was her. His white-dressed and barefoot love.

His blood surged with dread, and his chest erupted with razor-sharp panic, causing the temperature of the space about him to drop. With a blink of his eye, Sabina was gone. It was the shortest sighting Garence had ever witnessed, so it couldn't have been her. It couldn't. He hadn't seen Sabina in months, not since he learned of Chalise's pregnancy.

What was she doing here?

He swallowed his compacted fear, as rough and lumpy as it was, and walked down the frigid and unnerving corridor. He peered around the corner with chills stinging his spine and found no one there.

Garence didn't know whether to be relieved or disappointed. He had seen Sabina. He was sure of it now. Where had she gone? She had appeared after Wendy carried Luz off, which meant she was popping in on the babe. This idea calmed his anxieties. If anyone was going to over-see the care of his newborn, it was Sabina.

Garence stared out into the distance, and madness gripped his soul in its fist once again. Perhaps Sabina didn't want him to have a happiness that wasn't possible for them. Perhaps she wanted a child so badly that she wanted this one for herself. In every facet of Sabina's mental state, she desired a child even when she no longer wanted to try.

No. He couldn't believe Sabina would take his darling little girl from him; she would have known how much he wanted Luz. How much he needed this beacon of light in his dark existence, where the days repeated on and on like the voice that would never shut up.

The adrenaline associated with Chalise's delivery mixed with the elation Garence felt when he held Luz in his arms had taken its toll on him. His body and mind begged him to sleep and rest. Being close to Luz was soothing, but the knowledge that Chalise's flat was a mere ten minutes away was enough to make him sprint there. The new mother and their newborn were sleeping, and there was no reason for him not to do the same. Chalise had given him a set of keys a couple of months ago after he made a habit of visiting her; the corner of his mouth turned up with this reflection.

He stood in front of metal double doors and waited for the lift to arrive, then entered it; dead silence vibrated the air. Drowsiness called upon his eyes, and he looked forward to falling on the bed and sleeping hard for at least three hours. Then he would return to the hospital to be with his little girl.

As long as it had taken Garence to open up to Chalise and to let her in, he was glad he had. The affection he experienced with her was gratifying. Fulfilling, in fact. Watching a movie with his arm around her and her head on his shoulder, or reading on the couch together, or looking out a window with her enveloped within his embrace were treasures in a chest. He liked wrapping his arms around her tiny frame and squeezing her and caressing her silky skin. It amazed him how patient she was with him. Who else would have hung out with a depressed middle-aged man for months on end without receiving anything concrete in return? No one, and he knew it. Well, Luz was in the realm of being concrete, tangible, but he'd never once mentioned to Chalise his wanting to solidify their relationship because he wasn't ready for that commitment. He was certain Chalise knew this as well. Chalise was a blessing. He'd have to make a better effort in being there for her as much as she was there for him.

He ran his hand through his hair and itched his scalp. The longing to lie down was too much for Garence, and it threatened to take him down like a chain-sawed redwood. He yawned. His body swayed with exhaustion, and he jolted straight within himself; it was a miracle he caught himself before he passed out. The lift rang of his arrival to the main floor, and he exited the hospital.

His thoughts swam in the memory of holding Luz; he could fold his arms into the exact shape of her swaddled body to fit her tiny frame. He raised his arms above his head and stretched, took a deep breath, and exhaled. The precious face embedded in his mind forever stared back at him through his mind's eye.

He hailed a cab and gave the driver Chalise's address. He sat back and exhaled his relief. In a few minutes, he would be on Chalise's bed for the world's best power nap.

The phone rang.

"This is Garence."

His focus was intent as he listened to the nurse. Fifteen minutes later, he was hollering at Dr. Melo, a mustached gentleman in his early thirties, in an empty hospital room two doors from Chalise's. The door was closed, but anyone could distinguish what was going on if they peered through the glass inset.

"What do you mean she died?"

"Mr. Leitner..."

"I saw her," Garence exclaimed, raising his hand, trying to grapple with the time that had lapsed. "I just fucking saw her! How can she be dead? I thought this was an excellent hospital!"

He gripped his roots and growled. "Nooo! No! No! No! No! No! NO!"

"Mr. Leitner, if you would like to..."

He stared daggers at the obstetrician.

Garence mustered enough composure to utter one question before faltering. "Do you really want to know what I would like? I want my baby girl. I want... one."

His index finger was like a sword ready to battle the universe for all of the wrong in this reality.

"I want just one child. One bit of happiness!" he seethed.

Garence turned around, lunged forward, and punched through the glass in the door.

Chapter Fifty-One

PRESENT DAY

Garence raised his left hand and outstretched his fingers. The ones that used to be in a splint, skeletal and veiny, showed no sign of healing with their increased use to pack and write.

Luz died in hospital on November 1st at 1:11 a.m. It's ironic on so many levels, I still cannot decode the meaning behind it all. I suppose I should try.

Garence thumbed through the remaining blank sheets of writing paper.

There's still a bit of time left.

Let's begin with the more common fact that November 1st is Día de Muertos, a holiday celebrated throughout Mexico where the dead are honored. Not only did I have loved ones to celebrate, but I was mourning the loss of yet another loved one on the very holiday.

What a sick joke.

The next fun fact—forgive my flippancy—deals with repeated numbers. Remember, Sabina was intrigued by

*numerology, so I have some knowledge about the significance
of repetitive numbers. First off, one is a sacred number.
Its repetition, in this case, November 1st, represents the
manifestation of the Divine's power, and that the new path
you are on is being supported. How could this have been
possible? My new path was being dug up from beneath my feet
and backfilled with the soul of my darling Luz. I hate the fact
that for the past month, I have been forced to walk upon this
blessed path where the center is mounded over my daughter's
body. If I'm supposed to allow things to unfold, then where is
this new path leading me? I'm sorry, but I don't condone the
spiritual abduction of my little girl to steer me toward some
inexplicable fate.*

*Fate... She was born at 11:11 p.m. Alive for two hours. 11:11
is the most powerful pattern, as it carries the vibration that the
Divine being is alive. There are too many coincidences to ignore.
Blast, all of this means something! I can feel it!*

Garence dropped the pen and pinched the bridge of his nose. *Does it
matter?* he asked himself. Life wasn't worth living anymore.

*Maybe I'll never figure it out. At least not while I'm alive; for
the next few hours or so, I won't. I'm fed up, and I have no more
letters to read, and I have three more sheets to write upon. The
one thing stopping me is the fear I may not see Sabina in the
afterlife or in my next life, or whatever is going on in the universe.
I fear I will be lost to her.*

*I had been procrastinating, then the voices urged me to read
the letters from the luggage, Sabina appeared, and that was the*

game-changer. I participated in this jaunt toward my apparent
new path, expecting to arrive where I was meant to be, where
everything clicked into place.

Something else is nagging at me, though. It's a strong pull—
more like a windless sail, where I find myself gliding without
a destination in mind through the fog. I don't know. I can't
explain it any better than that.

He lifted his sore, sleep-deprived eyes skyward. He was too disheartened to appreciate his metaphorical evolution from the horrendous
mound that was Luz's death to the undisturbed waters where he no
longer looked forward to anything in life. These final breaths were ever
more valuable on his quest toward understanding the meaning behind
his heartache.

Too many patterns surround Luz's life for me to leave it alone.
I have to figure it out. What else am I missing?

With his palms over his eyes, he tried to recall all that he had learned
on his travels and what Sabina had said about the number one. Relationships came to mind first; each individual needed to be capable of being
true to themselves whilst being strong together—but that had nothing to
do with Luz! He was veering off course.

I want to say that repeated ones are also believed to open the
door to the other dimension. Is that right?

We are all made up of energy, and when we die, that energy
doesn't cease. Halloween is a celebration of that energy moving
forward. Pagans believed this was the time where the line
between the living and the dead was the thinnest, which aligns

with the Day of the Dead celebration. All three dimensions are
open: the lower world, Earth, and the upper world.

Garence rubbed his temple. More repeated numbers, or ones in this
case, presented the amplification of your direction. If all the information
was spread out in front of him and he moved the pieces around, then he
should be able to decipher what the hell was going on.

Luz was born at 11:11 p.m., and she died on November 1st at 1:11
a.m. during a time when some cultures celebrate the dead, and
where pagans believed that various dimensions were unguarded...
the gateway between the living and the dead was open.
  No, that's mental.

Then why did it feel right?

Something shifted the evening Luz died. Her energy went
somewhere, but it is the composition of her energy that baffles
me. If you recall my feeling, an energy shift the night Chalise
and I had sex, and its intensification upon Luz's birth. I'm also
baffled by the "why" behind her death and Sabina's connection.
  Perhaps someday I will understand this, but right now, I
am the living dead. I've felt like it for some time. Perhaps the
"middle realm" exists and I am stuck in it. It would explain why
our children—and Sabina—left it and why Sabina's apparition
visits me.

Chapter Fifty-Two

SIXTEEN DAYS AGO

It was a dreary November 11th, ten days since Luz's death. Chalise and Garence were tucked away inside a warm local, but neither of them removed their coats. They avoided each other's eyes as much as they clung to the shadows surrounding the pale light shining through the lead windows. Garence was slumped, yet he managed to lean his upper body away from Chalise whilst she sat erect and stiff as a raven.

Chalise ordered a glass of water upon taking her seat, as did Garence, and they waited in silence. Neither of them was eager to dance around the reason for their sorrow, so they said nothing.

Chalise had called the meeting and intended to say her piece once and for all. In order to cleanse her heart and soul of Garence forever, she'd have to dive into the deep end and expel a monologue that would be their ruin.

Their glasses of water were delivered a few seconds later.

Chalise took a sip. She placed the clear green glass upon the cardboard coaster on the scratched tabletop. She tapped her pinky finger upon the side, then leaped, calculating her target.

"I fell in love with you the moment I saw you in the Raucous Pint." She couldn't help but share a small grin; that life-changing instant was too great to disregard, and she found the courage to meet his forlorn eyes. "I was always struck by how you carried yourself. Your ability to stroll into any space, looking like David Beckham in black, and how you melted into your surroundings like any ordinary man. It was almost too good to be true, but I learned it wasn't a ruse and that you are an extraordinary man. I was glad to get to know you."

She looked away. Resentment crawled up her sleeve, but she would rather have honesty flow from her lips. "I was surprised by your humility, and I lusted after you even more for it. I knew you didn't love me in the beginning... but I didn't guess that you never would. I loved you even though I knew you would never care for me, not one smidgeon as much as you did for Sabina. I knew it, but I'm not going to lie, I had hoped, so I waited."

With every second, the growl in her tone grew. "I hate hope, and I hate patience. I hate how long I've stuck around you." She sniffled and conquered her anger. "Why did I bother latching on to you? I don't know why I tortured myself by being in your presence because nothing good has come out of it."

She was grateful for his silence because there was nothing he could have said to make her feel any better or to change the outcome of this meeting... but she did wonder if everything was meaningless.

She couldn't help but ask, "Do you ever think about that night?"

As if he could teleport back in time, he was taken to the night of her birthday. He'd rolled Chalise over and was on top of her; her mouth formed an O, and a strained breath escaped her lips.

"Yes," he admitted. "I care deeply for you... We shared a very beautiful moment—one that could rival tackling Everest. That moment created new life that I never thought I would encounter. A life that had rejuvenated me, and you were the source. You always were. Chalise, I wish I could have loved you. I still wish it, but I can't."

Her heart was breaking into a million pieces, and she was trying her hardest to battle the tears that threatened to gush. His candor hurt too much to hear, and his words stabbed her in the chest over and over again. *I wish I could have loved you.*

"I thought I could be your friend. I almost believed you when you said we could make this work. I thought I was going to be the mother of your child. I was so wrong," she shook her head, "and I've been wasting my time." She swallowed her pain, then looked at him dead-on. "I can't do this anymore." If only she could say she was sorry, but that would have been a lie.

Before the tears fell, she wiped them away. "I knew your heart was broken, but I was foolish enough to think it needed time to heal. I'd like to think that in another life we could have been together, but I know that kind of thinking is pure insanity; you belonged with no one else but Sabina, and I hope you meet her soon. I want nothing more to do with you. Don't try to contact me or think that we can mourn the loss of our child together some time in the future because it's not going to happen."

She rose from her seat and said goodbye without waiting for a reply.

Chapter Fifty-Three

PRESENT DAY

Chalise was my last outlet to any semblance of an existence in this life, and I let her walk away as if I never appreciated her. She loved me despite the fact that I couldn't let her into my heart even when we became pregnant.

When I first learned I was going to be a father, I was numb. Yes, I smiled at the news, but what was I supposed to do? That moment was supposed to happen over two years ago, and not with Chalise. I know that sounds so cruel, but it's the truth. I didn't want to be happy sharing a long-awaited child for a fleeting moment with another woman! Then I convinced myself that Sabina had sent Luz to me in her stead when in actuality, I had invented a reason to be happy without Sabina.

I was tired of being empty and alone—even though I was friends with Chalise for over a year—I couldn't live the way I had been much longer. When Luz's tiny hand wrangled my thumb, I was whole. I fell in love for the third time, and I never felt guilty for loving someone other than my wife. I knew from the depths of my soul that Sabina would have supported my feelings. She would have pinched my nipple if I didn't jump for joy the first day I heard the news, but as unexpected and quick as Luz entered my life, she vacated it. All I can do is hope that Sabina is taking care of her for me.

Garence's jaw tightened as he stared at the night sky through a window from inside the cottage. He wondered why the universe was cheesed off at him. Could it have been because he loved so intolerably? He was selfish for wanting Sabina and his four children in his life, but he wasn't apologizing for it.

He got up to use the loo and washed his hands. He shook them in the bowl, as there wasn't a hand towel available, while looking at a photograph taped to the vanity mirror of himself and Sabina; they were at a candlelit dinner in Singapore, celebrating their one-year anniversary.

He smiled at his girl when a dark figure appeared in the mirror and caught him off guard. He speculated how this man could have entered the cottage without his noticing him. This man's grueling appearance was stupefying. There was dried blood on his forehead and dark circles below his deathlike eyes. The man's dingy T-shirt drooped over his body as if his bones were a clothes hanger. The jeans that once embraced the hips were now too large and cinched to his waist by a leather belt that had seen the world, yet was still tough enough to hang someone. The man rubbed his eyes as much as he could with bruised fingers. He winced from the pain, but if he could dig and pick and scrape at the problem, he would feel better. Sleep would be a wise and a royal treat, but to be honest, there was no escaping misery.

Garence lifted his semi-rimmed, black glasses to get a better look at the semi-familiar man when he saw him lift his glasses as well.

That man was him.

Garence placed a hand upon his pallid cheek, stretching it as if it were drying paste. He hadn't been to the barber in some time, but he hadn't realized how unkempt he had become. The unshaved look that Sabina found sexy was unruly. His hair was slick with natural oils and longer than it had ever been, with the ends frayed to his shoulders like unraveling rope.

He peeled the photograph off the mirror, grabbed the bottle of hand soap, then walked to the kitchen. He peered into the icebox and the cupboards. They were all as empty as his stomach. He had forgotten there was no food. Then he remembered his sandwich from yesterday.

He went to the entry table at the front door where he'd left the café bag sitting on top of a moving box. He hadn't wrapped the sandwich when he last took a bite, so the bread halves were separated, and the lettuce and turkey were warm from being out. It was unappealing, so he left it. He moved the bag to the side, not realizing he was doing anything and everything to keep from packing Sabina's things.

Taking one last look at the photograph from the bathroom, he placed it inside the luggage with Sabina's letters. He tossed a log at the fire, and the weight of it crushed the charred ones; embers spewed like the burden of his anxieties and sparked bold new ones.

He settled into the armchair and watched the flames as he had done all weekend, but this time, Chalise was on his mind. His shoulders yielded to the guilt he had, but he was done with that emotion. He got up and leaned over the luggage, shifting and grabbing for the bundles that pertained to her, then tossed them into the fire. The edges went alight and were soon transformed into ash.

He slumped on the couch, and sleep took him. In his dreams, he heard his darling baby girl, Luz, older yet young at heart.

"Papa, I remember hearing your voice as I grew inside my womb-mother. I was over the moon with anticipation, knowing I would meet you at the end of this journey. I felt your love for me the second you held me in your arms and how massive your thumb was within my grasp. We hadn't met, in person, that is, but I knew you. Your love for me was as radiant as the sun, so that I couldn't help but shriek. Your smile warmed my spirit, yet I fell silent. I suppose I am quiet by nature, but I was starstruck by you. Your pinkish gold aura. The energy you were experiencing pounded upon my chest. As brief as my life was, I knew that no one could have ever loved me as much as you did—except for Mum.

"I sensed that my arrival mended your broken heart, and I didn't want to leave your side, but I heard Mum whispering to me. Calling me home to her. She said we would see you soon, and I had no reason not to believe her. I am grateful to my womb-mother. She took such good care of me, but I wasn't supposed to be in this world for long. I was meant to be Mum's such a long time ago. I couldn't wait another moment longer to be with her, but I had to meet you first, and I'm glad I did. I knew you had been through a lot, Papa, but you have to believe that this sadness will pass. Be strong. Stronger than you have ever been before. We will see you again. I promise."

Garence awoke from his dodgy sleep. His head ached from dehydration and a weekend of drinking, and his eyes were sore with the want of restful sleep. The smell of dew and wet grass filled his sleepy senses, and he knew the sun would rise in less than four hours.

He sat straight, wincing; his shoulder and back ached. He must have twisted and used his arm as a pillow. He ground his knuckles into his eyes and yawned. The fire had almost died out, but the charred log glowed. He looked across his left shoulder, and the fountain pen and embossed paper called for his return.

He obliged.

I am too weary to keep haunting this house. I don't want to keep waking up. For some reason, "Return to the light" is haunting my thoughts. I have done what the voice and Sabina wanted me to do, relive the past...

Garence pondered what it meant to relive the past and what purpose it served. The first thing that came to mind was learning from your experiences, which didn't apply to his predicament. That left appreciating all that had transpired. He repeated that realization. He had appreciated the opportunity to read the letters and relive some of the things that had happened. Like him and Sabina falling in love, getting married, and meeting Luz. But that was all he would hold on to. Everything else had done its worst and extinguished possibilities.

There was one sheet of paper left, and Garence was more than ready to call it quits. He surveyed the exposed beams overhead, amazed at how they stood the test of time; they had endured great weights as he did, but unlike himself, they would be here long after he was.

Sabina and Luz.

Their memories tug on the corner of my mouth. It's an odd sensation to be grinning after reading the memories that exposed my wounded heart, now that I am about to pack her things. And that means we're drawing to a close.

To you, my unbeknown reader: Thank you. You've been an unequaled presence. I have grown accustomed to the darkness that surrounds me, and I no longer need a light to guide me where I am bound.

At the start of this letter, I didn't recognize what I was doing by writing it. I said this wasn't a love story, but I can see now that it is.

And that makes this...

The End,

Garence

He folded the letter into thirds and placed it into the luggage. With the disposal of Chalise's letters, his binder fit on top of Sabina's letters, then all of their photographs. The lid closed without hesitation or force. He set the luggage by the door.

Garence walked down the bedroom hallway. He refused to see his wife on the bed in a terrible state, so he imagined her smiling at him, the sun catching the natural red highlights in her dark hair and her winking at him. Each of his steps was intentional, but he was more ready than he was aware.

He entered their bedroom.

Sabina's things were like the Beatles song "Here, There and Everywhere," and they had been waiting for him to get himself together. He went to the dresser and opened the drawers. A row of bras was in the first, knickers in the next drawer, then socks and trousers below those drawers. For a moment, he couldn't do anything but stare at everything, but he was out of time. He brought in a few of the large boxes from the car, built them, then secured the bottoms with packing tape. He placed the heavier items in first, then the lighter ones. As he placed each article into a box, he remembered the times she'd worn them.

He hadn't shed a tear since Sabina's death, but something about reading every single one of her words, followed by touching her things, chipped at the protective shield that was his depression. As he put more into boxes, he was turning a page in the book of life, and his grin faded. He went into the closet, and his demeanor turned grim.

There was the carnation-white, halter shift dress. The one from the photograph he'd been staring at all weekend. He lifted it off the hanger and brought it to his nose. After being locked away for two years, there was no scent on the material. Nothing clung to the fibers except his fingers. This dress had been present at the beginning of his happiness and every deteriorating stage from then on.

As he yelled, his veins popped from his neck and arms, then the dress ripped in half. The rules of time bent, and the minutes sat with him. A tear fell onto the dress, and, one by one, they were all absorbed.

He stole away from the main bedroom and returned with the duct tape and scissors. He tore a smaller piece of the dress and shoved it in his mouth. He cut three pieces of tape. Two small chunks, with the third much longer. The first strip went over his mouth. The second over his nose. The third around his right wrist, which was going behind his back and around his left wrist. It was tricky getting the end of the tape around himself, but he pressed his wrists against his back to seal the bond as much as possible. Reading the letters and packing all their possessions had put additional stress upon him, and touching Sabina's things had unraveled the tattered rope connecting him to this reality.

He fell sideways. A blurred image crouched beside him on the floor. He thought he saw someone, but he wasn't sure.

"Garence."

The voice was too muddied to recognize.

"Garence."

The person came into focus, their voice clearer. "Don't do this." Sabina was wearing the carnation-white, halter shift dress, but it was torn down the middle. She lay next to him, with her cheek against the floor. Her eyes were filled with tears.

"You promised."

I am suffocating without you.

With the smallest space between her hand, she caressed his jaw and the two flat moles like she always did. She nodded. "Break free from the darkness. Return to the light, *mi amor.*"

He wriggled his wrists with all of his strength, but he couldn't break free. The airtight tape sucked into his nostrils and his lips.

There was no incoming air.

"Return to the light."

He twisted his wrists and pulled at the tape to no avail. He met her pleading eyes, and he pulled and turned his wrists in the opposite direction, then jerked them the other way. He kicked at the floor with his heels, as if that would help the situation. He was holding his breath, but there was none to be held. The tape came undone. Garence sat up, and his fingers went to his mouth. He clawed at the ends and dug into his skin before the tape separated. He spat out the remnant and gasped for air. Inhaling and wheezing, he ripped the nose strip.

His mind spun in figure eights. He collapsed, willing himself to focus and calm down. He had come from such a fall that he couldn't believe he'd come close to achieving death. The one thing he desired since Sabina's.

Garence shot up. He turned left and right.

She was gone.

He grabbed two stacked boxes of clothes and left the house through the back door. With a grunt, he thrust the boxes to the ground a few yards from the rubbish bins. He ran inside and carried two more boxes, and repeated the process until the bedroom was empty. He took the box from the living room and threw in the items he'd used throughout the packing, including the sandwich, and projected it at the pile, growling with anger; the glass from the picture frames broke as the box tumbled from the pile. He went to the shed for the lighter fluid, then sprayed the boxes and threw a match to the mound. The bonfire lit his hollow face with a warmth he hadn't known since he last kissed Sabina.

He wavered as it all burned. It was dark, but the flames were now his light. It was cold, but the flames offered him warmth. Sabina's things burned, but the flames set him free.

Inside the cottage, Garence walked down the study's hallway and retrieved the rope and hunting knife hidden beneath the flattened boxes.

He gripped the blade, and his thumb rubbed the nonslip handle before placing it back into the box. The seven-inch blade was sharp. Sharp enough to slice tendons and muscles, and penetrate an organ.

Garence exited the house. The realtor would arrive in two hours, so he didn't lock the front door. He was dead set on his intent to kill himself, and there would be no turning back. He put the luggage in the passenger seat, then drove off without looking into the rearview mirror.

Chapter Fifty-Four

PRESENT DAY

It was drizzling, and the streets were empty. The townsfolk were tucked in their beds, fast asleep in their cozy worlds. The fuel gauge indicated the tank was near empty, but where Garence was headed wasn't far and he wouldn't need any petrol for the return trip home because it wasn't happening.

He tried to think of where he would do it. He didn't want to dwell on the trauma he would inflict upon a stranger when they found his lifeless body, but it could not be helped. But that eliminated the public park and the football field. He supposed there was no suitable place to kill oneself outside one's home; the option of killing himself in the cottage he and Sabina had built a life in was never on the table.

Driving, he now had too much time to think. He was better off making less of a scene and going near the authorities, but not by a hospital; he didn't want to be salvaged. He drove toward the police station eight kilometers away, and his ever-shattered mind recalled the sharp hunting knife. Yes, that was how he would do it. He would lie upon his coat and then cut into his forearms as his Sabina had done—a twisted homage to his beloved.

A little girl's voice erupted in the vehicle's cabin. "Papa, be strong."

Garence stomped on the brake pedal, and the wheels crunched on the gravel.

His eyes scanned the blackness surrounding him.

"I don't want this," he said out loud.

He pounded the steering wheel with both fists until his bones felt as if they would shatter. "I don't want this!"

Tears billowed from his weary sockets, and his jaw was sore from the force with which he was gritting his teeth.

Others were taken when they had so much to offer, whereas he had nothing. He should be allowed a reprieve from this undetermined life.

Although it was dark, Garence closed his eyes and began his breathing exercises.

In with the good.

Out with the bad.

Sabina's beautiful face flashed before him, a baby's tiny hand gripping his thumb, a memory of him sobbing every day, and him breaking the hospital door glass with his fist when he learned of Luz's death.

He felt for the knife with his hand.

"Keep the promise you made to me," said the resonating voice.

The memory of Sabina in the ambulance flashed in his mind. "Don't do it."

Don't kill yourself. That's what Sabina had been telling him as she lay dying. She foresaw what he would be pushed to do, an unimaginable act she had attempted herself.

Garence leaned against the steering wheel.

"I would give anything to see you again. The faintest opportunity to hold you in my arms. Who am I kidding? I want all of you. Your lips on mine. Your fingertips gliding up my back, then through my hair."

His imagination took sail. He'd draw her close enough to feel her heartbeat against his, warm her with his body, his hands upon her breasts and squeezing them. His thoughts could have continued, but everything simmered down to one simple truth.

In the most hushed voice, Garence whispered his greatest desire into the universe. "I want you by my side. Forever. I deserve nothing more, so I shall ask for nothing more."

He sat in silence… hoping for his one wish to be granted… for his life to be taken from him before he was forced to claim it.

He waited…

And he waited…

Nothing happened.

He continued to drive with his death wish for a passenger. Everything would click into place at the exact moment it was supposed to happen.

His conscience spoke, *You don't have to do this.*

Garence gripped the steering wheel with white knuckles. A growl rumbled through clenched teeth as he used the muscles in his right hand to beat the steering wheel. He replaced the pressure he had on the brake pedal. He didn't have to travel down this path, but he wanted to.

Then he heard, "Keep your promise."

Ripping into the steering wheel, he glared into the eyes of the black night that was now his salvation; death and a new life awaited. He ran his hands through his dingy curls and pulled on the roots.

He could turn his life around because Sabina and Luz would have wished it. The cottage was already sold and all its contents were gone; he had a clean slate. He could move to another town, perhaps in the Lake District. He could open those luxury bed-and-breakfasts with Ryo in Tokyo; that was a lucrative opportunity. Or move to a new city like Vancouver. Or Auckland. He'd always envisioned himself living in New Zealand, rappeling down canyons and waterfalls, kayaking across Waitemata Harbour, and learning to surf.

The corner of his mouth turned up.

He could circle back to the cottage right now and figure something out, start a new life. It was still possible.

Second by second, the Auckland move sounded like a good idea. A great idea, and then it turned into a plan. He didn't want to kill himself. He wasn't afraid of dying; there wasn't any need for it. There was no certainty of seeing his family again, and he couldn't say why, but he was sure Sabina's apparition would never return. She had led him to the luggage for a reason.

Things happen for us, he thought, remembering her voice.

Then a thought occurred to him. A huge thunderous thought, and he jumped.

He unlocked the luggage, pulled out the sealed envelope from Sabina he hadn't read, and separated the fold from the envelope.

Dear Garence,

I stopped doing it. Hurting myself. With my fingernails and the razor blades. It dwindled and then I stopped. There's nothing I can do to bring our children back and...

It's not my fault they didn't survive. I did everything I could, and they still died. It's not okay, but then it is. I am releasing the guilt and the pain I'm harboring one bit at a time. I know it won't ever go away, but I'm hoping it won't hurt as much as it does right now. Or as much as it did last month, or the moment I learned of their passing. I need to stop resisting what is and heal. With you.

You've been waiting for me to return to you. I know you've been in so much pain, and I'm sorry I wasn't there for you when you needed me. I'm so sorry, mi amor.

I am not sure I am going to hand this or the other two envelopes to you, so I don't know when you're reading this. We've always told each other everything, and I wanted you to know what's been going on with me. I'll leave everything up to Source. I know you'll read these when you're ready.

And when you do, mi amor, know that no matter how dark it seems or if it feels like a tower is crumpling, you will find clarity. I hope these words will find you in time or provide some sort of confirmation that you are on the right path. An open uncluttered mind and an open heart will allow energy to flow and balance your soul. It took me a while. Please don't waste another second on whatever isn't serving you. Stop resisting. It's time.

I love you,
Sabina

He gazed out into the black surroundings he had grown so accustomed to. He was out in the middle of nowhere, and he had been as alone as he had ever been in the bleakest of situations. Then he noticed the scattered luminescent perforations for the first time. He leaned over the steering wheel and saw that they had started to appear by the thousands. More and more stars appeared, and several more deepened in luster and reflected in his eyes.

Suddenly, "To Your Shore" charged the airwaves.

Garence's head jerked toward the phone sandwiched between the passenger seat and the luggage. He hammered the case away with his fist, and it hit the dash clock.

It was 5:55 a.m.

Garence saw the time, but he was too preoccupied with the song to realize he was being told there was an impending change. He stared at his phone. It was not on, the display light was off, but the phone was playing their song.

He reached over, but his fingertips pushed the phone away. It was now a hair away, and if he released his foot from the brake for a second, he could grasp it. One more try, and he extended his arm and twisted his wrist, but he was unsuccessful. His foot left the brake, and the car rolled forward. With his phone in his hand, he sat with his success when he realized the music had stopped playing. He pressed on the screen, but it didn't power on.

Before Garence could see or hear what was happening, a speeding car approached.

Click.

Chapter Eleven-Eleven

THE NEXT REALITY

A distortion of orchestrations descended upon the world only to be replaced by silence.

It was glaringly bright.

Garence was positive his eyelids were closed, but he couldn't explain the intensity.

The warm English sun scattered upon his skin, and he could smell the distinct group of flowers planted at his cottage in Bourton-on-the-Water. He believed he was standing, though he couldn't be certain because there was no pressure against the soles of his feet. He wondered if he was twiddling his fingers as he thought he was. Then, sensation in his fingers came to him, and relief.

He heard the faint yet distinct chirp of birds coming from the distant unseen hills, whose majestic presence he could sense. A pleasant warmth radiated over his body, but it wasn't from a single heat source. His entire body could feel the strength in his eyelashes, his back, his viscera, the minuscule peach fuzz nuzzling against his body hair.

He couldn't tell where he was, but he knew it was perfect.

He perceived inaudible footsteps coming from several hundred meters away, and even farther than that, he heard the pitter-patter of four sets of feet.

He stepped in that direction, as steady as if he could see them.

His sight blossomed, and he had the funny sensation he was coming out of a deep slumber.

Then he heard it for two spiraling seconds.

The resonating voices that had been haunting him split into two distinct voices... images became stronger and richer as their particles massed like clouds, stretching from the far-reaching horizon. If Garence sensed the hills and someone's distant presence, then he could decipher who was approaching.

He shook his head.

Within that whirling moment, he realized one voice had been Sabina's and the other had belonged to... Luz?

How could that be?

That voice had belonged to one that must have been three or so, an old-souled three-year-old at that, though no soul was new.

His head then seared with an ache that forced him to place his palms over what felt like bleeding ears.

Silence fell upon him for a fraction of a minute, like the amount of time that passes when adjusting the radio frequency. Then, he heard Sabina reflect upon the morning goings-on: "I pulled the morning eggs, fed the goats, watered the climbing roses. I still need to..."

Garence could almost see Sabina reviewing the checklist in her head.

The blood in his veins froze.

Checklist in her head? He could hear her thoughts.

Then he detected Sabina recognizing his, and his skin erupted with sensation when he felt her smile.

"Girls," she called out. "Your papa is home."

THE END

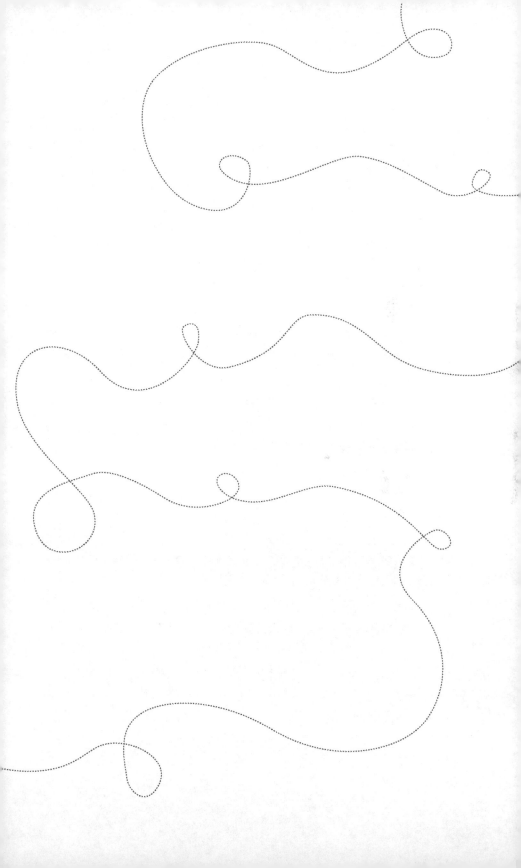

— ACKNOWLEDGMENTS —

From the moment this broken man popped into my head, I have been his champion, and many people have championed me and influenced *Story of My Life*.

Through the seemingly endless drafts, several unique individuals welcomed the opportunity to read this novel from its infancy to near-final draft. Thank you to my beta readers for your insightfulness: Donna Ames and Lisa Hagstrom, and a special thank you to Craig Smith for allowing me to bombard you with Spanish questions. Opening pages are important, and the following esteemed writers shared their wisdom with me: Reese Hogan, Adam Jones, Catherine Jones, Ken Hoover, Sydney Sinclair, and Sean Patrick. A heartfelt thank you.

After spending two years on this novel, I was inclined to make this story the best it could be. To my developmental editor Kyra Nelson, you provided the light I needed to dig deeper into the soul of this novel by offering me the tools and resources to take it to the next level. I thank you with all the stars, the sun, and the moon.

Thank you, Michelle Rascon, for polishing my debut novel with your crisp copy edit and making sure its complex timeline was as clear as intended. I am very appreciative of your talent and support.

Domini Dragoone, thank you for designing a beautiful cover and typography. I had a vision, and you brought it to life. I couldn't have asked for a more genuine artist to collaborate with than yourself.

Thank you, Sara Magness, for a meticulous proofread and ensuring this novel was as genuine as possible. Your keen eye elevated this novel's authenticity.

Thank you to my sister, Veronica Ramsak, my brother, David Baeza, my mother, Patricia Baeza, Lia Feliz, Kathy Bustos, Shauna Jim, Dean Hinds, and Jeff Clemens. Having you in my life has made me stronger.

Thanks to my boys, Ali and Carter, for being my cuddly writing buddies and pawing at me when I've spent an extensive amount of time writing in front of the laptop. You were the constant I needed during this time in my life.

Last but not least, you, my "unbeknown" reader. Everything I write is in some way personal, and that makes your support all the more meaningful. I look forward to sharing more stories with you.

Valerie is a natural storyteller and poet. She writes from the heart and draws readers in with a unique empathy for the human condition. She lives in Albuquerque, New Mexico with her dogs, Ali and Carter ("my boys") by her side, and she relishes the opportunity to hit mountain trails.

Visit her website at www.ValerieBaezaAuthor.com,
and follow her on social media.

Made in the USA
Columbia, SC
17 February 2023

12403601R00186